An odd expression crossed Nicholas's face as he looked at her.

Catrin followed his gaze and looked down. Her gown had slipped low over her bosom. Her face heated—no wonder he stared! She tugged the fabric higher and pulled her cloak tight about her.

A chill swept through her, washing away the pleasurable heat Nicholas had kindled. She must have been mad to let things go so far.

From the moment he had touched her, she'd had no control over the situation....

No control over herself.

She'd become a creature possessed by needs, needs she'd do well to ignore.

What had she been thinking, to fall into Nicholas's embrace so easily?

She hadn't thought at all. It seemed she could not trust herself in Nicholas's presence.

That would not do. She pushed the soft, wonderful feelings deep and tried to bury them beneath her usual prickly facade....

Dear Reader,

Sharon Schulze's very first book, *Heart of the Dragon*, gained her an RWA Golden Heart Award Nomination, some terrific reviews and a K.I.S.S. Award from *Romantic Times*. This month the March Madness author returns with *To Tame a Warrior's Heart*, a stirring medieval tale about a former mercenary and a betrayed noblewoman who overcome their shadowed pasts with an unexpected love. Don't miss it.

With *The Lieutenant's Lady*, her fourth book for Harlequin Historicals, author Rae Muir begins an exciting new Western series called THE WEDDING TRAIL. This month's story is about a hard-luck soldier who returns home determined to marry the town "princess," a woman who sees him as little more than a way out of an unwanted marriage. And *USA Today* bestselling author Ruth Langan is also out this month with *Ruby*, the next book in her ongoing series THE JEWELS OF TEXAS. *Ruby* is the delightful tale of a flirtatious young woman and the formidable town marshal who falls under her spell.

The Forever Man is a new title from Carolyn Davidson, the author of *Gerrity's Bride* and *Loving Katherine*. This emotional story is about a spinster who has given up on love—until a marriage of convenience to a widower in search of a new life for himself and a mother for his two sons heals her broken heart and teaches her to trust in love again.

Whatever your tastes in reading, we hope you enjoy all four books, available wherever Harlequin Historicals are sold.

Sincerely,

Tracy Farrell
Senior Editor

Please address questions and book requests to:
Harlequin Reader Service
U.S.: 3010 Walden Ave., P.O. Box 1325, Buffalo, NY 14269
Canadian: P.O. Box 609, Fort Erie, Ont. L2A 5X3

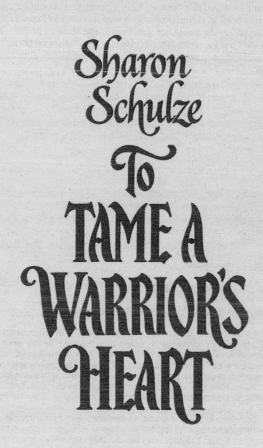

Sharon Schulze

To TAME A WARRIOR'S HEART

Harlequin Books

TORONTO • NEW YORK • LONDON
AMSTERDAM • PARIS • SYDNEY • HAMBURG
STOCKHOLM • ATHENS • TOKYO • MILAN
MADRID • WARSAW • BUDAPEST • AUCKLAND

ISBN 0-373-28986-3

TO TAME A WARRIOR'S HEART

Books by Sharon Schulze

Harlequin Historicals

Heart of the Dragon #356
To Tame a Warrior's Heart #386

SHARON SCHULZE

is a confirmed bookaholic who loves reading as much as writing. Although she has a degree in civil engineering, she's always been fascinated by history. Writing about the past gives her a chance to experience days gone by—without also encountering disease, vermin and archaic plumbing!

A New Hampshire native, she now makes her home in Connecticut with her husband, Cliff, teenagers Patrick and Christina, and their miniature dachshund, Samantha. She is the current president of the Connecticut Chapter of RWA; in her spare time she enjoys movies, music and poking around in antique shops.

Readers may contact her at P.O. Box 180, Oakville, CT 06779.

To the Connecticut Chapter of RWA—what a group!
Your friendship and support mean more than I can say.
Special thanks to my editor, Tracy Farrell, for her
patience and encouragement—and for recognizing
Nicholas and Catrin when she met them again.

Prologue

England, 1214

After a lifetime spent fighting for others in distant lands, he had finally returned to England to take his rightful place among his kind. Tall, strong, handsome—a warrior blessed with skill and grace upon the battlefield.

And between the sheets, rumor had it.

Lord Nicholas Talbot appeared the embodiment of knightly virtue, a nobleman born and bred.

King John knew better.

How it pleased him to bend Talbot to his will, to watch as the arrogant young lord danced warily through the intricacies of Court. Sooner or later, Talbot would trip and reveal his true self to the world.

That thought brought a pleasure of its own.

But until he did, his liege lord would make use of his skills, send him to the far reaches of the kingdom, if he wished.

And if Talbot did not obey, 'twould be an easy task to expose his shame to the world.

King John smiled. No matter what the deed, how could Talbot refuse?

Chapter One

The Welsh Marches

Hooves clattered against the rocky path, the sound echoing through the mist-shrouded trees. Catrin shifted in the saddle; the shiver that ran down her spine owed little to the icy moisture covering her like a blanket. Never had the journey to her cousin's keep at l'Eau Clair seemed so long—or so ominous. She pulled her cloak snug at the throat. Perhaps 'twas her impatience to arrive that made her nerves feel stretched to breaking, not the threat of an unknown menace hidden just beyond her view.

A pair of men rode ahead of her, another behind, to protect her. But she could sense their unease, hear them mutter low-voiced prayers as they scanned the thickening fog. She should never have brought them, the least skilled of her brother's guard; she feared they'd prove a meager defense.

A soft whine caught her attention and she drew her mare to a halt. "Idris, come," she called to the wolfhound who trotted at her side.

She surveyed the dripping trees as he rested his massive head against her leg. "Is anyone out there? Go see."

Idris nudged her, then dropped back to the edge of the forest, head moving from side to side, ears cocked.

Catrin urged her mount on before turning to the young man who rode beside her. Padrig's bony face appeared calm, though his skin looked pale as a fish's belly. His bright blue eyes perused the area as if he were already the warrior he hoped to become in Lord Rannulf Fitz-Clifford's service.

"Mayhap we should have waited for Ian," she murmured.

"Nay, milady, there was no need." Padrig sat straighter in his saddle. "Though Lord Ian's company would be welcome, of course."

Despite Padrig's brave words, he was afraid, to judge by his pallor. Though fourteen, nearly a man, he had led a sheltered life until he came to them. Yet he craved adventure, and the chance to become Rannulf's squire, with the same fervor she'd seen in her brother at that age.

She'd been wrong to leave without Ian, she'd realized as soon as they'd reached the forest. Her sense of unease had grown, so that now only her fear of retracing their tracks kept her moving onward, toward l'Eau Clair.

They'd have been safe with her brother's escort, for no one would dare threaten the Dragon—Prince Llewelyn of Wales's enforcer. But now...

She should never have risked Padrig's safety, nor that of the others, for her own selfish impatience.

Her cousin Gillian would give birth when God—and her body—willed it, whether Catrin was there or not. And likely manage just fine, despite Gillian's protestations to the contrary.

"You don't need the others, milady." Padrig looked

down at the gleaming sword at his waist, then glanced up, his cheeks red. "There are five of us, enough to protect you. Isn't that what you told Father Marc before we left Gwal Draig?"

Despite Padrig's tact, her face heated with shame. She'd fairly screamed the words at the hapless priest when he'd made a last, valiant attempt to stop them. Ian would berate the poor cleric yet again, no doubt, when he returned home and found her gone.

Padrig laid his right hand on the cross formed by his sword hilt. "I am yours to command, Lady Catrin. I will guard you with my life. I swear it."

She suppressed a smile at his fledgling bravado. Somehow the lad had managed to clutter his head with the foolish tales of chivalry so popular among the Normans. She didn't deserve such loyalty, but it would be cruel to spurn his gallantry. "I am honored, Padrig." She reached across the narrow space that separated them, not surprised when he grasped her hand in his and essayed a rough bow.

"Nay, milady, 'tis I—"

A muted sound captured her attention and she tugged her hand free. "Did you hear that?"

She halted her mount and waved Padrig to silence, but only the distorted clatter of hooves met her straining ears. Yet Idris bounded past them, just as she heard the sound again.

A flight of arrows!

"Hurry." She spurred her horse toward Padrig's and forced him to the side of the trail. "Come with me."

A muted cry echoed through the trees, followed by the clash of steel against steel. Catrin slid from the saddle, grabbed Padrig by the arm and pulled him into the forest.

The two rear guards sped by as she drew the boy deeper into the brush. Heart pounding, she dragged Padrig after her, paying no heed to the icy water and branches that pelted them as they stumbled though the leafless trees.

"Where are we going?" Padrig paused to disentangle his cloak from a bramble. "Shouldn't we help the guards?"

"'Twill do no good if we rush onto the trail and are attacked," she replied, bending from the waist to catch her breath. "Subtlety—"

A horse lunged past them, eyes rolling. One of her guards dangled from the saddle, blood streaming from his throat and mouth and dripping down his arrow-studded chest. The expression of surprise on his lifeless face would haunt her for a long time to come—assuming, of course, that she had any time left.

Padrig crossed himself, his expression grim. She had to get him away before yet another death stained her soul, but she knew he would refuse to leave her. Even as she struggled to form the words, he grasped her arm.

"Your pardon, milady." He tightened his fingers and pulled her along. "Fear not, I'll get you to safety."

Catrin tugged free of his hold and eased back toward the sounds of battle. He reached for her again. "We can do nothing for them. Come, 'tis best we leave while we can."

She reached toward him as though in supplication, then snatched at the sword hanging from his belt. The blade slipped free before he had time to do more than curse. "You've much to learn, Padrig." She closed both hands tight around the hilt and stepped away. He'd better not argue, for she hadn't the strength to heft the weapon for long. But he didn't know that—she hoped. "'Tis my fault we're in this trouble. 'Tis up to me to get us out." She motioned with the sword. "You must go for help. It's your duty," she added as indecision crossed his face.

"Did you not swear a solemn oath to me? You must go back and catch a horse, then ride for help. I will hide here until you return."

"I should not leave you," he protested. "Come with me."

"Nay, 'twill be easier for you to slip away alone, and you can ride faster." She brought the sword tip up to rest against his chest. "I order you to go—now, lest you incur my displeasure."

She could see that he believed she would use the weapon if he didn't obey her. He ducked his head and murmured, "God keep you, milady," before he darted into the bushes.

Catrin drew a deep breath and lowered the blade, her attention on the faint trail before her as she wove through the clinging branches. She had no idea of the enemy, their numbers or their strength. No more than three of her guard were left—and herself, of course, though she doubted she counted as much of an asset.

Who could have attacked them, and why? She'd brought scant baggage and rode surrounded by armed men. What possible benefit could they gain?

She reached the edge of a clearing. Setting aside the sword, she pulled up her hood to hide her face. Then, arms braced to stop their shaking, she took up the weapon once more and left the shelter of the forest.

As the wisps of fog drifted apart, she saw that only one of her men remained on his feet, surrounded by three tattered ruffians. They circled him like carrion crows round a dying lamb, blades and voices taunting his vulnerability. The bodies strewn over the ground bespoke her guards' valiant defense, but for naught. Her men had been outmatched by numbers alone.

She stifled a cry when her anxious gaze found Idris

draped over two men, their throats bloodied. Arrows protruded from his dark hide.

Anger and grief lent steel to her backbone and power to her arms. She held the sword before her and charged into the clearing, her voice raised in her brother's fierce battle cry.

The three men turned toward her and, ignoring the guard, stalked forward to encircle her.

Her hood had fallen, exposing her tangled braid—a banner proclaiming her sex, should there be any doubt. Too late to matter, she thought with a shrug, and tightened her grip on the sword.

"Here she is, men," said one, his filthy face twisted into a smirk. He pointed his knife at her. "Think this be the lady we's sent to fetch?"

Catrin stood motionless, only her eyes moving. She didn't recognize them. Who would want her this badly? "Who sent you?" she demanded.

"'Tis not for me to say." He motioned with the knife. "Come now, my pretty, put down the sword. Ye'll not be needing it."

"Aye. Only sword we'll be needin's right here," another added. The others laughed when he jiggled the front of his breeches.

Her stomach knotted. Please God, not that! Better to turn the blade on herself than allow these swine to touch her. But she'd take at least one of them with her, she vowed.

The men had relaxed their vigilance, and they continued to ignore the remaining guard. But though the man looked weary to her furtive gaze, she read a message in his eyes.

He would not fail her.

She swung her sword in a wide arc and ran toward the

ruffians as the guard rushed forward, slashing about with his weapon.

Her blade sank deep into the belly of the would-be rapist. Numbing pain shot through her fingers and up her arm, but she kept her grip. *I doubt your sword will serve you now, you bastard.* She smiled in grim satisfaction.

Her smile disappeared when the guard fell. She'd no one to depend upon now but herself. What to do? She braced her foot against her victim's chest and pulled the blade free, then backed up to maintain her defense.

The thunder of hooves split the air and horses burst through the mists. An armed man rode at their head, his battle cry filling the clearing.

Her attention caught by the sight, Catrin never heard the whoosh of arrows until their barbs sank into her flesh.

Nicholas wiped the beaded moisture from his face, though his glove felt just as wet from the clinging fog. He shook his head to clear the exhaustion from his brain and berated himself yet again for his stupidity. 'Twas foolish not to have accepted Rannulf's offer of a guide; it would have given him company to ease the boredom of the journey, as well as reassurance that he hadn't wandered away from the route to Dolwyddelan.

But he'd dared not linger at l'Eau Clair, not when Lady Catrin uerch Dafydd might arrive at any moment. Gillian's cousin was an enigma, a siren who drew him to her even as she sought to keep him away. Since he didn't understand her allure, he avoided her when he could.

Instead of lingering in comfort with Rannulf and Gillian at l'Eau Clair, he found himself camping along the trail, wet and miserable.

He should have learned patience by now, patience, and how to play the nobleman's game. But he'd angered his king once again. Look where it had brought him: plodding along a muddy trail through the backwoods of northern Wales. It seemed punishment for every sin he'd ever committed. God knew there were enough of them.

Rapid hoofbeats roused him. Three riderless horses appeared out of the fog, reins flying as they sped down the road toward him.

A signal set his stallion dancing sideways across the path to halt their headlong flight. He dismounted and sought to calm them. Though they accepted his touch, their foam-flecked hides and rolling eyes bespoke their terror.

Blood—a great deal of it—streaked the light gray gelding, although it appeared unharmed.

A strange cry pierced the air. He'd swear 'twas a battle cry, but the voice sounded feminine.

Someone needed help.

He grabbed the reins and tied the three horses together, then took up a lead rein and leapt into the saddle. Sword held high, he spurred his mount and raised his voice in a roaring bellow to accompany the thunder of hooves as they raced down the trail.

Too late!

A slight, dark-cloaked figure crumpled to the ground as he broke through the bushes. Even as he rode into the clearing, more ragtag fighters left the brush to add their numbers to the men already gathered within the clearing.

They beset him at once. As they reached to pull him from the saddle, he freed the string of horses and kicked out, sending one man to his knees with blood streaming down his face. He slashed with his sword and sent another to writhe upon the ground.

Perhaps he might escape this fiasco after all.

An arrow pierced his left arm, sending him reeling in

surprise. 'Twas all the distraction the ruffians needed. They attacked in force, cudgeling him with stout branches and pulling him from the saddle. His body jerked beneath the rain of blows.

He hit the ground with a thud and struggled against them, but he was no proof against their numbers. Someone stripped back his mail hood and they continued to buffet him about the head and body.

As his vision dimmed around the edges, his lips curled in a smile.

No one would ever believe Nicholas Talbot died doing a heroic deed.

Chapter Two

Catrin drifted in a cold, black void of confusion, meaningless words echoing in her head. She sucked in a breath, the inrush of air bringing with it the taste of fresh-churned soil and wet grass.

How did she come to be lying on the ground?

Raucous laughter sounded nearby, summoning up memories of the ambush. Fear held her motionless, lest her attackers notice her again.

Icy moisture dripped onto her face. As her senses sharpened, a wave of nausea swept over her, followed by fiery shards of pain radiating from her back. Gritting her teeth, she focused upon her surroundings.

The earth trembled beneath her cheek, and her ears picked out the muffled sound of retreating hoofbeats, but the voices remained—nay, they grew louder. She risked opening her eyes.

A small group of men, four or five, she thought, stood near a mail-clad body, their speech and gestures agitated. One man stepped away from the others and motioned them to silence. "I say we go after the horses," he said sharply. "That stallion alone'd fetch a handsome price, and the other mounts're finer than any of ours. With our pay for this—'' his arm swept out to encompass the slaughter ''—we can all live like kings.'' He moved out of Catrin's sight, then returned leading a horse. "Come on,'' he urged as he climbed into the saddle. "His lordship said we could have all the pickings from this job. That means the horses, too.''

"Aye, Ralph's right,'' another agreed. "We can come back for the rest later. They ain't goin' nowheres.'' He laughed and poked the body at his feet with a fine sword. "Best get what we can. We been cheated already—I had a powerful ache to ride a noble lady, not a damned horse.''

"Ye still could. She won't fight you any.'' They all laughed. Catrin tensed, the motion intensifying the ache spreading from her back.

"She's dead, you idiot. I'm not stickin' my rod in a dead woman! Christ, what fun is that?'' He gave a gusty sigh. "Come on, let's get the horses 'fore they're gone for good.''

To Catrin's relief, they mounted up and rode off, but she feared 'twas a temporary victory. She had to get away before they returned, else she'd be dead in truth.

Or wish she were, she reflected as darkness claimed her once more.

Nicholas lay flat on his back, grateful for the steady drip of cold water onto his face. It soothed his battered flesh and carried him away from the deadly black cloud muddling his mind. Groaning, he rolled onto his side.

A warm, foul breeze wafted across his face. He opened his eyes just as something hot, wet and raspy swept over his cheek.

Was he dead already, and Satan beginning his torment?

Only in the devil's pit would he find himself face-to-face—again—with Lady Catrin's hellhound.

Nicholas recognized Idris immediately, especially from this angle. At least this time the dog's teeth weren't sunk into his throat, and Catrin standing over him, laughing. He blinked in a vain attempt to clear his vision, then propped his head on his hand to stare at the beast. Idris lay sprawled beside him, maw agape and fangs glistening.

'Twas a wonder the dog could move. An arrow protruded from the hound's back, and numerous cuts marred his dark hide. Yet he'd managed to drag himself to Nicholas's side.

Could Nicholas do any less than to search for other survivors?

He shifted and raised his uninjured arm, surprised at how unsteady he felt, and reached over to rub Idris's head. "Why are you here, eh, fellow? Where is your mistress?"

Stomach churning, Nicholas sat up, blinking as his sight alternately blurred and sharpened. By God, he'd felt better after a night of hard drinking! But lying in the drizzle wouldn't cure his ills, nor protect him from the next knave to wander down the road. Cursing the weather, the king and the Welsh with equal venom, he rolled to his knees and pushed himself to his feet.

He had a bad feeling about this situation. If Idris was here, Catrin had to be nearby. Nicholas lurched across the uneven ground toward the fighter he'd seen fall. His balance shifted and he pitched the last few feet, to land hard on his side next to the cloak-covered body sprawled near the underbrush.

He slipped the hood back to reveal a mass of dark, tousled hair. His touch gentle, he eased her face toward him.

Catrin.

Her pale, delicate features, devoid of her usual defiance, brought death to mind. Yet she still lived, her breath a faint mist against his fingers when he touched her lips.

So cold! Her lips had been hot—both to hear and to touch—when last they'd met. The memory of her mouth, so soft beneath his own, had come unbidden into his mind far too often these months past.

He pushed the image aside and smoothed her hair from her face, then turned his attention to the three feathered shafts jutting from her back. "Holy Mary save her," he muttered. Crossbow bolts. Longbow arrows would have been bad enough, but these...

Too often he'd seen men suffer a lingering, pain-filled death from such wounds. He rested his throbbing head on the ground beside her and scanned her face once more.

How could he tell Gillian of her dearest cousin's death?

A moan, a mere wisp of sound, slipped from Catrin's lips, and she opened her eyes. Gone were the flashing silver depths he remembered. In their stead shone pain-glazed pewter, dull and gray. Her gaze flitted about before settling upon his face, so near her own. A spark of recognition flickered to life.

"Nightmare," she mumbled, her voice weak. Her mouth moved aimlessly before curling about the words. "Or death." She swallowed, her tongue darting out to capture a bit of moisture from her lips, as her eyelids drifted closed.

Nicholas pushed himself upright. Shoving the wet hair off his face with a shaking hand, he dragged his attention from Catrin and surveyed the clearing. The fog lent an unnatural glow to the carnage. Nothing moved. All was silent save for the steady drip of water from the trees. Yet he still should examine the bodies, for despite the amount of blood spattered everywhere, someone else might have survived.

Catrin's moan drew his attention once more. He dropped down beside her as she tried to roll to her side and, holding her steady, eased her onto her stomach. "Have a care, else you'll harm yourself more."

"This is real, isn't it?" Even as he nodded, her eyes begged him to disagree. "Cursed knaves attacked us. Not enough guards." She swallowed. "'Tis my fault—all my fault." Moisture pooled in her eyes, but the tears did not fall. "They've gone for the horses—south, I think—but they'll be back. I heard them say so." Her fingers clenched into fists, she sought to push herself up off the ground.

Nicholas grasped her beneath the arms and held her still. "You've three arrows in your back—how do you expect to move?"

"We must go." She sagged within his hold, hands clinging to him for a moment before she tried to shove free. "They'll kill us when they return. Mayhap we can find a horse."

"You're in no condition to ride—"

She pushed against him with more strength. "Don't you understand, you Norman coward? I'd rather die trying to escape than to chance certain death at their hands."

His fingers tightened about her ribs. "No one calls me coward, milady. We'll find a way to escape this place."

Determination steadying him, he gathered Catrin into his arms and carried her to a nearby tree. Though she held her lower lip caught between her teeth until she drew blood, she didn't make a sound.

"By Christ, I've never met a woman like you," he muttered as he set her down. Whether he meant it as a compliment or a curse, even he did not know.

"'Tis your misfortune then, milord." She wrapped her arms about the tree trunk and leaned against it.

Biting back a curse—did her baiting never cease?—he stepped back and eyed her pale face. She sounded more lively than she looked, but he doubted she'd fall into another swoon. "Will you be all right here? I want to see if anyone else survived. 'Twill take but a moment," he added as she nodded.

He moved swiftly about the clearing despite the fact that his head felt no better. The pain did not matter. If he didn't get them safely away soon, an aching head would be the least of his worries.

Only he, Catrin and Idris had survived the attack. Though it galled him to leave Catrin's men where they lay, he could not spare the time—nor the strength—to bury them.

As for the dead outlaws, they deserved their fate.

Catrin's packhorse must have bolted, for all he found were her guards' few belongings scattered across the blood-spattered ground. His own possessions were gone with his stallion, lost to him now.

Feeling like a grave robber, Nicholas removed the threadbare cloaks from Catrin's men. Further search yielded naught but their belts, a flint and a battered cup.

Something rustled in the bushes to his left. He reached for his dagger but came up empty. Before he had time to seek another weapon, a scrawny nag burst through the trees.

Ragged brown coat marred by narrow streaks of blood, nonetheless it appeared uninjured. A crude bridle drooped from its head, reins trailing, and a filthy sheepskin hung lopsided across its bony withers.

Nicholas made soothing noises and stretched his hand toward her. The mare halted before him, hooves shuffling upon the slick grass. After a moment the beast settled down, though her ears flicked back and forth as though she were uncertain whether to heed his entreaties.

Finally the mare heaved a ragged sigh and accepted his touch. Though naught but a rack of bones, she'd carry Catrin away from this abattoir.

"Come to me, my beauty," he coaxed as he grasped the reins. "There, my fine lady." Heaving his own sigh of relief, he laid his head against the mare's neck and stroked her wet, quivering hide. After a brief hesitation she followed him across the clearing to Idris's side.

At Nicholas's touch the hound tried without success to stand. He should have known the dog would share his mistress's stubborn nature. He could almost wish the dog had succumbed to his injuries, for Catrin would never agree to leave her companion behind. Cursing, Nicholas stilled Idris's struggles and hefted him up and onto the mare's back.

Blood trickled down his left arm as the barbed arrow shifted deeper into his flesh. Looping the reins through his belt, he pressed his fingers hard against the mail surrounding the shaft to stop the bleeding and led the mare across the clearing.

Still cursing, he dropped down beside Catrin. Jaw clenched, he gripped the arrow and tried to snap the wooden shaft. The arrowhead ground further into his arm.

Nicholas groaned, the sound piercing Catrin's pain-filled lethargy. She forced her eyes open. "Are you mad?" she shrieked when she saw what he was about. She reached out to stop him but could scarcely lift her arm. "You'll make it worse! You cannot pull—"

"Do you think I know so little?" He let go of the arrow and rose to his knees, shoving his fingers through the sweat-darkened blond curls plastered to his head. "I can't get hold of the damned thing to break it off."

"Lift my hand so I might help you," she said, struggling to shift to a better position.

He shook his head. "You haven't the strength for it."

"Stop wasting time, Talbot, and do it! I'll hold your arm while you snap off the shaft." He didn't appear convinced. "Come—I'm stronger than you give me credit for."

"No doubt you've the might of a warrior," he snarled. "There's little enough that's womanly about you."

"Is that why you kissed me when last we met?" She curled her lips into a shaky smirk. "I've heard that some nobles of the Norman court prefer a manly bedmate."

"Once we're away from here I'll show you what I prefer." Face flushed, he swept his gaze boldly over her. "It appears you have the necessary equipment."

His eyes had darkened to a deep violet, the pupils wide. They reflected more than temper; she'd seen that in his eyes often enough.

Was it pain that shadowed his gaze? Mayhap he'd taken a blow to the head. She doubted the injury to his arm would much affect so powerful a warrior as Nicholas Talbot.

The warmth of his fingers as they closed about her wrist made Catrin realize how chilled she felt. Though the cold had permeated her entire body, it did little to blunt her pain. When Nicholas lifted her hand, agony streaked across her back. She sank her teeth into her lower lip to stifle a groan and forced her fingers to close about his arm.

"If they'd left my knife I could have notched the shaft to weaken it. I need something to break off the arrows in your back, as well."

Catrin dragged her attention from the sinewy strength of Nicholas's arm beneath the cool, rough mail. "My eating knife is on my belt."

He slid the blade from its sheath. "This bauble?" Expression mocking, he examined the dainty, bejeweled dagger.

"Lift my skirts," she told him, her mouth dry.

"Under other circumstances, milady, I'd be pleased to oblige." His smile taunted her. "But now's not the time."

"Arrogant dolt!" Given a choice, she'd not permit him to so much as touch her hand.

But these were not normal times. Raising her chin, she cleared her throat and met his eyes. "Go ahead. I've a blade strapped to my thigh you'll not sneer at."

He held her gaze for a moment, his eyes burning with a strange light. "I doubt there's anything beneath your skirts I'd sneer at," he murmured, his hand already on the hem of her gown. "Which leg?"

"The right." She focused on a dripping branch as he pushed the wet fabric high enough to reveal the scabbard—and most of her leg. An icy weight settled into her stomach, threatening to break free when his knuckles brushed against her skin.

Startled by the warmth of his touch, she shifted her gaze to him. All she could see was the top of his head as he bent over her. "What are you looking at?" she snapped.

He slipped the blade from its worn leather casing, then eased her skirts into place before he glanced up. "'Tis indeed a knife," he said, testing the edge of the blade against his thumb. The corner of his mouth quirked into an uneven smile. "It should serve well."

Covering her hand with his, he tightened his fingers. "Hold fast," he told her. She saw a measure of trust in his eyes, and something more—something she'd never dare acknowledge.

She nodded and gripped his arm. His movements swift, he notched the wood and snapped the thick shaft, tossing it aside. Then, seemingly unaffected, he stood and turned to the horse.

Catrin's heart leapt with joy when she noticed Idris strapped onto the mare's back. Nicholas murmured to the animals as he adjusted the bridle and shifted Idris forward on the sheepskin, binding him in place with a sword belt.

Blood continued to drip from Nicholas's arm. "Shouldn't you bandage that?" she asked as he turned toward her.

"Nay, the bleeding has slowed." He wadded up a cloak and slipped it between her cheek and the tree. "And we must go." He reached behind her and grasped an arrow. "'Tis your turn now, milady. I dare not move you without first cutting back your plumage."

She burrowed her face in the musty fabric and sought to focus her mind on something else.

"Try not to cry out," he taunted. "Shall I gag you?"

Her attention captured—and her hackles raised—she drew a breath to speak, then gasped as molten fire shot through her back.

She clamped her teeth into the coarse material, fighting back a scream. How had he remained silent?

"Two more to go—" she heard before the darkness sucked her into its welcoming embrace once more.

"Thank God," Nicholas sighed, snapping the shafts. 'Twas nothing short of a miracle the damned woman had given in.

He eased her away from the tree, shaking his head at the cloak gripped between her teeth. He tugged the ma-

terial free, swung her into his arms and settled her behind
Idris on the mare's bony back.

After a moment's reflection he tied her on, as well. No
doubt she'd scream at him once she realized what he'd
done, but he'd rather face her wrath than risk her safety
further.

He murmured a swift prayer for the brave souls who
had died to defend their mistress, then added one for the
living for good measure. Scanning the copse once more,
he got his bearings. Catrin said their attackers had gone
south; he hoped to God she was right. Dagger in one hand,
reins in the other, Nicholas headed north.

Chapter Three

Padrig raced through the forest, dodging trees and boulders, paying little heed to the wet branches whipping his head and torso. The cold, damp air tore through his aching throat before settling into his lungs like a cloying blanket, stifling his efforts to breathe.

If only he'd caught the horse Lady Catrin sent him after! But the pain-crazed beast bolted and knocked him to the ground when he grabbed for the reins. Bruised and smeared with blood from the wounded animal, he had no choice but to continue on foot. Though it seemed as if he'd been running forever, he didn't dare stop, not when Lady Catrin and the others needed his help.

The invisible vise around his chest closed so tightly that he could ignore it no longer. Grabbing hold of a sturdy branch with both hands, he bent from the waist and sought to ease the spasms. His breath slipped through his lips in mewling squeaks, bringing tears of frustration to mingle with the rain and sweat streaming down his cheeks.

If he could have spoken he would have cursed. How would he ever become a knight? His body failed him at every turn.

His mind was little better. He should have known that

Lady Catrin—clever as always—would find a way to turn his own words against him. And now his lady suffered grave peril and he could do naught to save her.

He should have stayed with her, he knew it. Lord Ian would have found a way around his sister's dictates; Llywelyn's Dragon was the mightiest warrior in the land. Nor would he have allowed the Norman concept of chivalry to stand in his way, Padrig realized. The Dragon always knew what needed to be done and did it.

Curse his honor—he should have stayed to help Lady Catrin. A wave of guilt swept over him. He could do nothing now except obey her orders, for in his headlong dash through the woods he'd become completely lost.

After the paroxysm eased he filled his lungs, savoring his returning strength. He scanned the mist-shrouded forest to no avail. He'd lost sight of the narrow road almost immediately, and the sky, a solid gray, offered up no clue to direction. For all he knew, he could be near where he started.

What would Lord Ian do?

He might as well go on the same way he'd been headed. And mayhap if he eased his pace he wouldn't have such trouble breathing. Squaring his shoulders, Padrig wiped his face on the edge of his tunic and set off toward civilization.

He hoped.

Nicholas plodded along the faint trail through the underbrush, the mare following along with little guidance. Despite the chill air, sweat beaded upon his face as his head throbbed in a nauseating cadence.

His mail hauberk, usually no burden, seemed to have become heavier as the day wore on, adding to his discomfort. He should be thankful the bandits hadn't taken the time to divest him of it, for if they had realized he still lived, his life would have been forfeit. Why they'd left Catrin alone, he did not know, but he thanked God for it.

Not only had they spared her life, but they'd unwittingly left him the means to protect her, as well. He touched the dagger strapped to his waist—a fine piece, not the usual bauble a lady might wear. 'Twas their good fortune that Catrin was not a typical lady. Though why she felt the need to arm herself thus...

It couldn't replace his sword, or the other weapons his stallion carried, but mayhap it would suffice, should the thieving bastards catch up to them.

His gaze was drawn yet again to Catrin. She lay cradled against Idris's massive body—Nicholas could almost believe the dog held her nestled there apurpose—and though she moaned every so often, she did not move. While the fact that she'd remained in a swoon for so long could not be a good sign, nevertheless it allowed them to continue on their way uninterrupted.

As the gray daylight began to fade, much of the thick underbrush gave way to rock covered by a thin layer of soil. Tall, slim trees grew from seams in the rocks, filling in the spaces between towering firs. The trail rose steeply, and he heard the sound of rushing water nearby.

Catrin's moans grew louder, and he drew the mare to a halt, pulling the hood back from her face. "Damnation!" A rosy flush covered her cheeks and spread down to disappear into the neck of her bliaut. He yanked off his heavy leather gauntlet and laid his palm against her forehead.

Heat radiated from her skin. Though he knew next to nothing about sickness, he couldn't mistake her condition. Catrin needed help.

Tucking the cloak about her, he cast a swift glance at

their surroundings. He had to find shelter, food and water before it got dark. God help them if their attackers were on their trail, for he could ignore Catrin's injuries no longer.

He led the mare toward the sound of running water. As soon as he found a defensible place to set up camp, he'd stop.

The mare's ears twitched forward as they crested the hill and found the stream. She picked up her pace and nudged Nicholas in the shoulder as if urging him to greater speed, not stopping until she bent to drink.

Catrin slipped sideways, but Nicholas caught her before she fell. Her eyelids fluttered open and she looked about in confusion before focusing upon Nicholas's face. "Where are we?"

He slid his hand beneath her head to support it. "I wish I knew. I tried to head north, though there's not much to go by for direction."

"My back is afire."

Her back was not the only thing afire. Her fever raged—the flesh beneath his palm felt hot, and her lips were dry and cracked. "I'll get you some water," he said, easing her head onto Idris's back.

He knelt beside the stream to fill the cup, pausing to splash the icy water over his aching head. When he returned to Catrin, he found her scanning their surroundings with a surprising intensity, despite the pain that still clouded her eyes.

She gulped the water as soon as he raised her head to drink, then drained the cup twice more before indicating she'd had enough.

Idris lifted his massive head and whined, eliciting a faint smile from Catrin. "Don't forget about him," she whispered.

As if he could, Nicholas thought as he tended the dog. So long as he and Catrin were in the same place and Idris yet lived, the beast would protect his mistress.

Though the dog's vigilance might stand them in good stead.

Nicholas cast another glance at the darkening sky. He could delay no longer. He drew Catrin's hood about her face and bound her more tightly to the mare, then took up the reins and headed upstream.

If they couldn't find shelter somewhere along the stream, he could build a lean-to. He began to gather branches and sticks from beneath the trees along the path—'twould do for a fire, at the least.

Awake now, and refreshed by the water Talbot had given her, Catrin peered out from beneath her hood, concentrating upon their surroundings. What she saw made her heart beat faster.

"Talbot," she called. He didn't answer—no surprise, since her voice had come out so weak she'd scarce heard it herself. She cleared her throat and tried again. "Damn you, Talbot. We must stop."

He dropped an armload of wood onto the ground and spun to face her. "Must we indeed, milady? There is much we must do, aye—find food and shelter, tend your wounds—but I doubt that stopping here will accomplish anything. Lest it escape your attention, 'tis nigh dark, and I've no place to—"

"I think I know where we are."

Talbot stalked toward her, stripping off his gloves and tucking them into his belt. "You know where we are." He slid his hands—so cool against her heated skin—over her cheeks and sank his fingers into her hair. "When did you intend to tell me?" Leaning close, he stared into her eyes. "Or do you enjoy wandering through the forest with arrows in your back?"

Catrin moistened her lips. His expression frightened her nearly as much as the feel of his flesh against hers. But she held his gaze. His violet eyes took their intensity from the lengthening shadows, she told herself. And 'twas the chill air that sent a shiver sweeping over her, nothing more.

She swallowed, her fear a choking lump slipping down her throat to weigh heavy in her stomach and gnaw at her mettle.

But she'd not permit Nicholas Talbot to see her fear.

Never would a man make her cringe and cower again.

His mouth was so close to hers, she felt every breath he took. Her own breath shuddered in her chest. She wet her lips once more. "I may know this place, but I cannot be sure. Pray lift me up so I might see."

Talbot released her with an alacrity she might have found amusing if she hadn't been so relieved. His movements jerky, he went to tie the reins to a tree, then returned to her side.

He pushed aside her enveloping cloak and slipped his hands about her waist. "I know how you hate to depend upon anyone," he taunted as he lifted her. Thankfully his voice masked the whimper she couldn't suppress. "But you'll have to lean on me. It seems you have no choice."

How she hurt! Catrin caught her breath as Talbot settled her against the rough mail covering his chest, one arm beneath her breasts holding her upright. "There's always a choice," she mumbled. "Unless you're dead."

Though his arm tightened about her, he made no reply.

The trees spun before her for a moment, then righted themselves as the dizziness passed. "Was there a cleft rock to the right of the stream, with a rowan tree growing out of the crack?''

"I saw such a stone. I don't know what kind of tree grew from it," he said, "but how many such could there be?"

"You don't know the rowan?" she asked, unable to resist taunting him. "'Tis said to protect against demons—I'm surprised you're not more familiar with it."

"If you don't cease your prattle, woman, you'll soon wish you were in a tree. Mouthy wench!" He drew his hand through his hair, smoothing back the damp blond waves. "What would it take to quiet you?"

She smiled at the question she'd heard countless times before. "Short of death, nothing."

"Your brother should take you into battle with him— he could use your tongue as a weapon. I'd wager 'twould serve as well as a sword." Talbot shook his head. "You could cleave a man in two. 'Tis no wonder you're not wed."

Catrin seethed with frustration. "If I had my knife—"

"'Twould serve you naught. You cannot even hold a knife, let alone use it. Besides, you couldn't harm me—" he cast a look of distrust at Idris "—even if you weren't wounded."

"I'll show you what I can do once I'm well," she growled. He'd be surprised if he knew just what she was capable of. A wave of cold passed through her, making her shudder. Not that she'd ever tell...

"That will give you reason to recover, I've no doubt." His smile faded. "Enough of this. Do you recognize this place or not?"

She glanced around once more. The area looked familiar. It reminded her of a place where she and Ian had waited out a violent summer storm years before. "I believe there's a rock cairn up ahead, at the top of this rise. The cave in the hillside should do for shelter. 'Twas a shrine long ago, a place sacred to the Old Ones. No harm will come to us there.''

She regretted her last comment when she caught Talbot's piercing look, but he said nothing as he eased her back down onto the mare and took up the reins. After one last, lingering glance at the sky, he gathered up his meager pile of sticks and continued along the trail.

Once more Catrin cursed her impetuous tongue. Talbot had told her without words that they'd lingered to bicker too long. She still couldn't be sure she knew where they were, but, please God, let her be right!

Now that she was no longer distracted by Talbot's barbs, her injuries reclaimed her attention. Flames seemed to radiate from the arrowheads, sending waves of heat to flow over her entire body, leaving a pulsing pain in their wake.

She snuggled against Idris's coarse coat and took comfort from the steady beat of his heart beneath her cheek. If they did not starve to death, at least her faithful companion might survive once Talbot saw to his injuries. Though she lacked the energy to lift her hand, she twined her fingers into the dog's fur. Idris whined in response. He was more than a pet, he was companion, guardian, confidant—the loyal repository of all her hopes and fears.

There were some things Catrin could never share with anyone, not even Gillian or Ian. The shameful secrets from her past would distress them, and for naught. She could not change what she had done—would not, even if she could. But neither would she endanger those she loved by stirring up things better left alone.

Yet her actions today had endangered other innocent souls, caused the deaths of several people. Had her past taught her nothing? Uncharacteristic tears ran down her cheeks to soak into Idris's curly hide. Her mere presence posed a threat to anyone near her.

Even Talbot, aggravating as he'd been in the past, didn't deserve to be saddled with her now.

She could change—nay, would change—if she survived this latest coil. 'Twas more likely she'd die and burn in hell for her sins. At the very least, God in his vengeance would want her to suffer; a swift, clean death could not possibly be punishment enough.

It mattered naught.

'Twas no more than she deserved.

Chapter Four

The bandits met on the trail in late afternoon. Their leader, Ralph, sat atop the knight's stallion, a fine embroidered tunic pulled over his filthy, ragged shirt and leggings. The remaining garments in the knight's pack tempted him mightily. Soft, bright-colored wools and silks, of a quality he'd never seen even in those far-off years when he'd been a tailor's apprentice.

But the take belonged to them all, and though nominally the leader of this ever shrinking band of outlaws, Ralph knew he couldn't bedeck himself in the finery unless he wanted a revolt on his hands. And he'd no intention of losing his neck over a shirt and a pair of hose.

"'Tis a fine day, lads, a fine day indeed," he said, the three remaining fingers of his right hand caressing the jeweled sword laid across his lap. What a pity he couldn't wield the weapon, but 'twas too big for his maimed grip. Ah, well, no use crying over what he couldn't change. "We've ne'er taken such a prize as this."

"Aye, 'tis fine for you, Ralph," Ned piped up, shifting his gaunt frame atop an equally scrawny palfrey. "Look at all you've got."

"What are you worried about?" Ralph asked. "Everyone'll get his share, same as always. 'Tis good pickings, the best we've seen in a long time. And now there's fewer of us, there's more to go around. Once we collect the rest of it, we'll go see his high-and-mighty lordship and get paid what's owed us." Tugging on the reins and kicking mightily at the stallion's ribs with his soft-soled shoes, Ralph urged the horse into motion and led the way to the clearing.

Confusion reigned as they burst into the meadow. Not one of them had ever handled a mount with any spirit—indeed, some could scarce ride at all, a fact that had already cost the lives of two of their band. Fortunately the horses, foam-flecked and blown, had passed from rebellion to exhaustion. Even so, Ralph and his men had learned to be more cautious now.

"Quiet," Ralph bellowed. "Come, let's be about our business and be on our way. I'm frozen to the marrow."

Ned hopped down from the saddle and ran across the clearing. "By Christ's balls, they're gone," he cried as he darted from one spot to another. "Look, you, the knight and the wench both. The bastard took the hauberk, too." He bent to examine two of their fallen comrades who lay in a pool of blood. "Even the damned dog is gone," he said, his squeaky voice rising higher still.

He stopped beside the dead guards, nudging one body with his foot, then kicking it. "Nothin'. We already took what they had." He turned to the others, standing silent now in the middle of the clearing. "Weren't much, neither. But I wanted that hauberk."

"Would've been too big fer ye anyway, Ned. Got no more meat on ye than a chicken," Alf said. He staggered about as though carrying a great weight on his shoulders. "Can't ye just see it, lads?" Everyone laughed but Ned. "You wouldn't've been able to move."

"Someone else took them while we were gone. Robbed us, they did," Ned said. He turned to Ralph. "How're we goin' to get paid without the wench?"

Ralph ignored Ned's whining and walked around the meadow, stooping every so often to examine the ground. "Someone rode out—one horse," he told them. "'Twas that rack o' bones you 'ad, Ned, what looked like you. I'd recognize that track anywhere. No one took 'em." He shook his head, laughing at Ned's ire. Likely no one but himself would see the humor in robbing a thief. "Mayhap that knight carted the woman and dog away to bury them. I hear tell the nobles are odd that way, always doin' things the way the priests tell 'em."

Ned looked up at the darkening sky. "Ye mean we have ta go after him? We can't track him in the dark," he added. "I don't want ta tangle wi' him again, not over a bloody corpse. Took all of us ta nab him before, and there ain't so many of us now."

The others greeted Ned's words with a chorus of agreement. Ralph shook his head and grabbed Ned by the front of his tunic. "What are you, a mouse? He's naught but a man, same as us." He tossed Ned to the soggy turf and eyed the others. "If I say you go after him, you will. D'ye understand?" He gave the nearest man a shove. "But it so happens we won't. We weren't hired to kill him, so there's no sense bothering with him. He can't get far anyway—his head's likely cracked like an egg."

He pulled a fine dagger from his belt and began cleaning his nails with it. "Besides, the wench was dead. We all saw her." The men nodded. "So we tell his lordship she's dead. He couldn't expect us to stroll into his keep with her body, now, could he?"

"What if he don't believe us?"

Ralph shrugged. "We tell him to come see for hisself.

Of course, it ain't like to be a pretty sight once the wolves get to her, eh, lads?'' He snorted. "He won't bestir himself. Wants to keep his hands clean—'tis why he hired us. Can't have it said he murdered his kin, after all.''

"But what if he wants proof, Ralph?"

"Christ, Ned, can't you do anything but complain? Keep it up and we'll be splitting your share, as well," he warned. He turned to the overburdened packhorse hitched to the stallion's saddle and began removing bundles. "Anyone find the lady's baggage?"

"There's some clothes in the big pack on the bottom, and that small wooden box is full of dry leaves and smelly potions.'' Alf pulled the packs from the horse and opened them. "This be enough?"

Ralph pawed through the garments, frowning as his rough hands snagged the finely woven silks. "Aye, take out a couple gowns—not the best ones, mind you—they'll fetch a good price in Chester. No sense wasting it all on his lordship. He'll have to take our word for it the wench is dead, or come see for himself. And he won't." He stuffed the remaining clothes back into the pack and laced it tight against the damp, then hoisted it onto the horse.

He stretched, grimacing at the pain burning in his joints. "I'm getting too old for chasing through the wood in the cold and wet. Mayhap after today's work we can retire. We could live like kings on the jewels from this sword alone."

Spying the wooden box on the ground, he picked it up and opened it. "Pah—what a stench!" he gasped. Worse than a midden in the summer sun. Why a noble lady would cart such as this around, he didn't know. He dug through the contents, then dumped everything out and examined the inlaid lid. "'Tis a pretty piece—it might fetch something if we can get rid of the smell."

He tossed it to Ned. "Put it with the rest. Then you, John and Alf take the good horses and head for Chester. We don't want his lordship to steal our hard-earned booty—and he would, the scum. 'Sides, there's no good way to explain how we come by it, short of the truth. I'd just as soon not hang. I've learned my lesson 'bout thieving," he said, holding up his hands. "Don't get caught at it."

The others laughed, but he could sense their fear. "Have a care," he warned. "Them horses're more than you're used to. We don't want to lose them. The rest of us'll go get our pay, then meet you in Chester."

Ned snatched up the reins and stood scowling. "What's to keep you from makin' off with our money?"

Ralph shoved him to the ground and kicked him in the ribs. "Don't be a fool." He nudged him again. "What you're taking with you is likely worth a hundred times more than what that little prick is payin' us."

Casting a last, longing look at the stallion, Ralph went instead to one of the poorer horses and mounted up. "We'll see you in Chester," he said, waiting until the three rode away before heading southeast for a confrontation with his bloody lordship.

The last rays of the setting sun broke through the clouds as Nicholas and the mare topped the hill. He hoped the sudden burst of light was a sign their luck was about to change. God knew they needed fortune to smile upon them; he had much to do, and next to nothing with which to do it.

A cairn stood before a stone-framed opening in the hill tall enough to admit a man. Moss-shrouded dirt, lightly studded with bushes, covered the crown of the hill, and a spring—the origin of the stream—spilled from the ground near the entrance. It looked like something from the land of fairy, the stone portal shimmering through the mist. Though not a fanciful man, Nicholas hoped they'd find some magic here, if such a thing existed.

He dropped the wood he'd gathered near the cave, then tied the mare to a sturdy bush before turning to Catrin. When he drew the hood away from her face he spied the tear tracks on her cheek. His fingers crept out of their own volition to smooth the marks away. She'd made no sound—even in her current state, she'd too much pride to let him hear her cry.

Pride he understood, being overburdened with it himself. How else had she found the strength to lash out at him? Any other woman would have remained in a swoon since the attack, or at the least complained of the pain. Though he wouldn't have thought less of her had she reacted thus, he was grateful she had not.

Lady Catrin might be the most aggravating woman he'd ever encountered, but he could not deny the exhilaration he felt whenever they clashed.

He refused to permit the bright glow of Lady Catrin uerch Dafydd to fade away.

Dirk in hand, he clambered over the rock-strewn mouth of the cave and stooped to pass through the doorway. In the faint light he discovered a stone-lined chamber tall enough for him to stand upright, the remnants of a fire pit in the middle. The dirt floor felt smooth and even, as though it bore the imprint of countless feet.

They'd be safe here while he fought the battle to save Lady Catrin's life.

Reassured, Nicholas hurried to move her inside. Hands numb with cold, he fumbled with the wet leather until the knot gave way and she slid from the mare and slumped against him. Even her slight weight sent a jolt of pain through his upper arm, reminding him that his own wound would need tending eventually.

But he had more important work to do for the nonce.

She moaned as he shifted her in his arms. He could almost believe she'd reached the end of her mettle—almost, but for the fact that he'd never dare underestimate her strength of will. And though 'twould be easier to treat her injuries if she remained in a swoon, he doubted he'd be so fortunate. More likely she'd awaken in a moment, ready to flay him with her tongue.

She felt so small, so dainty as he carried her into the cave. He'd forgotten that she barely reached his shoulder, for the force of her personality made her appear taller, stronger than he knew her to be.

Nicholas wrestled her cloak around to place beneath her and eased her onto her stomach, bringing her arm up to cushion her face. Straightening, he wiped sweat from his brow and went outside for the dog.

Somehow Idris had managed to get off the horse. He leaned against the mare, legs aquiver, his massive head drooping almost to the ground. Nicholas rushed toward him in time to catch him as he fell.

Cursing his two stubborn charges, Nicholas hefted the dog into his arms and lugged him inside. When he laid Idris down on the far side of the fire pit, the dog stared at his mistress and whined. "Don't worry, I'll take care of her," Nicholas said, ruffling the animal's coarse fur.

He worked swiftly in the dying light to gather kindling and arrange it beneath the wood in the fire pit. Then, scarcely able to see, he tended the mare, murmuring praise all the while. She'd borne a heavy burden today—had likely saved their lives. He wished he could give her grain and a warm stable to reward her as she deserved. Instead he led her to the stream to drink, then rubbed her down with a handful of dry grass and left her to crop beneath the trees. They'd have need of her again, of that he had no doubt.

He only hoped 'twas a living woman she'd carry back to civilization.

Hands shaking with weariness, Nicholas paused just inside the cave and took a deep breath. In his present state, he feared he'd do naught but harm Catrin in his attempts to help her.

But without his help, she would surely die.

He groped his way to the fire pit and fumbled with the flint and steel until he managed to wheedle a spark from it. After several tries the tinder caught; he hovered over the tiny blaze, tending it carefully until the flames licked at the small mound of wood.

Catrin mumbled something, the words indistinct. The flickering light glinted upon her sweat-dampened brow and highlighted the pain etched upon her face. He could delay no longer.

Taking up a pitch-covered branch he'd found outside, he held it amidst the flames until the end glowed. Thrust into a crack in the stone wall, it cast a bright light throughout the entire cavern.

How should he proceed?

Calm spread through him as the fire began to warm the chamber. Hands steady, he gathered his meager supplies and sought to draw his wits together, as well. Two knives, flint and steel, cup, belt, a cracked wooden bowl he'd discovered in a corner.... Were these enough to save Catrin's life?

Even a simple barber had better tools than this.

Had Catrin worn a purse upon her belt? Though he had not noticed, what woman left her chamber without one, fairly bulging with God knew what?

She moaned as he eased her onto her side and moved her nearer to the fire. Just as he'd suspected, a soft leather pouch hung from her leather girdle by a silver chain. Afraid to let his hopes rise too high, he unhooked the chain and loosened the drawstrings.

He hesitated but a moment before he tipped the contents onto the floor. A surprising assortment of items spilled out. Most looked useless for his purposes, but a small wooden case, smoothly carved with fanciful designs, caught his attention. Lady Gillian carried her needles and pins in a similar box. A spindle of thread lay beside it.

He fumbled to loosen the lid and sent the contents showering onto Catrin's cloak in a shimmering cascade.

She cursed, capturing his attention. He hadn't realized she was awake. "Have a care," she whispered. "Needles are costly, and easily lost."

"Aye, milady." Squinting as his vision blurred, he bent to pick them up. "At the moment they're more valuable to me than all the king's riches." He dropped the last pin into the box and replaced the lid. "Now I can care for your wounds."

Her eyes widened, a spark—of fear, perhaps—making them shine silver in the firelight. "You do know how to sew, don't you?"

Nicholas's lips curved into a genuine smile. "I've seen it done before." He shrugged. "Perhaps it's time I learned."

Chapter Five

"What do you intend to do?" Catrin asked. Panic lent her the strength to move so she could better see his face.

"I must remove the arrows from your back, and soon," he said as he pawed through the contents of her purse. "You've a fever, if it's escaped your notice. And I doubt you could remove them yourself, at any rate."

A shudder racked her body, whether from fever or the thought of Nicholas Talbot wielding a knife upon her flesh, she could not say. She doubted he'd ever performed surgery on anything other than some hapless fowl at table.

And her back was no sampler for him to display his prowess with a needle!

But what choice did she have?

Impossible as she found it, she had to entrust herself to a man; a man, moreover, more confusing to her than anyone she'd ever met. This could only be reparation from a vengeful God for every sin she'd ever committed—and possibly some she'd only contemplated.

Sweat beaded upon her forehead, and a flood of heat poured through her veins. She could withstand this—she'd suffered worse before and survived.

At least Talbot meant her no harm.

"There's a small pouch—the green one—it holds a mixture of herbs. 'Tis good for pain or fever." She nodded when he picked it out of the pile on the cloak. "You must steep it in hot water."

He wavered as he rose to his feet, and his eyes closed for a moment as though his head pained him. "You should take some, as well," she added.

Talbot set both knives to heat in the fire, then took up the cup and a bowl and left the cave. Catrin stared at the flames leaping merrily before her and tried not to worry as she considered what Talbot must do. She had removed arrows from hardened warriors, some of whom had screamed worse than a woman in childbirth. And though she prided herself upon her control, her strength of will, she had no idea whether she could withstand Talbot's surgery without shaming herself before him.

She feared such weakness more than the pain.

Talbot knelt beside her, startling her. "What should I do?" he asked.

"Add three pinches to the water, then stir it with the knife."

The water hissed as he plunged the blade into the cup, and a bitter scent filled the air. Talbot wrinkled his nose, but wrapped his fingers about the mug for a moment. Still grimacing, he held up her head and brought the draft to her lips.

She swallowed the potion swiftly, grateful for even so foul a drink as this. 'Twould not take long before she began to feel the effects....

She wrapped her fingers about his brawny wrist when he lowered her to the floor. "Best if you wait to take some," she cautioned. "It might make you sleep."

"Will it make you sleep?" He set the cup aside and brushed her tangled hair away from her face. His fingers felt blessedly cool, hard yet gentle against her heated flesh, and his eyes glowed pale lavender against his tanned skin.

Never had he turned so tender—so pitying—a look her way. She wasn't sure she cared for the way it made her feel.

"Perhaps," she whispered. His pulse beat strong and sure beneath her fingertips, making her more aware of his nearness, his size. She opened her hand and released him. "It matters naught—just do what you must."

The light went out of his eyes at her tone and he turned away, leaving her bereft. She rested her head on her arm and watched Talbot's preparations. Mayhap the potion had affected her after all, for a strange, calm sensation seemed to flow through her body.

The firelight shimmered upon Talbot's golden hair and threw the angles of his face into sharp relief. When had he become so appealing? She'd always known he was handsome—she wasn't blind—but something about him had changed.

Or perhaps she had changed. The potion blurred her mind, 'twas all. Never had she taken it when fevered... Mayhap it had addled her brain.

"The needle will do no good if I cannot thread it," he muttered in Welsh. "Finally," he cried, his voice rich with satisfaction.

"What did you say?" She frowned. Had he spoken to her in Welsh before?

"I said..."

"Nay." Her lips curled carefully about the word, slow to respond. "Have you been speaking Welsh?"

"I have." He knelt beside her. "Does it matter?"

"Didn't know you could." When he reached out to

push her hair away from her face she leaned into his stroking hand like a cat.

His gaze met hers. Amusement lit the depths of his eyes, their color darkened to indigo. "There's much you don't know about me." He eased her over onto her stomach and helped her rest her face on her folded arms.

Catrin fought the shadows taking hold of her mind, but the battle was nearly lost. Her limbs felt heavy, weighted. "Can't think. This never happened to me..." Warm and relaxed, she sank further into the comforting darkness and thought no more.

Nicholas sent up a prayer of thanks as he watched her slide into sleep. He'd feared she might lay there, awake and watchful, while he sliced away at her flesh—finding fault with everything he did, no doubt. As it was, he felt a fool. A knight—a former mercenary, by God—who had done his best to skewer the enemy at every turn, hesitant to use a knife to save another's life.

He had to work swiftly, for he'd no notion how long she might sleep. His fingers felt clumsy as he struggled to knot the thread. Vision gone blurry once more, he closed his eyes and willed himself to stillness. If his hands didn't stop shaking, he'd do her more harm than good.

Feeling somewhat better, he took up the cup and returned to the stream. It was full dark now. A crescent moon hovered over the horizon, playing amongst the clouds scudding across the sky. Somewhere in the forest an owl hooted, perfect accompaniment to the howl of the rising wind.

'Twas a night made for magic; he hoped 'twould help him in his labors. He knelt beside the spring and slaked his thirst, then scooped water over his aching head. The shocking cold helped clear his senses. Casting a last look around, he went back to the cave.

Catrin slept on undisturbed while he built up the fire and prepared his meager supplies. Idris remained against the far wall where Nicholas had placed him, his gaze fixed with steadfast devotion upon his mistress. Nicholas shifted the torch to a better spot, then settled down at Catrin's side.

He could delay no longer.

He eased off her cloak, slipping the fabric over the broken-off arrows before turning his attention to the laces on each side of her bliaut. Even after he loosened them, he couldn't remove her gown, so he cut a neat slit down the back. 'Twas ruined anyway, but he tried to preserve it enough for decency's sake. Her undertunic laced up the back, simple enough to roll down over her arms to her waist.

When he loosened her chemise and pushed it aside, still another layer of fabric covered her from armpit to waist. Now he understood why her wounds had not bled freely; this garment—whatever it was—was wrapped so tight, it acted as a bandage.

"Thank God you're not awake," he murmured as he reached beneath her in search of the fastenings. "Please stay that way." A twist of his hand and he found the knot and loosened it.

Soft, yielding flesh sprang free as he tugged the stiff material apart.

If she woke now, he was a dead man.

His fingers brushed against an ample pair of breasts. He grinned. Never would he have imagined that such bounty lay beneath her modest gown.

Enough! he censured his unruly mind. He was no green boy, to be set off by a bosom, no matter how impressive. Frowning, he turned his attention to working the binding over the arrow shafts.

The garment had likely saved Catrin's life, for the stiff fabric had kept the arrows from sinking too deep. And despite the rusty streaks of blood that marred the smooth ivory skin of her back, the wounds had bled little.

One arrow tip lay half-buried in her flesh, its barbs still exposed—a simple matter to remove. The other two, unfortunately, were embedded to the shaft. He'd have to cut them free.

Red streaks ran from the crusted wounds, and the flesh around the crudely molded arrowheads felt hot and swollen. Nicholas drew the cloak up over her and sat back upon his heels, cudgeling his scrambled brain for any knowledge he could use.

There had been an incident in the Holy Land. Though he'd been little more than a lad, he had never forgotten it. A Saracen healer of great renown had traveled with them for a time, bartering his medical skills in return for their protection. Nicholas had watched, fascinated, as he removed a deeply embedded crossbow quarrel from a soldier's back, a man who survived to die in an angry whore's bed not six months later, he recalled wryly.

What had the healer done?

The Saracen had washed his hands, the knife and the injury, then passed the knife and needle through a flame before he used them. Nicholas had never seen any barber or chirurgeon do that before or since. The bandages had been clean, as well, he recalled, the white fabric a startling contrast to the victim's sun-browned skin. And after cutting the arrow loose, the healer allowed the wound to bleed freely before he sewed it closed, applied an unguent and bandaged it.

Though Nicholas had no salve to soothe Catrin's wounds, the rest he could manage. His spirits lighter, he hacked a wide strip from the hem of Catrin's chemise and tore it into strips. He set the bowl of water beside the fire to warm, then took the knives outside and scrubbed them—and his hands—as best he could in the icy stream.

When he returned to the cave he plunged both knives blade-deep into the glowing coals, pausing a moment with hands outstretched to the fire's warmth while he reviewed his memories yet again. But he remembered nothing more.

A sheen of sweat dampened Catrin's brow, and the flush upon her face owed little to the fire's heat. She hadn't moved since he'd loosened her clothing. He'd get no better chance than this.

But she stirred when he folded back the cloak and began to wash the area around the arrows, her low-voiced moan sending a chill up his spine. What if she struggled once he cut her? He had worries enough without having to wrestle a pain-maddened woman into submission. Hesitating but a moment, he bound her wrists together with a lace from her gown.

If that didn't work, he could always kneel on her.

Nicholas drew a deep breath and let it out slowly, readying himself in the same way he would prepare for battle. Eyes closed, he concentrated until a sense of calm flowed through him. Breathing deeply again, he snatched Catrin's eating knife from the fire and set to work.

The shallowly embedded arrow popped free with but a nudge of the blade, leaving a faint trail of blood in its wake. Should he make the wound bleed more? Could he halt the flow once it began?

If only he knew what in God's name he was doing!

If cleanliness had been the key to the Saracen's success, he'd follow its dictates completely. Muttering a plea to the Virgin, he pressed on the cut until a bright trickle oozed forth to wash out the wound.

Lower lip gripped tight between his teeth, Nicholas

bent closer to Catrin's back and slipped the slim blade into her flesh next to the shaft. "Don't move," he muttered, pushing the knife deeper despite the way her back tensed.

Blood spurted free and ran in a rivulet over her ribs. When he pressed a wad of fabric against her to stanch the flow, she arched her back and screamed.

"Stop, Catrin," he said. "You must not move." She continued to squirm, so he pinned her down and swiftly extended the cut. He tried to work the arrow loose, but 'twas difficult to grasp the short, slick shaft—he'd cut off too much, leaving scarcely enough to grab hold of.

Catrin continued to writhe beneath him, mumbling and moaning as he fought to remove the arrow. Her struggles he could deal with, but to hear her distress... He snatched up one of his leather gauntlets and stuffed it between her teeth.

The arrowhead ground against bone, feeling much the same as ramming a blade into someone's gullet. Cursing, Nicholas took up the knife once more and, still tugging at the shaft, widened the cut until the arrowhead broke free.

He blotted away the worst of the blood and pressed on the cut as he heated the needle in the flames, nearly scorching his fingers in the process. When he turned back to Catrin he found her staring at him, her eyes awash with tears. But he saw no recognition there, only anger and pain.

'Twas just as well she didn't recognize him—her opinion of him had been low enough before the day's events. Christ only knew what she'd think of him after this.

It mattered not, so long as she survived.

Squinting, he focused his still-blurry gaze upon the oozing wound. "Pretend 'tis a shirt," he ordered himself as

he stabbed the needle into Catrin's flesh. She gave a muffled shriek. "Not bloody likely."

He set the stitches with mechanical precision, doing his
best to ignore the way she flinched with each jab of the
needle. By the time he finished he was nearly sitting on
her legs to hold her down, and still she squirmed beneath
him.

She must have the strength of a warrior to put up such
a struggle. And he could well imagine the litany of abuse
she called down upon him. At least he couldn't understand
any of it.

Still sprawled over her, he made short work of removing the third arrow. Hands shaking, he wet a rag in the
bowl of water and swabbed away the last of the blood.
The warm cloth seemed to soothe her, and she ceased her
struggles.

He ventured a glance at her face; eyes closed, mouth
silent, she seemed to have finally reached the end of her
endurance. He made swift work of bandaging the cuts,
then tugged her shift and tunic up over her back with a
sigh of relief.

Legs shaking, Nicholas went to check on Idris. The dog
slept, apparently resting comfortably despite his injuries.
He decided to leave him thus till morning.

His own wound could be left till then, as well, but he
had to get out of his hauberk. Having slept in it before,
he knew he'd regret doing so again. He bent at the waist
and tugged the neckline over his head to allow the weight
of the mail to pull it off.

A wave of dizziness washed over him. Arm aflame,
head reeling, Nicholas pitched forward onto his hauberk
and knew no more.

Chapter Six

Bryn Du, Northern Wales

Lord Steffan ap Rhys jerked the bedcovers up over his shoulders and burrowed his head beneath the pile of bolsters, but the pounding at his door did not cease. He poked at the woman sprawled beside him. "Answer that, you lazy bitch."

The slut moaned, rolled over and slid her leg over his hips as she edged closer to him. "Get up," he snarled, grabbing her by the leg and thrusting her aside. Lips curled in a frown, he shoved the blankets away and climbed from the bed.

A slap on her fleshy buttocks worked well enough to move her off the mattress. "Why are you still here?" He snatched up her gown and threw it at her. Judging from the leisurely way she dressed, his displeasure didn't disturb her one whit. He'd teach her better next time, he vowed, blood heating at the thought. "Answer the door on your way out."

She tossed her tangled hair over her shoulder and sent him a gap-toothed grin. "Aye, milord." Hips swaying, she ambled across the room, then spun about to face him. Her avid gaze caressed his body, lingering on his engorged manhood. "Certain ye want me to leave just yet?"

Did she count herself responsible for this, his usual morning state? Witless bitch! He stepped into his chausses and pulled them up. "Do as I said and go about your duties," he snarled.

Jerking the door open, she flounced past Huw, the captain of the guard.

"There's a fine piece," Huw said as he entered the chamber and shut the door behind him.

"You're welcome to her." Steffan slipped into his shirt. "She hasn't a brain in her head, but she's skilled enough between the sheets."

Huw smirked. "She don't need a brain for what I have in mind. So long's she's got the right parts, she'll suit me fine."

"I assume you've a reason for dragging me from my bed. And you needn't look so pleased with yourself, you fool—I'll not tolerate your arrogance for long." Despite his displeasure, Steffan kept his tone bland, but something in his voice must have alerted the other man. Huw's expression grew serious and he straightened, assuming the mien of subservience.

Steffan permitted himself a faint smile.

"That fellow Ralph is here, milord, with two of his men." Huw spoke in a flat tone quite unlike his previous jocularity. "Says he's got something for you."

"Indeed." Being forced from his bed at dawn just might have merit after all. "Bring them to me." He paused, waiting until Huw was ready to go out the door. "Bring me bread and wine, as well."

That order did not sit well upon him, Steffan noted as Huw fled the room.

'Twas clearly time to show him who was master here.

Steffan scratched at his chest and savored the successful completion of his latest strategy. He'd tried three times to bring Catrin within his grasp, and three times he'd failed.

This time he would succeed.

Since subtlety hadn't worked in the past, brute force might—nay, would—grant him a full measure of success. Rumor had it that the scum he'd hired were the best.

Catrin would be within his grasp soon.

He did hope they hadn't killed her. There were so many experiences he wished to share with his dear cousin before she died.

The mere thought cheered him immensely.

He'd had little time to put his plan into motion, but the idea had been stewing in his mind for months— ever since his faithless cousin Gillian had escaped him. He rubbed the back of his head. It had taken nearly that long for the lump Gillian had dealt him to disappear. But time had not eased his anger at her perfidy, nor Catrin's part in it.

Gillian stood beyond his reach for the moment.

But Catrin...

He settled into the commodious seat of a thronelike chair, fingers gripping the carved armrests. By Christ's bones, he could scarcely wait to get his hands upon the traitorous bitch.

A racket at the door brought his pleasant dreams to a halt. Huw shouldered his way into the chamber, tray in hand, clearly unhappy with the menial chore. Three men followed him into the room.

"Leave that here and get out," Steffan told him.

Once Huw left, Steffan lounged back into the cushions and gazed at the men. They appeared nervous—not a good sign. However, Ralph stepped forward easily enough at Steffan's signal.

"You've something for me, Ralph?" He could scarcely contain his anticipation.

Ralph took a rough cloth bag from one of the men, opened it and pulled out a woman's bliaut.

"What is this?"

"'Tis one of your lady's gowns, milord." Ralph removed another from the sack and held it out. "There's two of them."

"And what does this mean?" Despite his mounting frustration, Steffan ignored Ralph's offering and sipped at his wine as though he hadn't a care in the world. "I told you to bring me the woman, not her clothes."

Ralph flung the gowns to the floor. "Would you rather we'd carried her lifeless body through your bailey for all to see?"

Outraged by the man's gall, Steffan leapt to his feet. "I wanted her alive, you fool!" He snatched a bliaut off the floor and tore it in two. Perhaps there was still a chance... He thrust the garment toward Ralph. "This proves nothing. It could belong to anyone." Flinging the fabric aside, he snarled, "Bring Lady Catrin uerch Dafydd to me."

Though Ralph stood his ground, it appeared his courage had fled, for he wouldn't meet Steffan's eyes. "It couldn't be helped, milord. In the thick of battle she took an arrow—a couple of arrows—in the back." The others nodded agreement. "It'd be more'n our lives're worth to carry her in here like that." His face grew pale. "What if that hell-spawned brother of hers found out? All the gold in the world couldn't save us from the Dragon!"

Ready to howl his frustration, Steffan dragged his hands through his hair. "What must I do to get anything done properly? I'd wager you never even saw the bitch." He swept his arm across the table, sending food and wine flying against the wall with a satisfying crash. "I didn't pay you to spend the night in some tavern—warm and lazy in your doxy's arms."

Ralph's cohorts sidled toward the door. "Get back here," Steffan demanded. "I didn't tell you you could leave." They stopped in their tracks, legs aquiver. "Sniveling cowards," he muttered, turning to Ralph. "Well?"

"Truth to tell, milord, you haven't paid us yet." Ralph smiled—smirked, more like. Steffan's hands itched at the provocation, but he restrained himself. He wasn't done with the man quite yet. "But you should," Ralph continued. "Indeed, milord, though we couldn't capture the lady like you wanted, we got the job done. She'll ne'er cause you trouble again."

One of the others stepped forward, much to Steffan's surprise. "Aye, milord. Deader than a haddock, she is. Seen it wi' me own eyes. Weren't no help fer it, sir—she attacked us." He hitched up his breeches and nodded. "Right fearsome bitch, weren't she, Ralph?"

Blood afire, Steffan lunged forward and struck him across the face, knocking him to the floor. "How dare you speak so of a noble lady?" 'Twas his right to speak of her however he wished—she was his kin and his equal. But these scum...

"See here, milord—" Ralph said.

"Get out, all of you!"

Ralph drew himself up and stood his ground. "You owe us, milord. 'Tain't our fault things didn't go the way you planned. Lady Catrin is dead—go see for yourself if you don't believe us. 'Course, by now the wolves've likely been at her, but what can ye do? 'Tis too risky for us to be trottin' through the woods wi' a dead noblewoman. By the rood, we'd be dead men ourselves fer that."

Steffan stared at Ralph's misshapen hands. "Been caught at mischief before, I see."

Ralph held up his hand and wiggled his three remaining fingers. "I have. And that's why I don't plan on getting caught again. Be my neck, the next time." He motioned his man up off the floor. "We killed her, 'tis true, but we lost eight men ourselves. You can't expect us to take a loss like that for nothin'. We came for our money, and we aim to get it."

He'd had enough of these fools. "You'll get nothing from me until you can prove to me that she's dead—or bring her to me alive. I'll not accept that she's gone until I see her corpse for myself. I'll pay you then, and not a moment sooner."

Cursing, Ralph snatched the gowns off the floor and stuffed them in the sack. "Come along, lads. 'Tis plain his lordship's in a right foul mood. Be wasting our time trying to make him see sense." He slung the sack over his shoulder. "You know how to find me, milord, should you change your mind." Turning on his heel, he led his men out the door.

Steffan stomped out after them and paused on the landing. "Huw," he yelled once they'd started down the steps. The soldier crossed the hall and stopped at the foot of the stairs. "Get up here."

Looking much put-upon, Huw climbed up to join him at a leisurely pace. "Now what, milord?"

Though tempted to knock Huw back down the stairs for his insolence, instead Steffan motioned him closer. "Find a man you can trust and send him to follow those jackals," he said in a low voice. "I want to know where they go and who they speak to—as soon as possible."

"Aye, milord." Huw sent him a mocking salute as he left.

Steffan lingered at the railing and watched his impertinent servant's slow descent, vowing to light a fire under him at the next opportunity. For the moment he needed Huw, but another chance would present itself soon, no doubt, since Huw irritated him with annoying regularity. "Escort those vermin from the keep," he called after him. "Don't let them in again until they bring me what I need."

Waving his acknowledgment, Huw fell into step behind the three men as they left the hall.

More inept bandits he'd never seen! Steffan stormed into his chamber and slammed the door.

It seemed that no one he hired ever did an adequate job. Something was always lacking, some vital spark necessary to ensure the success of his ventures.

Perhaps he should take care of his concerns himself. He couldn't depend upon anyone—his schemes always ended up in ruins.

Look at this situation! He snatched the wineskin off the floor and drank deeply as he considered how it had gone wrong. Such a simple plan, to abduct Catrin from her meager guard.

He'd nearly shouted with joy when his spy at Gwal Draig sent word that Catrin had set out for l'Eau Clair with so little protection. No one there knew she was coming, and Ian wasn't expected home for another week, at least. Plenty of time to make her pay for the loss of Gillian and l'Eau Clair.

If only Catrin had minded her own business he would be lord and master of l'Eau Clair now, a powerful Marcher lord. His noble cousin Llywelyn—even King John of England himself—would have danced to his tune. The beautiful Lady Gillian would be his bride, although that didn't seem such a prize now that he'd come to know her better.

Still, to hold l'Eau Clair within his grasp would be more than sufficient to compensate for her willfulness.

And he'd have shown her who was master soon enough.

Catrin had ruined it all with her concern for Gillian. "I've heard that my dear cousin has come to stay with you," she'd said after Huw had stolen Gillian from her own keep and brought her to Bryn Du. "You must let me visit her."

He'd had no choice but to allow Catrin to see Gillian, not without rousing her suspicions. He'd known Catrin was a bold, daring wench, but he'd never have suspected her to be in league with Rannulf FitzClifford. She hated Normans!

"She is ill, Steffan—let me bring a physician to examine her," she'd offered.

Ill! The perfidious bitch wasn't ill.

She was pregnant with another man's child.

He'd have taken Gillian to wife as soon as she'd been rid of her bastard.

Indeed, he'd planned to free her of the Norman whelp sullying her womb as soon as possible.

But Catrin's "physician" had been Gillian's lover, FitzClifford. They'd wrested her from him and spirited her away from Bryn Du. His dear kinswoman Catrin, allied with the Normans to spoil his plans.

Nay, his destiny.

With their royal blood combined, he and Gillian would have been equal to—nay, superior to—anyone in Wales.

Even Prince Llywelyn himself.

Catrin had done him ill so often, she could never make

it up to him. Could he but get her into his grasp, however, he'd derive some recompense.

And by Christ, he'd enjoy it!

Catrin still lived, he could feel it. He'd know, somehow, if she were gone.

And if those fools could not bring her to him, he'd go out and find her himself.

Ralph and his men pushed their scraggly mounts until Bryn Du was little more than a blur against the sky. He couldn't help but yearn for the smooth-gaited steed he'd taken from the Norman knight. Every bone-jarring jolt of the mount beneath him served to remind him how unprofitable this venture had proven thus far. Lord Steffan wouldn't pay them; he'd seen that clear as day in the arrogant bastard's face. And since it wasn't easy to dispose of stolen goods, they weren't likely to get anywhere near the real value of the items.

They stopped alongside a rushing stream. Ralph dismounted and stood for a moment with head bent, pondering what to do. It wouldn't do to show a mite of weakness, else he'd be dead in no time.

"What do we do now?" Will asked. He hopped down from the saddle with surprising vigor considering how hard Lord Steffan had hit him. "I say we go back and try for the money again," he added, fingers caressing the knife at his waist. "I'd like to sink my blade into that strutting cock."

"Get yourself killed, more like," Ralph told him. He bent and scooped water over his head—all he could do to cool his anger for now. "Here, Will, come stick your head in the water—your nose is still dripping blood. Mayhap the cold'll put some sense in your noggin."

Diccon knelt beside them, pausing to drink before offering his opinion. "I'd like to make that weasel pay. All the work we did, and he won't pay." He shook his head. "Can't trust no one."

Ralph settled back against a tree and nibbled on a dry crust while Diccon and Will bandied plots back and forth. 'Twas best to let them go on until they ran out of ideas— it wouldn't take long. It was comfortable here in the forest, and he wasn't in any hurry to leave.

A rustling in the bushes caught his attention. Will and Diccon bickered on, their voices masking his movements as he rose and slipped into the brush.

The spy never had a chance to cry out. Ralph wrapped his arm about the young man's neck and stuffed a cloth into his mouth, then lashed his wrists together with a piece of rope.

Ralph dragged the youth by the tunic through the underbrush and shoved him to the ground at Will's feet.

"Where did he come from?" Diccon asked as he whipped his dagger from his belt.

"Found him in the bushes there." Ralph removed his prisoner's knife from its scabbard and pointed the blade toward the path they'd made through the brush. "Spying on us. Will, go find his horse—and have a care, in case he brought company."

Ralph nudged the youth onto his back and twitched out the gag. Eyes fixed upon Ralph's misshapen hand, he gulped for breath. "What are you going to do with me?" he asked, voice faint.

"Depends on why you were watching us. Don't suppose you'd care to tell me?" Ralph grinned in a friendly manner, though he kept the dagger in plain sight.

"My—my name's Prys. I'm nobody important," he stammered. "A poor farmer—"

Ralph turned Prys's hands palm up. No farmer had

hands that pale and soft. "I doubt it." At the sound of muffled hoofbeats he turned and watched Will lead a saddled horse into the clearing. "And no farmer would own so fine a beast."

Now that he thought about it, Ralph could see that his captive's clothing looked like livery. He pressed the knife against Prys's throat. "Did you follow us from Bryn Du?" he growled.

Prys trembled, but made no reply.

Ralph shoved the blade harder, until blood seeped from the shallow cut. "Answer me."

"Huw said to follow you," Prys replied quickly. "See where you went. Lord Steff—" The word ended in a croak. Ralph eased up on the blade and Prys tried again. "Wants to know where the woman is."

Ralph moved the knife and sat back on his heels, allowing Prys to wriggle away from him. "I know nothing else, I swear! I only came because Huw made me. Let me join you," he pleaded. "I can't go back now. They'll kill me."

Will stepped closer. "'Tis a good idea, Ralph. We need more men."

"Aye, Ralph," Diccon piped up. "Lord Steffan'd never know. 'Sides, he owes us—since he won't give us our money, we'll take his servant."

Hope brightened Prys's wan face, but Ralph refused to be swayed. Leaning forward, he grasped the youth by the shoulder. "Sorry, lad," he said as he plunged the dagger to the hilt.

"Ralph," Will gasped, mouth flapping. "What did you do that for?"

"Are you mad?" Ralph asked. He wiped the blade against Prys's tunic, then stood and dragged the body into the bushes. "What if he went back to Bryn Du once he knew what really happened to the woman? Could be that Lord Steffan ordered him to find a way to join our band. 'Tisn't a risk I wanted to take.''

He'd had enough of this, and these fools. "Come on— time to go. We've lingered here too long.'' His movements jerky, he untied his horse and swung into the saddle, then snatched the reins of Prys's mount from Will's grasp. "This has been nothin' but trouble from the start,'' he said with disgust. "Least we've got the loot from the ambush. Should be worth somethin'.''

Not bothering to wait until Diccon and Will mounted up, Ralph urged the horses along. "On to Chester. I never want to see this benighted place again.''

Chapter Seven

Saint Winifred save her—vermin had nested in her mouth. Catrin tried to swallow, but her mouth and throat felt dry as dust, and it seemed her tongue had swollen to at least twice its usual size.

Fiery heat scorched her side and imps stabbed at her with tiny pitchforks.

Had she passed on to hell?

Her wrists were bound. When had that happened? The last she recalled she'd been draped over a bony nag, arguing with someone. Stormy violet eyes, smooth, deep voice with a sardonic edge... 'Twas Nicholas Talbot.

Why did it have to be him?

And how did he dare tie her up?

She needed water so badly she'd beg if she had to, though it galled her to ask Talbot for anything. Mentally elbowing her pride out of her way, she forced out the words.

"Talbot." Her voice sounded little more than a hiss. "Talbot," she repeated. Why didn't he answer?

Her back screaming agony, she turned her face toward the fire. All she could see of him was a boot-clad foot protruding from a filthy cloak. "Damn you, Talbot. Wake up."

She shifted her legs until she connected with something soft, eliciting a moan. Must have been his head. Despite her pain, she smiled.

"Wake up, you Norman idiot." Her voice grew stronger with every word. She nudged him again. "Lazy fool." A bead of sweat ran down her nose and plopped onto her sleeve. Though she tried, she couldn't raise her bound hands enough to wipe her face.

"Talbot!"

A stream of curses, interspersed with moans and grunts, told of her success.

"Unless you'd like me to stuff that glove down your throat again, be silent." Talbot sat up and faced her. Pale and whisker-stubbled, eyes red-rimmed and puffy, he still looked far better to her than any man had a right to.

Obviously her brain had been affected, too.

He squatted beside the fire pit and stirred up the coals. "Are you mad?" she asked as he piled on more wood. "It's hotter than hell itself in here."

"It only seems that way to you—you have a fever." He held his hands out to the growing flames. "I'm so cold I doubt I'll ever feel warm again." His gaze rested upon her face. "Do you remember what happened?"

"Not since we stopped by the stream." His earlier words came back to her. "What did you mean, stuff a glove in my mouth again?"

"You screeched something fierce last night. Yon beast—" he pointed to Idris "—didn't care for it. Nor did I." He held up his glove, teeth marks still visible in the battered leather. His smile, so fleeting she almost missed it, sent a strange feeling to lodge in the pit of her stomach. "'Twas the only way to quiet you—other than kissing you. But it wasn't the right time for that, alas," he added, amusement lighting his eyes in contrast to his solemn tone.

"Norman swine!" Her blood nigh boiled. "How I wish I could give you what you deserve." She held up her wrists. "And what is your reason for this?"

"'Twas necessary." He busied himself with something beside the fire. "You moved so much when I cut the arrows from your back, I feared you'd do yourself further harm."

Now she knew why she hurt so much! But other than sore muscles from journeying slung over a horse like a sack of meal, only her back pained her. She'd suffered worse in the past—and survived.

However, that knowledge did nothing to ease her pain. Fire raged through her blood, radiating out from the wounds.

She hoped Talbot didn't intend to go on today.

But the least he could do was free her. "You do intend to untie me, I trust." A strange hissing distracted her from haranguing him further. She looked up and bit back a cry.

Stripped to the waist, Talbot tended to his own injury. His upper arm looked swollen, and blood seeped from around the hacked-off arrow.

"Why didn't you care for your own wound?" She focused her curious gaze upon his broad shoulders and well-muscled chest. Clearly Nicholas Talbot was no stranger to pain. Several scars marred the smooth, tanned flesh of his torso. The two on his left shoulder looked to have been severe.

Mayhap he considered his present injury a mere trifle.

He watched her while he prodded at his arm. "After I finished wrestling with you, I wanted nothing more than to rest. It feels no worse now than it did then," he added with a shrug. "Compared to your back, 'tis naught."

Unwilling to bear the weight of his scrutiny, Catrin glanced away. She did not believe him, for she'd seen how his lips tightened when he poked at the shaft protruding from his arm.

Her heart sank further within her chest. How much suffering had she caused through yesterday's foolhardiness?

He shouldn't have ignored his own needs to tend to hers.

She rested her cheek on her folded arms and settled her gaze on his face once more. "What are you going to do?"

Talbot wasted no time with words; breathing deep, he pushed the shaft through his arm.

Now she understood why she'd left teeth marks in the glove—and why her throat felt so raw. Sweat beaded on the taut planes of his face, but he made no sound. She bit at her lip to stifle her own cry when the arrowhead broke through his flesh in a gush of blood.

He flung the arrow aside and mopped at the blood dripping from his arm. His lips twisted into a rueful grin. "That's a relief," he said, wiping his brow against his good arm.

The urge to smile in return died a swift death as she considered her own lack of control. "You didn't even need a glove," she muttered. Though he could not know it, the loathing in her voice was directed at herself, not him.

He tied a scrap of cloth about his arm, then slid closer. "This is but a trifle compared to your wound." He reached out and cupped her cheek in his palm.

"Don't patronize me." She jerked away from the comforting warmth of his hand, wincing as the movement pulled at the stitches in her back. "Just untie me, if you please."

That he dared to touch her should anger her. But 'twas her own reaction to him that fired her temper.

She liked the way it felt—and she should not.

Her gaze lowered, Catrin held out her wrists. The cool steel slipped between them, the well-honed blade slicing through the bonds in an instant. As soon as she was free she curled her hands close to her body to hide how they trembled.

Talbot touched her face again. "Be still. You've blood on your cheek." His fingertips stroked along her cheekbone, then lingered there to hold her captive. With a sigh he bent so near that his breath feathered across her lips. "You believe I mock you?" He sat back and released her, then raised her hand to a large, puckered scar to the left of his collarbone and pressed her palm to the mark. "You'd have enjoyed how I screeched when I got this."

Did he think her so heartless?

Was she?

'Twas possible, but... "Nay, milord. I take no pleasure from another's pain."

"Not even mine?" Amusement lit his eyes, and she felt laughter rumble beneath her hand. "You cannot deny your delight when that beast—" he nodded toward Idris "—pinned me to the muddy ground of l'Eau Clair bailey, his teeth at my throat."

"'Twas your pride he hurt, nothing more. God knows you've an abundance of it."

As did she.

And she could not deny that a blow to her pride stung at least as much as a wound to her body.

The strong beat of his heart beneath her fingers jolted her. His warm skin felt far too good against her own.

Closing her eyes to shut out his face, she tried to slip her hand free, but Talbot held it fast.

Did he seek to torment her?

Or did he enjoy her touch, as well?

"Aye, 'twas my pride he hurt, nothing more," he said, his voice soft, beguiling her to watch him yet again. "Even as he held me pinned to the ground, I could appreciate your control over him. In that moment, you might have held my life in your hands." His eyes darkened. "Is it a game you play, to show your disdain for men?" His fingers pressed hers tight against his heart and his gaze held hers captive. "Or is that honor mine alone?"

She wished she could look away, but she refused to permit herself that act of cowardice.

Yet she could not still her tongue. "You flatter yourself." She felt his pulse quicken.

"Do I? Since we first met you've drawn my attention, Catrin. Whether you meant to or not—for good or ill."

"I don't even like you," she whispered. Her own heart thrummed faster—in fear?

"Nor I you." Talbot bent close, until his lips brushed her cheek.

His touch caused a strange pang in her stomach. Her mouth dry, she forced her eyes closed to free herself from his gaze.

It made no difference.

If she never saw him again, his face would remain etched upon her mind.

Nicholas eased her hand from his chest and rested it beside her flushed cheek. If he wasn't careful, he'd find himself forcing his attentions upon her, her injuries be damned. With a curse, he wrenched his gaze from Catrin's delicate features and sought to slow his racing heart.

He rose to his feet and turned away from her, lest his

body betray him. "Are you hungry?" he asked. "After I take care of the dog, I'll go out and find food."

"I'm thirsty," she replied, looking as if food mattered not a whit.

Nicholas all but gnashed his teeth as a familiar tide of frustration swept over him.

The woman had pride enough for God Himself!

'Twas a stupid question he'd asked, at any rate. Since asking her anything had never earned him an answer, he'd do better to simply care for her as he would any stranger, and save himself the aggravation of treating her as though there had ever been—or ever could be—anything more between them.

He tightened the bandage about his arm, the twinge of pain a welcome distraction from the fire raging through his blood, and hastened from the cave.

For once he savored the chill bite of the air against his sweaty chest. He filled the dishes at the stream, then immersed his head in the icy water. His skull felt as if it had been clubbed with a battering ram, although his vision remained clear this morning.

When he returned to the cave, he mixed more of Catrin's medicinal powder with the water in the cup. She lay sprawled on her stomach as he'd left her, her head resting upon her folded arms, her eyes closed. He placed his hand on her shoulder lest he startle her, waiting until she opened her eyes before raising her from the pallet and bringing the cup to her lips.

Though she grimaced, she drank the foul potion without protest. Heat fairly radiated from her skin. She groaned as he eased her onto the cloak, then pillowed her head on her arms without a word and closed her eyes.

Catrin with the fight drained from her was a sight he'd never thought to see—nor did he wish to.

He wiped her face with a damp cloth. He never should have sparred with her, not in her present condition. Had he no honor?

And his response to her...his response shamed him. Had he become an animal, that the mere sight of her could heat his blood?

He didn't even have to look at her! The merest hint of challenge in her voice made his body spring to attention. Never had he reacted thus to so little provocation.

He'd always prided himself upon his control with women, but with Catrin, it appeared he had none.

Injured, ablaze with fever—she couldn't even sit up!

It mattered naught. He wanted her anyway.

Nicholas rubbed absently at his bristly face. Such arrogance, he thought with a grimace. Covered in gore, battered and bruised—and in all likelihood he smelled worse than a rutting goat. Even if she were well, she'd find him no prize.

At any rate, so far as he knew, she cursed the very ground he trod upon. Doubtless the fact that he'd saved her life, should they survive, would weigh little with her.

Besides, Lady Catrin uerch Dafydd wasn't like the sluts at court, jumping from bed to bed for sport.

His willful body was doomed to disappointment. He had no place in his life for a lady.

Idris yelped, startling Nicholas from his fruitless musings. Yet another sin to lay at his feet; the poor creature still suffered, while he sat there lecturing himself.

He gathered together his meager supplies and approached the dog. Though he could no longer put off treating the beast, he didn't look forward to it. Injured animals could be unpredictable, and Idris had never liked him to begin with.

He sank to his knees and ignored Idris's low growl.

None of the many cuts scattered over the dog's rough coat seemed serious. Only the arrow needed attention.

The dog remained still, though he followed Nicholas's every move with his gaze. Nicholas could have sworn that the intelligence of a man lay captured within Idris's dark eyes. He could almost understand why Catrin treated Idris like a person: he found himself talking to him as though the beast knew what he said.

Perhaps he did, for he remained sprawled on the smooth dirt and permitted Nicholas to care for him. The dog's acquiescence made it an easier task to cut the arrow free and set stitches in its place.

Nicholas gave Idris water and turned gratefully away from those disconcerting eyes. As he stretched the kinks from his back, his stomach rumbled, reminding him that another chore remained before him.

The light that streamed into the cave had dimmed, taking on an odd, purplish tinge. And it sounded as though the wind had picked up, as well.

He slipped his shirt on. Despite the weather, he planned to hunt. The mare needed attention, too. He snatched up the bigger knife and left the cave.

Dark clouds scudded across the sky, and thunder boomed in the distance. The mare whinnied a greeting, hooves shuffling nervously as she tugged at her tether. He cast another look at the sky and decided to hobble her, lest she become frightened and pull herself free. He couldn't risk losing her. Moving swiftly, Nicholas led the horse to drink, then tied her beneath the firs again.

Though he didn't have any rope, he'd noticed vines hanging from the trees. 'Twas a long climb up to where the vines twined around the branches, but it took no time at all to slash them loose and drop them to the ground. He scrambled down after them.

He wove several lengths together and wound them about the mare's dancing hooves, then gathered together a mound of vines.

Good luck had come his way, for once. His venture up the tree had yielded more than rope, for dried grapes hung in clusters from the vines. Nicholas quickly gathered several handfuls of the fruit, then realized he'd need something to carry them in.

Thunder rumbled, nearer all the time, and lightning flashed bright against the roiling clouds. The storm was nearly upon him. Hands full, he bent from the waist and wriggled within the loose shirt, but he couldn't get the neckline to slide over his head. He grabbed the fabric with his teeth and squirmed until he could inch the shirt over his head.

The rising wind whipped his hair about his face as he stripped the vines and piled the raisins on his shirt. The cold air didn't feel so wonderful now. Fat, icy droplets pelted him as he gathered up the shirt and raced toward the cave.

He didn't make it.

A bolt of lightning split a massive tree and jolted him flat onto his back before the thunder could echo through the rocky hills.

Chapter Eight

Nicholas's ears rang as he lay upon the wet ground, stunned and blinded by the flash of lightning. A strange sensation tingled along his skin and scalp, then faded away.

His lungs felt squeezed empty. He gasped and wheezed, trying to suck in air.

A sharp stench bit at his nostrils—fire and brimstone, perhaps? It wouldn't have surprised him to see the devil himself standing over him, laughing.

Nicholas inched back and propped himself against a boulder, blinking until the rocks and trees came into view.

Moving like an old man, he stood, but his legs would scarcely support him. By Christ, but that had been close! Scattered pieces of a huge oak lay about him, shredded by the lightning's force. Smoke rose in wisps as the rain fell on the scorched remains.

He shuddered and crossed himself. A few steps closer to the tree and he'd have been reduced to a smoldering lump, as well.

Each step toward the cave came easier as he shook off the effects of the lightning, but he couldn't escape the feeling that he'd led a charmed life till now. He'd rather encounter a rampaging army of infidels than the whirl of hazards he'd faced of late. Even nature herself conspired against him!

Frenzied barking greeted Nicholas when he entered the cave. Catrin had moved off the pallet and dragged herself across the floor on her stomach, from the look of it. She lay sprawled alongside the fire pit. By some miracle her clothes hadn't caught fire. The eating dagger clutched in her hand, she stabbed at the floor.

Idris stood over her, barking and trying to shove her away from the flames.

"Nay! No more!" She sobbed as she slashed at the space before her. "Not again...I won't let you!"

Nicholas tossed the shirt aside and hurried to her. "Let be," he murmured to the dog, urging him away from his mistress. "Go lie down." Idris whined pitifully and nudged Catrin once more before slinking off to his place by the back wall.

Dropping to his knees, Nicholas grasped Catrin about the waist. "Hush, milady." She squirmed within his hold with surprising strength and whimpered as she continued to strike out with the knife. Ignoring her struggles, he pulled her away from the fire. "That's enough."

Sparks smoldered along the side of her gown. Cursing, he slapped them out, then grabbed her by the wrist and wrenched the dagger from her. "No, damn you!" she screamed. Her fingers clawed at him. "I'll see you pay." Her gray eyes wide, she stared at him, but he didn't think she saw him. "Don't touch me!" Panting, she attempted to rise to her knees.

"Catrin." He touched her cheek with a gentleness at odds with his harsh tone. "'Tis all right—you're safe here."

"Keep away," she snarled. She seemed aware of his

presence now, though he couldn't be certain she recognized him. Her head jerked to the side, as if to avoid a blow. She crept backward until she bumped into the wall. "Come near me again and I'll see you in hell!"

Thunder boomed nearby. The earth shook and fine dirt rained down from the ceiling. As the sound echoed through the cave, Catrin's body convulsed and she slumped back, eyes closed.

"Lady Catrin." Still on his knees, Nicholas lunged forward to catch her.

Nicholas rolled to protect her as they tumbled to the floor. They lay there for a moment, motionless.

Her faint groan vibrated against his chest. "What are you doing?" She stared down at him, her gaze measuring.

He squirmed from beneath her and eased her onto the ground. "Not what it looks like, unfortunately," he muttered.

"What do you mean?"

His lips curled in a wry smile. "While I wouldn't mind having you atop me in other circumstances—" he pushed her disheveled curls back from her face "—now is not the time."

"Lustful pig." Panic darkened her eyes once more, before she closed them and turned her face away.

Her expression now appeared as it had been during her dream—if her confusion had been a dream. Whatever she'd imagined had not been pleasant, that much was clear. He would never have expected to see her show such fear.

He never would have expected her to *feel* it.

Retrieving his shirt, he settled down, cross-legged, beside her. "I found us something to eat." He spread the material open with a flourish. "At great personal risk."

Catrin's eyes remained closed, though she propped her head on her folded arms. "Stir up the fire, then."

"I doubt you'll want this cooked." His stomach growled. Unable to wait any longer, he picked up a handful of raisins and tossed a few into his mouth before holding his hand out to her. "Have some. They're delicious."

A scowl marred her delicate features. Catrin raised one eyelid, then both eyes popped open. "Raisins? You were in grave danger gathering *raisins?*"

"Aye." What did it take to make her laugh? Did she have no sense of fun, of the ridiculous? He'd not bother to explain. It would make no difference. He stuffed more food into his mouth, then leaned back against the wall and folded his arms.

The injured expression on Talbot's face made Catrin want to laugh, though her back hurt like the devil. He looked like a sulking little boy—though she'd never considered him in that light before. His reaction touched her, swept the effects of her dream away. The mighty warrior was no different than any other man, it seemed.

She could stroke his pride. She'd had plenty of practice at that, with her brother and his men.

But 'twould be so much more fun, and distracting, to plague him. He deserved it, after his remark about rolling on the floor with her. She didn't know if he'd meant it. Indeed, 'twould be best if he did not, for both of them. She had nothing to offer him—or any man.

However, she'd always found badgering Talbot a most enjoyable diversion. And at the moment, anything that might distract her from the shadows in her mind and the pain in her back would be a blessing.

She propped her hands beneath her chin and raised herself enough to meet his gaze. "So tell me, milord—did you use a dirk on the beasts, or did you wrestle them into submission with your bare hands?''

A hint of surprise crossed his face before his lips firmed into a thin line and his eyes darkened to a deep purple. A giggle escaped her before she composed herself. ''Henceforth you shall be known as Lord Nicholas the Raisin Slayer.''

''You honor me, lady,'' he said, his grave tone at odds with the sparkle in his eyes. He held out a sticky mass of the fruit. ''Please accept this token of my regard.''

How should she take that remark? she wondered as he held the raisins to her lips. His fingers brushed against her mouth, their hard warmth discernible despite the heat radiating from her skin. The warmth his touch generated 'twas different from any she'd felt before, a glow from within the depth of her being.

She pushed away that disturbing thought and turned her attention to the food. Idris provided a blessed distraction, creeping forward and nudging her with his nose. Praise God, he appeared on the mend; he flopped in a heap beside her and allowed her to scratch his head. He eyed the food spread out on Talbot's shirt, but he made no move to touch it.

''I doubt he'll want them,'' Talbot said, then surprised her by pushing a few raisins toward the dog. Idris sniffed at them and, after her nod of approval, lapped them off Talbot's palm.

They ate in companionable silence, the rain and thunder a soothing backdrop now that the storm had moved away. She hadn't realized how hungry she was until she started to eat, but now she felt ravenous. She savored every bite Talbot gave her and watched with regret when he wrapped the shirt around the remainder.

"I'll find us some real food tomorrow," he said. "But 'twould be foolish to eat all we have now."

He gave a muffled shout of laughter. She looked up, then joined in, wincing at the pain but unable to resist.

Idris chewed at the wad of raisins in his mouth—and chewed. "They must be stuck in his teeth," she said, chuckling at the sight. "Idiot," she murmured as Idris swallowed and gave her a tooth-filled grin.

Talbot left the cave, returning almost immediately with a cup of water. "I thought dogs only ate meat," he said as he handed it to her.

She held the cold cup to her face for a moment, then drank. The water felt so good pouring down her aching throat! All too soon, she handed the empty cup to Talbot. "That falsehood exists only because no other hunter has ever had the courage to seek out and subdue the frightful raisin."

"I see." His lips twitched, but he didn't laugh.

When he left to refill the cup, she thought she heard him chuckle, though she could not be sure. However, his face showed no emotion when he brought her more water. After handing it to her, he returned to the doorway and stared out at the forest.

Her back had begun to throb. "Would you mix in some of the powder?" she asked. Let him think whatever he would of her request; she felt too tired—too drained, suddenly—to care. And she knew that, despite her exhaustion, the pain would not let her sleep.

Not without sending her back in time on a journey she did not wish to take.

She held the cup to her temple and closed her eyes. What would she do the next time the past claimed her? Would she stab Talbot when he sought to help her? Set herself ablaze?

She had no idea what she was capable of during the confusion of her dreams.

Mayhap she should ask Talbot to tie her up or clout her aside the head. She watched as he crossed the chamber. He'd enjoy that, no doubt.

He took the cup from her hand and gave her a wet cloth in its stead. "I gave you the potion already." Sighing, she swabbed it slowly over her face and throat. "I put it in the water you drank before I left the cave."

"How much did you give me?" She should be sleeping like an innocent babe, if it was the proper dose.

"The same as last night." He knelt beside her and, placing his fingers beneath her chin, tilted her face toward him. Uncomfortable with his scrutiny, she closed her eyes. "Nay, open them," he demanded.

Bracing herself, she watched him as closely as he did her. It didn't seem to bother him, to her dismay; would that she had the same reaction to him!

"The drug should be working." He tightened his fingers on her chin, then released her. Perhaps her gaze disturbed him after all, she thought with satisfaction.

But then he cupped her chin in his hand and brushed his thumb beneath her eye. "Your eyes look strange, wide and dark. 'Tis from the potion, I imagine. Do you still have pain?"

A shiver shot down the back of her neck and along her spine as he continued to draw his rough, callused thumb over her skin. How could she be so susceptible to so little provocation?

She doubted he intended to provoke her.

"A little," she lied. Though if he continued to touch her, her body's response would likely drown out any pain.

"Should I give you more?"

More? Her reaction to him was already more than she

could endure. "Nay. 'Tis too dangerous." She squirmed, trying to find a more comfortable position—and evade his torment. "It matters not. I've suffered worse than this."

"But if it will ease your—"

"Let be! I'm no puling demoiselle, to whine over some trifle."

"Your injuries are far more than a trifle. By Christ's blood, woman..." His gaze focused on her bosom, half-exposed by her unlaced tunic. "Your actions aside, I cannot deny you *are* a woman. But I've seen fierce soldiers howl over lesser wounds than yours."

Catrin lowered herself further onto the cloak and tried to tug her gown closed. Damn him—and herself—for this insidious warmth stealing through her veins.

"No doubt they were Norman soldiers." As soon as the words left her lips, she regretted them. How had she come to this—to stoop so low?

Whatever else she might think of Nicholas Talbot, she had never questioned his valor.

If not for him, she'd likely be dead now...

Or wish she were.

Apologies were a sign of weakness she promised herself long ago never to reveal.

She forced herself to meet Talbot's steady gaze, to hold it with her own and reveal not a whit of the turmoil in her mind—to hide how tempted she was to break her vow.

"I can withstand this," she said. "At least if I feel the pain, I know I'm alive. 'Tis something to rejoice in."

"Do you never give in?" He took the tattered cloak he'd used as a blanket and wadded it up. "You're more stubborn than an ass."

"Thank you." She smiled at his look of confusion. To her his comment was high praise, though she doubted he meant it that way.

He slid close to her. "Come here." Resignation colored his voice, but it could not mask the weariness. He couldn't have rested much himself, the night past. Though why he wanted her to...

He scooped her into his arms. Ignoring her protests, he wrapped the cloak about her and settled her on his lap. "There. Is that better?"

"Aye," she whispered against his chest. She was too tired to fight, for the moment. Talbot made a much more comfortable bed than the floor, and something about his nearness made her feel safe.

He could protect her from her dreams, she thought as he enfolded her in his arms.

Shielded within this warm cocoon, his heartbeat strong and steady beneath her cheek, she nestled closer.

But how could she protect her heart from him?

The light had brightened and the rain stopped completely by the time Nicholas awoke. Catrin slept on in his arms, snuggled against him. It appeared that no dreams had marred her rest, for she had not stirred.

He couldn't say the same for himself. Even in slumber, his body recognized hers and reacted to it. Three times he'd awakened, disturbed by the scent and feel of the woman draped over him like a blanket.

Somehow her breasts had come to rest upon his bare forearms. Her gown might as well not exist, for all the protection it gave. She shifted in his grasp, the sweet weight of her bosom driving a shaft of desire straight to his vitals.

If God were merciful, there would be a warm and willing woman lurking just outside this cave. He reluctantly eased his arms away from Catrin. But 'twas his misfortune that the woman he wanted lay within his reach already, her head cushioned against the pulse throbbing in his neck.

Even the whisper of her breath across his throat stirred him!

It wouldn't have surprised him if he'd found himself already buried to the hilt in her feverish body. He'd done that—and more—in his dreams.

And his desire was stronger still, now that he was awake.

Was he going mad?

She was injured, perhaps unto death.

But even were she well, Catrin was not for him. No matter what his errant body demanded, he had no place in his life for a pure and innocent noblewoman.

Not that she'd want him, if she knew the truth of his past.

The sooner he got her away from here—and away from him—the better it would be for both of them.

Nicholas turned his thoughts to a more important path. He needed to discover who had attacked Catrin, for he had no doubt she had been the target. She could be annoying, 'twas true, he acknowledged with a grin.

But he found it difficult to believe that someone wanted her dead.

Catrin's hand slid across his stomach and settled in the juncture of his thighs. He leaned his head back against the wall, eyes squeezed shut.

Dear God! Don't tempt me further. I cannot withstand much more.

With a sigh of regret, he lifted her hand from his lap. It appeared so dainty within his own battle-scarred fist. He looked closer. Reddish marks mottled her palm, and her skin felt even hotter than before.

He gently turned her around till he could see the flesh

exposed by the drooping neckline of her gown. Her face and throat were bright pink, and though heat radiated from her skin, no sweat had risen to cool her.

Nicholas laid Catrin down on her stomach and drew her gown away from her back. Fingers trembling slightly, he unwrapped the bandages.

"Blessed Mary save her."

A foul yellow fluid oozed from her wounds, and red streaks marred her ivory flesh.

What should he do now?

Chapter Nine

Shame washed over him. While he lay there, thinking with his cock, her wounds had festered. Nicholas shifted his gaze from Catrin's back and stared, unseeing, at the light-filled doorway.

There must be some plant, some treatment... He refused to believe they had escaped certain death, only for Catrin to perish of her injuries in this godforsaken wilderness.

She crept closer to him, moaning softly. Perhaps she knew of something he could do. He wasn't too proud to ask for her help, not when her life might hang in the balance.

"Wake up." He placed his hand on her shoulder with a gentleness at odds with his harsh tone. "Catrin—you must help me."

She turned her head toward him. "What?" she whispered. She stared his way, eyes unfocused.

He pushed her hair aside and cupped her face in his hands. "I need your help."

She squinted, though he leaned so near she couldn't help but see him. "What do you want?" A glimmer of awareness lit her eyes. "I feel so strange."

Nicholas moved back. "Your wounds have festered, and I don't know what else to do for you. I know nothing of herbs and such. Is there something I could use, some remedy I might make?"

"Did I kill him?" she asked urgently. "I cannot rest until he's dead."

Did her dreams still hold her captive? He would have sworn she was awake....

She closed her eyes, then opened them to stare at him intently. "Your pardon, milord. My mind is a bit muddled."

"Do you recognize me?"

"How could I forget Lord Nicholas the Raisin Slayer?" Her lips curled into a weak semblance of a smile.

"I wish you might forget that." Nothing could hinder her tongue, it seemed. He found a certain reassurance in that fact. "Your wounds are infected," he told her, "and your fever has worsened. Is there anything else I can do?"

She stared at the wall in silence, then met his searching gaze. "There is a plant that grows near water, though it might be too early for it yet."

"Describe it for me," he urged, afraid her mind might drift away again.

Though he could see she scarcely had the strength to speak, she gave him the details he needed. After making her as comfortable as he could, he set off to search downstream.

Catrin listened as Talbot left, then sighed with relief. It had taken her last reserves of strength to keep her eyes open, to think clearly enough to give him the information he sought. Once again the shadows closed in, and she feared she could hold them at bay no longer.

Phantoms awaited her there, ghosts she'd faced too

many times before. "Go away!" She brushed away a tear. "Begone!"

If she shut her eyes, the demon from her past would come for her. How could she face him?

This time, she might not escape.

She knew he was there.

He stood just beyond her vision, his voice rich and smooth—and malevolent. "'Tis your choice, my beauty. Your decision."

"Just let me go," she pleaded, despising her cowardice. "I won't tell anyone."

His low chuckle sent a ripple of fear down her spine. "I'm not through with you yet, my dear."

Her muscles tensed as his footsteps came closer to the bed. She was helpless to do more than squirm, and she refused to give him even that small victory. He enjoyed her struggles far too much for her to indulge his sickening appetite.

It galled her to lie there on her stomach, motionless. But she had already learned the futility of tugging at the coarse rope that bound her to the bed frame. All she'd done was chafe her wrists until they bled.

Doubtless that would please him, as well.

She forced her breathing to slow, and tried to relax. The slim rod hurt much worse when she tensed in anticipation of the blows.

As she lay there in the twilight gloom of the tower, she concluded that the expectation of what he might do was part of his torment. She never knew from one time till the next whether she'd be forced to endure pain or his peculiar ideas of pleasure. Both were repugnant, though she found a beating far preferable to his perverted sexual attentions.

How could she have guessed his true nature? Madog ap Gerallt was respected by the Welsh nobility, a friend of Prince Llywelyn himself. Though he ruled a small estate, men of power and influence valued his opinion.

Even she had been taken in by his charm—God save her from her folly.

No one would ever suspect that Madog had taken her, or the things he'd done.

Why had she assumed that evil wore an evil face?

Someone entered the room. "Put the tray near the bed," Madog ordered.

Footsteps shuffled nearer, and she looked up at Madog's servant, Mab. The poor boy—for despite his amazing size, the lad couldn't have been more than thirteen—hung his head and stared down at the floor.

Madog laughed and sauntered into view. "Go ahead and look at her, Mab. Don't be shy." He reached up and grabbed Mab's chin, forcing the boy's gaze toward her naked form.

"Would you like her?" Madog used his free hand to flip her hair out of the way. "You'd enjoy her, I'm sure."

Mab trembled, his gaze darting nervously away.

Madog shook the boy's head and drew him closer to her. "Look at her, I said!" His eyes began to glitter. He released Mab and untied Catrin's feet.

Her heart pounded wildly as she considered what Madog might have in mind. Not the boy, too, she pleaded with the same god who had turned a deaf ear to her earlier pleas. Mab looked to be a decent lad, but that would not prevent Madog from forcing him to do his bidding.

She suppressed a moan when he undid her wrists and turned her onto her back until she lay exposed to them. Madog had seen it all before; there wasn't an inch of her he hadn't subjected to his loathsome attentions.

He moved a branch of candles closer to the bed and stared at her as though she were a choice morsel for his delectation. Though she wanted nothing more than to shrink away and try to cover herself, she did not, for she knew he would enjoy that more.

"Think how I honor you, boy." A flush stained Madog's face, and the glimmer in his eyes intensified. "A noble lady—so delicate, so fine. She's yours, to use as you wish."

Mab leapt toward Madog, a knife clutched in his hand.

The dagger went flying in the struggle as Mab grabbed Madog by the throat. It landed on the bed. Catrin reached painfully for the knife, her fingers closing about the hilt.

Mab's size made up for his lack of skill, and he now held his master pinned to the floor.

Every movement agonizing, Catrin pulled the sheet from the bed and wrapped herself from throat to ankles. She managed to take two steps before her knees gave out and she landed in a heap on the floor, the dagger still clenched in her hand.

Madog lay motionless, his eyes closed.

"Is he dead?" she asked.

"I don't know, milady." Mab sat back on his heels. He still would not look at her. "Did he really mean for me—"

She took a deep breath. "Aye, he did. He's an evil beast." Catrin dragged herself closer and felt for a pulse.

Mab retreated farther. "My ma was so proud, me workin' for the master." He hung his head. "But I couldn't do what he wanted."

"You will before I'm through with you," Madog roared as he sat up and spun to face them.

Catrin screamed and fell back. With a curse, he grabbed for her, but she wrenched free and raised the knife.

"Nay." He reached for her again.

She eluded him. "Never again, you bastard," she swore, and found the strength to plunge the knife up into his chest.

His fingers grabbed at the hilt. "No," she sobbed. She slapped at his hands. Mab sprang into action then, seizing her by the shoulders and pulling her away, then jerking the blade free.

Eyes wide, Madog stared down at the rush of blood from his chest. He crumpled to the floor.

Mab gaped at him. "They'll hang us for certain, milady."

"No, they won't." Determination lent her the mettle to pick herself up off the floor. Her mind raced with possibilities. "Your master was a careless man."

Mab stared at her, uncomprehending. "You've done well, Mab," she reassured him. "You've a place in my household for as long as you wish." She nudged at the body with her toe. "But first, we must dispose of this filth."

The servant positioned Madog on the bed as if he were asleep. Meanwhile, Catrin gathered her tattered clothing from a chest against the wall and dressed. "Will we be able to leave here without being caught?" she asked, gathering the food Mab had brought into a bundle.

"Aye. There's a passageway that leads to a postern gate. 'Tis how the master slipped in here when he had company."

"Good." She dragged the stand of candles close to the bed curtains. "Are you ready, Mab?" He nodded, then took up the bundle and unlatched the door.

Catrin touched a candle to the hangings. "May you burn in hell," she vowed as she stared at Madog's face through the flames.

"Come along, mistress." Mab took her by the arm and drew her away. "We must leave."

He tugged at her arm again, harder this time. But his voice grew deeper. "How the hell did you get over here?"

Madog's deceptively charming visage still swam before her eyes. "You can let go of me, Mab. Come, we must flee." She blinked to clear her vision.

Mab no longer stood beside her. Instead, Nicholas Talbot held her, his hands harsh on her shoulders. "Where is Mab? We must go now, else we'll be trapped by the fire. Will you help us?"

Strong arms lifted her from the floor and carried her a short distance. "Not on my stomach," she cried out as he lowered her to the pallet. A sigh of relief escaped her lips when he placed her on her side. "Are we safe now?"

A cool cloth smoothed across her aching brow. "Aye, you're safe. Sleep now."

The voice wasn't Mab's, but something about it heartened her. She could sleep with this man by her side; he'd chase the demons away. She grasped the hand that soothed her, content.

Nicholas slumped against the rough stone wall, his eyes closed. What he wouldn't give for a horn of strong brown ale, or better yet, an entire jug of fiery Irish usquebaugh. It wouldn't help their situation, but it might provide a brief respite.

No use wishing for the impossible. Besides, there were any number of things he'd rather have, things more useful than strong drink.

He wasn't likely to get any of them, either.

Once he settled Catrin on the pallet and poulticed her back with the herbs he'd found, he could not rest. She hadn't moved, even when he cleaned her wounds. At least the treatment had helped, for the swelling had gone down and the red streaks faded by the time he replaced the bandages.

He ached with weariness, body and soul. He'd never been responsible for anyone but himself, not in so intimate a fashion. He couldn't remember a time past when so many thoughts whirled through his brain.

And now he wondered if Catrin had gone mad.

Christ's bones, he'd heard her screams and curses halfway up the hill!

Resting his arm on his upraised knee, he dangled the dagger loosely from his fingers and stared out into the murky night. "What is it that I guard her from, the dangers of the forest or the anger within her?" he asked Idris. At the dog's questioning whine, he reached over and scratched the beast behind the ears. "Your mistress is a puzzle. The more I learn, the less I understand." Nicholas examined Idris's wound. "At least you and I are nearly well."

The dog licked his hand, then went to lie beside Catrin. Still asleep, she cuddled up to Idris with a sigh.

A much safer bedmate for her, Nicholas thought as he wrapped himself in a cloak.

Dawn tinted the sky a delicate peach when Idris nudged Nicholas awake. Every muscle screamed a protest when he rose from his rocky bed and stretched, then followed the dog outside.

Catrin was awake when he returned. "Did you find the herbs?" she asked as soon as he stepped into the cave.

He swept her a mocking bow. "And good morrow to you, as well, milady. I trust your sleep was restful."

"Why are you so cheerful?" she snapped, dragging her fingers through her tangled hair.

Nicholas ignored her foul mood and dropped to his knees beside her. "What do you think you're doing?" she shrieked when he tried to push aside the back of her gown.

He sat back and studied her face. "To judge from your vigor this morn, I believe you're getting better." He touched a finger to her cheek. "But your color is still terrible, and your flesh is hot. You are sick, milady, and I need to look at your back. Unless you don't care if you recover."

"Of course I want to get better." She fairly flung the words at him. "How else can I get away from you?" Scowling, she turned onto her side and pushed her gown off her shoulders.

After examining her back, he replaced the poultice with a fresh mixture of herbs. "The poultice is working well." He drew her gown up, and she huddled into the fabric. "It would serve well for battle wounds. What are the plants called?"

"Shall we exchange recipes? Or discuss the best way to remove wine stains from fine linen?" She folded her body more tightly into a ball and glared up at him. "Don't waste your charm on me. Save it for someone who will appreciate it."

He leaned over her. "I believe you would appreciate my 'charm' just fine, milady." He moved closer, until his lips hovered over hers. "But I'll save it until you're in a better mood." Drawing away, he added, "The only claw marks you'll put on my hide will be from passion, not spite."

Disregarding her curses, he stood. He dressed quickly, stuck the dagger in his belt and snapped his fingers. Idris came to his side at once, earning him another frown from Catrin. "Come along, boy. Perhaps a decent meal will put your mistress in a better mood.'' The dog at his heels, he passed through the doorway, laughing when the cup flew past his head.

His step jaunty, he headed down the trail, Catrin's shriek of outrage speeding him on his way.

Chapter Ten

Could she screech!

Likely she'd frightened off all the game, and he and Idris would need to range far afield to hunt.

Although the sun remained trapped behind a heavy bank of clouds, the air was dry, and the rain had already dripped from the budding leaves. Catrin had riled him so, he'd forgotten to take a cloak, but he wouldn't need it. Between the hike through the forest and the way his temper rose every time he thought of Catrin's odd behavior, his blood flowed hot enough.

"What is wrong with her?"

Idris stopped and looked up at him with those odd, knowing eyes, head cocked to the side as though considering the question.

Nicholas sat on a large flat stone alongside the trail and rubbed Idris's ears. "I know women are prone to odd starts, all sweetness one moment, screaming shrews the next...and the things she said the other night—they made no sense."

The dog lay down beside him and placed his head in Nicholas's lap. "I don't understand her at all."

He'd had little experience with noblewomen, Norman

or Welsh. In truth, he'd had little contact with the gentry at all. Mercenary troops were made up of the refuse of every level of society, but mostly the lower classes. His father had been a classic example of a higher-born mercenary, a second son at odds with his family who had hied off to the Holy Land to hire out his sword. The noblemen reduced to such straits were hardly among the better specimens of nobility—though he hadn't found their more "honorable" counterparts much better, now that he'd inherited Ashby and returned to England to join their ranks.

Of highborn women he knew next to nothing. He did realize that those ladies he'd encountered at court could not be typical of the breed. He'd never seen a more brazen, amoral group of sluts outside a Parisian whorehouse.

However, living with Gillian de l'Eau Clair had shown him a different sort of lady, one who took the responsibilities of her station seriously, whose concern was for others before herself—or her passions.

Catrin must be that type of woman. She bore no resemblance to those whores at court—and she was Gillian's kin, after all.

Perhaps he simply didn't understand women, no matter their place in the scheme of things.

Perchance that would explain why she confused him so.

Something told him it wasn't that simple. Even with his limited knowledge of the weaker sex... He shook his head. No man in his right mind could possibly believe women were weak.

And however he thought of other women, he knew that Catrin was nothing like any other woman, in any way.

Should he mourn that fact, or rejoice that it was so? It didn't matter anyway. Lady Catrin uerch Dafydd, blood kin to Welsh royalty, cousin to Prince Llywelyn himself, was not for the likes of him. If she knew the truth of his origins, or how he'd lived until four years ago, she'd likely spit upon him.

He deserved nothing less.

He should be beaten for even daring to think of her as he had the past few days—nay, since the first moment he'd seen her. And it didn't seem right to lust after a decent woman, although that thought flew straight out of his mind when he was near her. If her brother—the Dragon—discovered the liberties Nicholas had taken with his sister...

Likely he'd slay him on sight.

Idris whined.

"You're right, we should be about our business." He stood, shaking his head. It wasn't his way to ponder life, or to find himself awash in maudlin thoughts.

As he looked down the hill at the scene spread out before him, he felt a familiarity about it. He shrugged; mayhap 'twould come to him later.

To catch anything substantial, he needed a weapon. Catrin's dagger was a fine blade, but not enough for what he had in mind.

He set several snares in the bushes along the trail, fashioned from bits of thread and supple branches. With luck—and time—they'd catch something there. For now, though, he'd try for something larger. Perhaps a young boar; all he'd need to fell one was his knife and a stout, sharpened stick.

He found just the right stick beneath an ancient oak and sharpened it against a rock. He hefted it, tossing it in the air, and shaved a bit off the end until he was satisfied with its crude balance.

The past few days made him question his ability as a

warrior—Catrin's tongue alone could do that to a man. He was ready to pit himself against an adversary, to test his skill and cunning. Grinning, he sent Idris in search of prey.

The dog soon picked up a scent. Blood warming to the chase, Nicholas set off after him.

Catrin dragged herself from her resting place and snatched up the cup Talbot had left filled. Her arms trembled, she noted with disgust. She had turned into a weakling!

Ignoring the way the movement pulled on her wounds, she sat up and raised the cup to her lips. By sheer determination she drained the water without spilling any, though it was a near thing. Minor though the feat had been, she counted it as progress.

The poultice seemed to have helped her back, for though the wounds still hurt, they no longer throbbed so badly. 'Twas good, for she could not linger here for long; Gillian would need her help soon, and she intended to be at l'Eau Clair to give it.

She wished she could remember what she'd done when Talbot found her wandering earlier. The present had become twisted up with the past, and she couldn't unravel the memories.

No doubt Madog had gone straight to hell after she and Mab had helped him on his way. She hoped he burned there still. The dream had seemed so real. She shuddered in remembrance.

For a long while after she had escaped Madog, little things—a sound on the edge of her awareness, a scent, a man's touch—jolted her back into the horror. In recent months, thank God, her reaction had eased. But last night, she'd endured it again, every detail the same.

Would it ever end?

The experience colored everything she'd done or felt since. Even after four years, she remained convinced that she could never share her life with a man—not that any man would want her, after the things Madog had done.

She could live without a man in her life.

But she wanted children.

Whenever she saw Gillian and Rannulf, their contentment so clear as they awaited the birth of their child, Catrin felt a hunger so deep it hurt. She did not begrudge them their love, their joy.

But she hated the emptiness she felt in the dark, lonely depths of the night—nights when she ached for a lover, and the child they'd hold safe between them.

As she'd done so many times before, Catrin folded her arms across her chest and forced her longings deep inside. She knew better than to dream of what she could never have.

Perhaps she should blame Talbot for making the yearning reappear.

Since she met him last year at l'Eau Clair, something about him had held her thoughts, her attention—made her uncomfortable whenever he was near. Though she hadn't the sweetest temperament to begin with, in his presence she often became a veritable shrew. He brought out the warrior in her, made her challenge him, clash with him.

She didn't care who won their battles; 'twas the exhilaration of the fight she enjoyed.

She pulled her cloak about her shoulders, frowning as she considered that startling thought. When they sparred with each other, she felt alive, more alive than she'd been since Madog took her captive.

Was it right that she feel life so keenly, when she had killed a man?

Madog deserved to die. She felt no guilt for killing him—nor remorse, either. 'Twas that which gave her pause.

Shouldn't she feel regret for what she had done?

Nicholas Talbot made her remember what had happened to her, but she feared he also had the power to make her forget. When she matched him taunt for taunt, when he drew her eyes to his in the heat of battle, the past ceased to exist. Her blood rushed through her veins, the tumult of sensation overwhelmed her judgment. She ached with the desire to touch him—with her hands, her gaze, her words.

She couldn't permit it to continue. She didn't deserve the pleasure she felt in his presence.

He deserved better than a woman like her, a woman with a past she carried within her like a canker eating away at her soul.

Her attention should be focused on other things—such as who wanted her dead. Only by the grace of God and Nicholas's arrival had she escaped that inept crew of bandits. They'd have finished what they began if Nicholas hadn't come along.

But she couldn't think about that—about anything—anymore. Weariness drained her; her body ached with it.

She dragged herself near the fire pit and pushed more wood on the dying flames. Arm outstretched to pillow her head, she stared into the glowing coals until, with a sigh, she settled into sleep.

The swish of a tail woke her, that and the clicking of claws against stone. Nicholas and Idris, back from the hunt?

She forced her eyes open. The gathering gloom of dusk made it difficult to see. She sat up, tucking her legs beneath her, and scraped her hair back from her face.

A low growl sounded outside the door. "Idris? Come, you cannot still be growling at Talbot. Behave yourself, you old beast!"

Catrin stretched her hands toward the dying blaze, then stopped in midmotion when she saw the compact gray creature lurking just beyond the doorway. Her breath caught in her throat and her stomach tightened with fear.

A wolf stood silhouetted against the darkening sky.

The beast moved closer, into the doorway of the cave, its ruff bristling and its teeth bared. It growled again.

Shadows skulked behind it, no doubt its brethren waiting outside. The wolf came forward, teeth still bared as it surveyed her with glinting yellow eyes. It stopped just inside the cave.

She eased her right hand away from her body toward the pile of sticks Nicholas had left for the fire. There looked to be enough life left in the glowing coals to rekindle a flame.

"Begone!" she cried, outrage lending a knife's edge to her voice that almost hid its quavering. Closing her hand about a stout branch, she drew it toward the fire. The wolf's gaze remained fixed upon her face. "Begone, I say! Get out of here," she ordered as she slipped the stick into the coals.

She groped at her waist for the eating knife, certain she'd tucked it into her gown before she settled to rest earlier. Her questing fingers found it, and she gave a silent prayer of thanks.

Her nostrils flared at the feral stench rising from the wolf's shaggy body in the warmth of the cave. She suppressed a nervous chuckle. It must really stink to overpower her own smell.

The scent of burning wood cut through the other odors as she sat there, still captured by the wolf's avid gaze.

He believed he knew where they were.

It had been a wonderful day. Nicholas laughed for the sheer joy of it.

As they entered the cluster of trees surrounding the hilltop, Idris stopped in his tracks and dropped the rabbits. All his attention focused on the yet unseen clearing ahead.

Nicholas dropped to his knees beside the dog and placed a hand on his shoulder, reaching for his knife with the other. "What is it?" he murmured.

The mare let out a squeal of terror, the sound followed by an unmistakable howl. Nicholas tossed the pig aside and ran, his blood frozen in his veins. Idris raced after him.

One word throbbed through Nicholas's head in time with his pounding feet.

Wolves.

She darted a glance at the stick and saw a thin smoke rise from it before the wood caught fire.

Thank God! She doubted the animal's curiosity— tience—could last much longer.

Nor could she.

Her fingers tightened about the stick as more snar shadows crept forward. What should she do? She da not sit here, waiting for Nicholas Talbot to rescue her again.

The blood of warriors flowed in her veins; now was the time to use that fact to her advantage. A man would not wait for deliverance...he would act, no matter how uneven the odds.

She had complained about that particular masculine trait often enough. Perhaps it wasn't so bad a habit, after all.

Catrin snatched the burning stick from the fire with one hand and whipped the dirk from her waist with the other. Despite her trembling limbs, she leapt to her feet, thru the stick before her and screamed as loud as she could.

Nicholas climbed the path to the cave eagerly. Blo streaked his chest and chausses, and he carried a yo boar under one arm. He couldn't hold back a grin could not recall ever enjoying a hunt so much.

But then, it had been a long time since his stomac been so empty.

Idris trotted at his side, a brace of rabbits carrie derly in his massive jaws. He'd earned his keep to magnificent hunter, he was surprisingly stealthy, ering his size, and alert to the faintest hint of pre

Nicholas's spirits were high for another reason They'd traversed far afield, and he was almost c recognized the terrain.

Chapter Eleven

Gwal Draig, Northern Wales

As the walls of Gwal Draig came into view on the crest of the hill, Lord Ian ap Dafydd spurred his mount into a ground-eating gallop. His battle cry bursting from his lips, he bent low over the stallion's neck, the cloak billowing out behind him giving him a heady sense of freedom. His hair whipped about his head, the long dark strands lashing his face as he savored the familiarity of his surroundings.

Home.

Now all he needed was a tongue-lashing from Catrin to make his homecoming complete.

The gates clanked open before him, the guard's shout nearly lost in the hollow clatter of hooves over the drawbridge. His troops thundered after him.

Ian tossed the reins to a stable lad and searched the gathering crowd for his sister. She was usually among the first to greet him, but he didn't see her anywhere.

"God save you, milord," someone called across the courtyard.

Father Marc hurried from the keep, wending his way

through the chaos. Lines of worry etched the priest's usually cheerful face. Ian knew a moment's panic as he wondered what predicament Catrin might have fallen into in
his absence.

Though only two years her elder, he had always looked
after his sister, even before their parents' death six years
earlier. And though her years now numbered four and
twenty, he had no desire to break the habit—most of the
time.

Father Marc joined him at last. "Thank goodness
you're here, milord." The priest wrung his hands, then
shoved them into the trailing sleeves of his coarse brown
robe.

"What has she done this time?" Ian removed his cloak
and tossed it to a passing servant. He should likely dis-
count the man's distress, since Catrin's actions almost always had this effect on him. At times, Ian wondered if
she did it apurpose, simply to jar the serenity of Father
Marc's existence. Fighting back a grin, he asked, "Is my
sister afraid to face me?"

"'Tis far worse than that, milord." Father Marc stared
down at the muddy ground.

Ian ran a hand through his tangled hair and sighed.
"Tell her to meet me in my chambers, then. I can await
her pleasure more comfortably there," he said, thinking
longingly of a steaming bath and a horn of hot spiced
mead.

He turned to leave, but Father Marc grabbed his arm.
"She cannot, sir. I'm sorry to say—"

At Ian's look of surprise, the smaller man released him.
"You can tell me the particulars inside." Ian headed for
the keep. "Although it's probably too late, I'd rather not
air our dirty linen in the bailey, if you don't mind."

"Lord Ian."

Ian stopped. Never had he heard such demand in the priest's voice. Hands on hips, he turned, giving Father Marc a stern look. "Out with it, Father. I can see I'll not have a moment's peace until you've had your say."

"Lady Catrin is not here, milord."

"What? I left strict orders that she not leave Gwal Draig without me." Frustration lent an edge to his voice. Why hadn't the priest said something before now, instead of hesitating? "Where did she go?"

"She left for l'Eau Clair two days ago."

Ian's exasperation disappeared, replaced by icy tendrils of dread. The niggling signs of threat toward Catrin might have no source save his imagination, but he'd learned to trust his instincts.

They seldom failed him.

Damn her!

"Dai!" he shouted, scanning the knot of men near the stables for some sign of his second-in-command.

"Right here, milord." The voice came from behind him.

Ian turned. "Have fresh horses readied, and provisions for several days. We'll take six men with us—that should be enough." With a glance at the gray sky, he tried to gauge how much daylight they had left. A few hours, no longer. "Be ready to set out in an hour."

Dai grimaced, but his pale blue eyes held resignation. "Going after your sister, milord?"

News traveled swiftly. "Aye. It seems she couldn't wait to visit Lady Gillian."

Dai nodded and headed for the stables, leaving Ian to question the priest.

"I tried to stop her, milord. I told her she should wait—"

"I'm sure you did," Ian reassured him. "I also know how stubborn she is."

Father Marc's expression eased. "If you've no further need for me, milord, I'll return to my duties."

"Nay—come with me. I want to know who went with her and where she planned to go, among other things."

There was no time to waste. He should have warned Catrin about the rumors he'd heard. But telling Catrin she was in danger was tantamount to issuing a challenge. He'd hoped to avoid involving her at all—or at least until he had the situation in hand.

It was too late for regrets now.

But he wouldn't rest until he saw that Catrin had arrived safely at l'Eau Clair.

Nicholas raced toward the cave, Idris hot on his heels. He took in the situation at once. Two shaggy wolves harried the mare, nipping at her throat. But Idris leapt into the fray and turned their attention toward him.

Nicholas left the dog to deal with them and went to the mare. Her eyes rolled wildly, and blood and foam flecked her coat. She had several slashes along her neck, but the injuries didn't seem bad. She'd weathered the attack well.

Thank God they arrived in time! He would hate to lose her. Though she didn't look like much, she had heart; she'd proven that already. And he would need her plucky determination again soon, to carry Catrin away from here.

He had just cut the hobbles and jerked the reins free when a scream split the air.

Were there wolves in the cave?

Tugging the mare along behind him, he swiftly looped the reins around a tree near the cave. Two more wolves skulked away from the doorway as he drew near. The screaming did not cease.

Dagger in one hand, stick in the other, he crept into the cavern.

One wolf remained, larger than the others—clearly the leader of the pack. He stood halfway across the room, fangs bared, his lean body poised to attack. All his attention centered on Catrin, crouched on the other side of the fire.

Catrin looked like a warrior woman, a diminutive Valkyrie come to dispatch her enemy to hell. She held a dirk in her left hand, a burning brand in her right. Her lips were drawn back in a fair approximation of the wolf's snarl.

Even as he feared for her, Nicholas couldn't help but be moved by her wild beauty.

She tossed her hair back over her shoulder. "Come to me, you bastard. Go ahead—jump. You'll get more than you bargained for, I swear it." She feinted with the flaming stick, forcing the wolf back a step, but he remained vigilant. "What do you want me for, you bloody beast? Take a bite of me, and you're like to die on the spot."

Nicholas held back a chuckle at her words. He didn't want to distract her attention, make the beast pounce.

"Come on, you coward," she coaxed. "You want me, come and get me. I'll not make it easy for you—I'm damned tired of being attacked."

The beast seemed bewitched by her voice, for he didn't move, not even when she jabbed the stick toward him. Nicholas, heart climbing into his throat, watched her edge nearer to the wolf, still thrusting with the stick. The wolf snarled and drew himself into a tighter crouch.

He looked ready to leap.

There'd be no better chance. Nicholas clutched the sharpened stick in his right hand and launched himself onto the wolf's back just as the beast lunged.

He heard Catrin scream, but all his attention remained upon the snarling, squirming bundle of fury caught in his arms. He dropped the stick and scrabbled for a firm grip in the animal's thick, shaggy pelt.

A claw raked his face. The slash burned, lending him strength. Nicholas leaned his weight onto the wolf's back, clamped his arm around its neck and slashed his knife across its throat.

As a warm stream of blood poured over his arms and thighs, Nicholas felt the life drain from the beast. The body twitched once, then slumped in his grip. Dropping to his knees, he cast it aside.

"Nicholas." Tears streamed down Catrin's face. She knelt beside him and wrapped her arms about him, blood and all.

Nicholas held her trembling body, shaking himself from exertion—or was it from relief? Careful of her wounds, he cradled her against him.

"Did he harm you?" Her tears alarmed him. He hadn't seen her cry, not through the pain she'd endured. That she would do so now concerned him.

She cuddled closer. "No." Shuddering harder, she looked down at the body, then buried her face against his bare shoulder. "A noise woke me. I thought it was Idris, but when I looked up, 'twas the wolf." She raised her head and looked over his shoulder at the door. "There were others." She tried to move from his arms. "Where is Idris? The mare…"

He tightened his hold. "Several ran off, and Idris will keep them away."

Mumbling disjointed protests, she made as if to rise, but he refused to release her. "Hush, Catrin." He wiped away her tears. "They're fine. Idris can take care of himself, and I left the mare tied right outside."

Her skin felt soft beneath his fingertips, and her moist lips glistened in the fading light, tempting him. He couldn't resist. He tilted her chin up with his free hand and lowered his mouth to hers.

Her lips felt as delicate as they looked, like the petals of a rose. After a trifling hesitation they moved against his. He slid his hands from her face to cradle her head, sinking his fingers into her tangled curls.

Catrin's hands clung to his shoulders, moving against his skin in a delightful caress. Shivers glided over his back and chest in their wake.

He drew a shaky breath and fought the urge burning through his veins—to lower her to the floor and ease his aching body. Instead, he contented himself with seducing her mouth.

He hadn't realized how enjoyable building that ache could be. Had his entire body become more sensitive, more attuned to Catrin? The slight increase in her breathing, the almost imperceptible tremor running along her skin...subtle signs of arousal he'd never noticed before.

Catrin's response vibrated through him, intensifying his own desire. He eased her closer, until her unbound breasts pressed into his chest. Only a single layer of cloth separated them, a barrier so thin it might as well not exist. He could almost—almost—imagine staying like this, savoring the exquisite sensation.

But there were so many other possibilities to explore. Catrin's hand crept into his hair, her fingertips kneading at his scalp. He drew a deep breath. The caress shimmered along his spine to settle into the growing heaviness in his loins. 'Twas a heady torture.

When Nicholas's tongue swept into Catrin's mouth, it sent a bolt of heat quivering over her skin. She wanted to burrow closer, absorb him into her very being. Her tongue ventured out to imitate his, stroking his lips, savoring the difference in texture between his satiny mouth and whisker-stubbled face.

A moan shuddered through him. Her heart tripped with pleasure.

She had caused that sound—a reaction to her.

Opening her eyes, she searched his face. His eyes were closed, and a flush rode high along his cheekbones. "Come back," he whispered, his mouth seeking hers.

Power surged through her, kindling a strange warmth deep within her. *She* could make this mighty warrior moan. She kissed him again, eager to see what he would do.

Almost as though he sensed her gaze, his lashes swept open. Heat flooded her face as she stared into his eyes.

She had considered violet a cool, emotionless shade; she would make that mistake no longer. Passion flared from Nicholas's eyes, sending an answering fire surging through her.

Something cold and wet touched her neck. "What was that?" She plastered herself more snugly against Nicholas.

He looked over her shoulder and laughed. "Your dog is jealous."

Idris bumped Catrin on the arm with his nose, then shoved his head between them to lick her face. "Stop it, you slavering idiot!"

"He's only trying to stake his claim." Nicholas reached up and rubbed Idris's neck.

She swiped her hand across her cheek. "That's disgusting."

Nicholas grasped her about the waist and settled her in his lap. "He's doing what I did. Did that disgust you?"

Did he want to discuss this...now? She wasn't ready for that.

When she looked away and slipped from his grasp, he didn't stop her. Instead he helped her settle on her pallet.

"At least you didn't drool on me," she mumbled.

An odd expression crossed his face as he looked at her. "'Twas a near thing."

She followed his gaze and looked down. Her gown had slipped low over her bosom. Her face heated—no wonder he stared! She tugged the fabric higher and pulled her cloak tight about her.

A chill swept through her, washing away the pleasurable heat Nicholas had kindled. She must have been mad to let things go so far.

From the moment Nicholas touched her, she had no control over the situation—

No control over herself.

She'd become a creature possessed by needs, needs she'd do well to ignore.

Thank God Idris interrupted when he did. What had she been thinking, to fall into Nicholas's embrace so easily?

She hadn't thought at all. In her relief that Nicholas had destroyed the wolf, she'd simply reacted. It seemed she could not trust herself in his presence.

It would not do.

She pushed the soft, wonderful, *woman's* feelings deep and tried to bury them beneath her usual, prickly facade.

She couldn't do it.

The sight of the wolf carcass sprawled on the floor sent a chill through her. "You might have been killed." Her voice shook. She stared at the blood spattered across Nicholas's arms and chest. Her stomach twisted, and dizziness washed over her. "'Twas my fault the wolf got into the cave."

Nicholas looked up. Where was the warrior now? He knew as well as anyone the unsteadiness that followed battle. Mayhap 'twas why she had allowed him to hold her.

He shouldn't assume 'twas anything more.

After a swift look at her wan face, he turned his attention to cleaning the knife. "How is it your fault?" He stood and tucked the dagger into his waistband, frowning as he tugged at his blood-soaked chausses.

"I wasn't ready, hadn't paid attention," she said, her breathing uneven. "That cursed beast would have eaten me for his supper if you hadn't come back when you did."

"Nay. You'd have taken care of him yourself if you had to." This wasn't like Catrin at all, he thought, concerned. Why didn't she insult him for not being there when she needed him, or rage at him for taking advantage of her?

He knelt beside her and drew her back into his arms, surprised when she offered no protest, no resistance. Instead she seemed to welcome his embrace, for she slid her arms around him in turn.

Though he didn't understand why she held him, nothing on earth could keep him from her now.

God only knew how long such peace would last.

Chapter Twelve

They sat huddled together until it was nearly full night. The fire had dwindled to little more than a heap of coals, and Nicholas could scarcely see. It would be so easy to drift off to sleep, comfortable with Catrin held snug in his arms.

But a multitude of tasks awaited him. He fought the temptation of her embrace and tried to ease away, but she clung to him, her arms wound about him like a vine. "I have to get up," he whispered into her hair. "Look, 'tis cold and dark—I need to build up the fire."

Murmuring drowsily, she pressed closer to him. He slipped her arms from about his shoulders. "I brought you a surprise, if the wolves didn't steal it. Come, milady, let me up. 'Twill take but a moment."

Finally, a sleepy smile curving her lips, she released him. He carried her closer to the fire and eased her back to rest against the wall. She felt limp, and he knew she'd lost weight. She needed to eat.

At least now he had something substantial to feed her.

He stirred up the coals, watching with satisfaction as the flames licked at the wood. By the time he got rid of the wolf and looked after the mare, the fire should be just right to roast a tender haunch of pig.

He lit a torch and stuck it in the wall, then turned to discover Catrin watching him, an unfamiliar expression in her eyes.

He pretended not to notice, for her scrutiny made him uncomfortable. There was a warmth in her gaze he'd never seen before.

'Twas truly surprising, considering his present state. Filthy, blood-smeared and rank, he could scarcely stand himself. Perhaps he should bathe in the stream—the cold water would be welcome to cool his blood.

He rubbed his fingers over the raspy beginning of a beard. The dagger would serve as a razor—no sense scraping Catrin's delicate skin...

He had no sense at all.

Have I gone mad?

An icy flood of reason rushed through him, ebbing the still-warm glow of desire until nothing was left but self-disgust. In the past he'd scoffed at any man who let his rod rule his brain. Now he seemed in danger of making the same mistake.

He needed a cold bath, all right. He only hoped 'twould jolt some sense into him.

He grabbed the wolf by the hind legs and dragged it from the cave.

"Don't be long," Catrin called after him.

Completely uncertain how to deal with her, Nicholas fled the cave.

Catrin awoke to the ambrosial smell of roast pork.

"Decided to join us?" Nicholas asked, his voice curiously flat.

"Is that real food I smell?" She untangled herself from

her cloak and shoved it aside. When she sat up, a groan escaped her lips before she could hold back the sound. Earlier she'd felt little pain; her attention had been on simply staying alive. Now she would pay. She felt as if she'd been beaten, and her wounds pulsed with a fiery throb.

Squeezing her eyes closed, she shifted until she could rest one shoulder against the wall.

Nicholas brought her water. "Do you want the powder mixed into this?"

She shuddered at the thought of enduring more of the potion-induced sleep. "Nay. Sometimes it gives me bad dreams."

"This is no dream, I assure you." He moved back to the fire and turned the meat. Fat crackled and snapped as it dripped into the flames, making her mouth water. "It's nearly ready."

He handed her a damp cloth to wipe her face and hands. "How do you feel—truly?"

She darted a look at his face. He didn't meet her gaze, his expression one of studied indifference.

Good. Perhaps he was as ready as she to forget their earlier madness. "As well as you'd expect, after the past few days."

"That's not what I asked."

Why did he continue to press her? "I feel like something scraped from beneath the wheels of a baggage wain—after ten teams of oxen trod over me." She scrubbed at her face with the rag. "And I smell worse than the bottom of a midden." She flung the cloth at him. "Satisfied?"

He snatched the rag out of the air, a grin lighting his face. "Not quite...but getting closer." His smile disappeared as swiftly as it came, his expression settling again into the distant look his face had worn before. "I asked for a reason. I traveled far today, into an area that seemed familiar. I believe we're not far from my keep at Ashby."

"Ashby is yours?" She hadn't realized that. But then, she knew little about Nicholas Talbot—save how he made her feel.

He glanced away. "Aye."

"You could be right. Is that where you were headed when we were set upon?" She had wondered what he was doing, wandering the Welsh countryside on his own.

"No. King John sent me to see Llywelyn. Otherwise I would have stayed at l'Eau Clair until after my godchild's birth. I've not been to Ashby in a long time." He looked grim. "I'd rather not go there now, either, but we need better food and shelter than we have here. And your wounds should be examined by someone who knows what they're doing."

"Could we try for l'Eau Clair? I promised Gillian I would be there to deliver the babe. That's where I was going."

"Nay, Ashby is closer. And we aren't as likely to run into our attackers. I'd rather not face them now, unprepared. I'll deal with them later," he vowed.

Catrin stared down at her fingers, knotted together in her lap. "Ian said he'd escort me to l'Eau Clair, but I refused to wait. All those lives lost—their deaths are my fault."

"Did you know you'd be attacked on the journey?"

Her head jerked up. "Of course not!"

"Then how is it your fault?" he asked impatiently. "People are beset by robbers everywhere. 'Twas just your misfortune that they were an overeager lot. Mayhap they panicked when your guards fought back."

A huge lump settled into Catrin's throat; she could scarcely speak. "Nay. 'Twas me they wanted."

"What?"

"Someone hired them to kill me, or take me captive." The doubt in his eyes acted as salt upon her lacerated emotions; her only outlet was anger. "Do you doubt me? *I heard them say it.*" She dashed away an errant tear. "Just before they debated whether to use my body to appease their appetites before they left."

"Foul knaves." The lean planes of his face settled into a warrior's mask. "Who would want you dead?"

"Any number of people, I'm sure," she said bitterly. "You're not the only person I irritate."

His smile surprised her. "I wouldn't call it irritation, exactly." His expression became serious once more. "Besides, that's no reason to kill someone. At least the bandits were unsuccessful, thank God."

"Whether they killed me or not is unimportant. But the others who were killed—their deaths matter. There was a boy, Padrig. He was a good lad. Rannulf said he'd train him, let him be his squire."

"I didn't see a boy's body among the dead."

"Before they got to us I sent him for help, but I doubt he knew where to go. I hope someone finds him before he comes to harm. He didn't deserve this, any more than the guards did. They were good men, with wives and families." Tears rolled unchecked down her cheeks. She swiped them away. "I failed them by my selfishness. They were doing their duty, obeying my orders. I failed in my duty to them."

Nicholas came closer and tried to take her in his arms, but she pushed him away. "Nay, don't comfort me. This pain is no more than I deserve."

"At least allow me to look at your injuries," he said

quietly. "Will you let me do that? You needn't refuse to care for yourself in punishment for what happened."

"Don't mock me."

"I'm not." His hand settled on her shoulder, offered comfort. Catrin shrugged it away. "I honor your concern for your people."

His sympathy was unbearable, reminding her of her folly. "Let me be," she snarled, striking out at him with her fist. She connected hard with his face.

Pressing her throbbing hand against her lips, Catrin watched in horror as the area around Nicholas's left eye began to swell.

"I'm sorry, Nicholas." Never had she meant an apology more. The area where she hit him had already begun to discolor, a dark purple bruise rising to mar the flesh beneath his left eye.

Ignoring the injury, he glared at her. "Why, Catrin? I meant you no harm. I only wished to comfort you."

Flames flared up around the roasting pork, and he snatched it from the fire and set it aside. "Sometimes when I'm around you I feel like this piece of meat. If I come too close to you, you scorch me with your anger, an anger I don't understand."

Leaving the fire, he sat near her, forcing her to face him—and his words. "What is it about me that provokes you?" he asked, his eyes intent. "You judged me and found me lacking the first moment we met. Nothing you've said or done since has shown that your opinion has changed, unless 'twas for the worse." His gaze shifted from hers and he toyed with the lacings of his shirt.

He lowered his hands to rest upon his thighs. "Likely there's little that's good in me. But why do I anger you?" She felt his question—and his confusion—to her very soul.

But Catrin didn't want to lay bare her darkest secrets, her deepest shame.

How dare he ask for the weapons to destroy her?

As was her habit when threatened, she kindled the anger burning within, summoned her temper to a fiery conflagration. But as she gazed at the intensity in Nicholas's expression, all his attention centered on her, an icy douche of self-reproach doused her anger, leaving in its wake the bitter ashes of shame.

She lowered her gaze, stripped naked without the cloak of anger to protect her. Once she pushed the haze of ill temper aside, the meaning of his words finally seeped through. "How can you say there's little good in you? You've the patience of a saint, to suffer my provocation without strangling me. And you saved my life, at the risk of your own—for which I thank you. These are the actions of a decent man."

Nicholas's gaze shifted to hers, then slid away. The arrogant Lord Nicholas Talbot, uncomfortable with praise? Catrin reached out and touched his cheek, turning him toward her. "You don't believe me, do you?"

"Don't." He jerked away from her hand when she would have held his face still.

"Nicholas?" She reached out and stroked her palm across his cheek, noticing for the first time that the skin beneath her hand was now smooth shaven. Along with everything else he'd accomplished while she slept, he must have shaved, as well.

But he still refused to meet her gaze. It seemed he had troubles of his own.

Perhaps she shouldn't burden him with her secrets, too. "The fault is with me." She strove for a light tone. "You know that I possess a sour disposition. Don't blame yourself for my bad temper," she said, trying for a careless laugh.

He brought his hand up to cover hers, holding it against his face. "Don't think to put me off with falsehoods, Catrin. There has been something wrong between us from the beginning. Do you remember how it was at l'Eau Clair? By the time you left we were at each other's throats like wild dogs."

His eyes glowed like amethyst in the flickering firelight. Catrin stared into their smoky depths, mulling over how much she dared reveal. Her stomach knotted, as if to hold all her vile secrets deep inside.

The fault lay not with him, but within her. She was a coward, hiding behind arrogance and ill temper to avoid the demons who tormented her. Awake or asleep, she couldn't escape them.

Perhaps the time had come to face those demons.

Stiffening her spine—both mentally and physically—Catrin closed her eyes and breathed deeply.

"What are you doing?"

Her eyes snapped open at the sound of his voice. Catrin stared at him, enjoying the harmony of his features, avoiding the bruise she'd given him. A feeling of security settled over her. The shadows enclosed them in a soothing cocoon, the sensation heightened by the warm glow of the fire.

She'd never have a better opportunity than this. He'd already seen her at her worst. She doubted she could shock him, no matter what she said.

Inhaling deeply, she said, "I'm preparing myself to meet my enemy."

He took her hand in both of his and lowered it to rest on his thigh. "I'm not your enemy."

Her lips curled into a trembling smile. "I know you're

not." Now that the time had arrived to finally speak of it, she didn't know if the words would come. "My enemy has no form, no substance. I cannot face it with knife and sword, to battle it into submission."

"You speak in riddles," Nicholas said, weaving their fingers together. "If you'd rather not tell me—"

"Nay," she whispered. Clearing her throat, she raised her voice. "Nay, I must. The past is my foe. I cannot fight it, or alter it, yet it shapes my life—my very being."

"Everyone has things in their past they'd rather forget. But those same things shape the person you are now."

She tried to pull her fingers free, but he wouldn't allow it. "Exactly. My temper, the way I react to you, has nothing to do with you personally. 'Tis a result of something in my past."

Perhaps he'd be satisfied with her vague reply.

Nicholas slanted her a knowing look. How could she imagine he'd be appeased with so little? "What you said doesn't explain a thing." He grasped her chin with his free hand, staring into her eyes. "I deserve more than that, don't you think?" He stroked a finger over her cheekbone, noting the way her gray eyes darkened at his touch. "You cannot convince me you react the same to everyone. I know you do not. Your response to me is stronger—in every way."

A flush mantled her cheeks. Nicholas knew she understood his meaning. "Tell me," he added mockingly, raising his fingers to lightly touch his swollen cheekbone, "how many men have you punched in the eye?"

Again, she tried to wrench her hand away. "Let me go!"

"So we're back to that." He tugged her closer, until she squirmed against his chest. "What will you do if I don't release you? Hit me again?"

Catrin ceased her struggles, though the look she gave him might have slain a weaker man. But they'd gone too far for Nicholas to be satisfied. He didn't want her compliance. He wanted—no, he needed—an explanation.

How else could he help slay the phantoms that haunted her?

"Why do you taunt me, why do you strike out at me every chance you get?" Nicholas grasped her upper arms to hold her still. Beneath his palms her muscles tightened as her tension grew.

"Do I make you feel trapped?" he asked, dragging her up so close to his face that every panting breath she took blew across his lips. "Do I threaten you in some way? Is it me, or is it because I'm a man?"

Her eyes grew frantic, and even as he watched he saw her begin to distance herself, escaping to a place deep within her where he knew he couldn't reach. "No you don't," he said, shaking her. "Stay here."

A whimper darted through her lips and her eyelids closed. "No, Catrin. You cannot run away. Look at me." Nicholas eased his grip when she whimpered again, but he refused to release her. "Look at me," he growled when her eyes remained closed.

"Let me go!" She turned into a writhing, fighting fury within his arms. "Let me go, don't touch me," she repeated, her voice as fierce as her struggles.

A reaction! Nicholas would have fallen to his knees and given thanks if he hadn't been otherwise occupied. But Catrin in a frenzy was a formidable opponent, requiring all his attention.

He let her lash out, easily evading the worst of the blows. Eyes still shut, she squirmed and clawed at him. As he dodged her fist before it connected with his nose, he wondered if she even knew who she fought. All her attention seemed focused within.

He gradually became aware that the breathless cries she made were words, words that made his blood run cold as their meaning became clear.

It was the only explanation that made any sense.

She'd been raped.

Chapter Thirteen

So much became clear to him now, especially Catrin's strange behavior when the fever held her in its grip. At the time, he'd wondered whether her words and actions were part of a fever-induced dream.

It was far more likely she'd been reliving a nightmare.

And he'd forced her to relive it now. Nicholas released her and, shifting to sit beside her, wrapped her in his arms. "Hush, Catrin, hush. No one will harm you ever again," he soothed, scarcely aware of what he said as he sought to haul her back from the nightmare. Clearly it was a place of terror and fear for her, and he'd driven her to it.

His arms crossed over her chest, he held her to him, brushing his lips along her brow as he murmured comforting nonsense. Eventually he felt the fight go out of her, leaving her slumped back against him. Drawing a deep, shuddering breath, Catrin brought her hands up and clasped them around his forearms. When he tightened his embrace she sighed and turned her head, brushing her cheek along his throat where his shirt was unlaced.

"I'm sorry," Nicholas whispered into her hair. "I didn't mean to push you so hard."

He felt her near silent, mirthless laugh. "Didn't you?" she asked in a weary voice.

"Aye, I did. But I didn't realize what your reaction would be." He leaned back against the wall, settling Catrin more comfortably across his lap. "I only wanted you to tell me why you respond the way you do to me."

"It's not you, Nicholas." She brushed her hand along his forearm, absently stroking the blond hair growing thickly there. "Well, perhaps it is you, though not the way it might seem."

"I don't understand. You've attacked me from the moment we met. I hadn't even had a chance to open my mouth and show you what a dolt I am."

Under normal circumstances his comment would have lured an answering insult from Catrin, but she only ducked her head. After a moment he heard her murmur against his neck, "It was because you're so handsome."

"I'm pleased you think so, but what has that to do with insulting me?" Since his looks had never mattered much to him, he was surprised to discover that her compliment did please him.

"I didn't want to be attracted to you," she said in a small voice, burrowing deeper into his lap as though trying to escape some danger.

If she kept that up, he'd be the menace, for she'd soon be sitting atop an ever growing threat. He liked the feel of her slight weight snuggled against him too well.

After chastising his single-minded body for its rebellious behavior, he forced his attention back to her words. "If I allowed myself to like you—" she sighed and tightened her fingers, her nails biting into the muscles of his arms "—it might be harder to resist the temptation to know you better."

"There's nothing wrong with that."

"There is for me, Nicholas." Her voice was laced with pain. "I have nothing to give anyone."

"How can you say that? You're beautiful, brave, and you have a mind that would put most men to shame—"

Catrin shoved aside the joy his compliments gave her. "And a temper that would drive most men to murder." Her nails dug into his arms so deeply, she wouldn't be surprised to find she'd drawn blood. She eased her grip. "But those things mean little when weighed against the rest. I'm no virgin."

He cradled her within his arms. "But you weren't willing. From what you said, you were—"

"I was raped." Such a simple word for such a horrible act. It would have to suffice, for she doubted she could be more specific than that. It should be enough to silence him, at any rate, and to bring an end to the burgeoning attraction between them.

She prepared herself for the moment he'd push her away. No good could come from self-pity; 'twas a lesson Catrin had had plenty of opportunity to learn. Raising her chin, she forced a thread of steel into her voice—and her spine. "It doesn't matter how it happened. No man wants another's leavings."

There. The simple truth, ungarnished with excuses or prevarications. Surely he could accept it.

"And how do you know that?" Nicholas asked, his tone as harsh as hers. "Have you allowed any man close to you since it happened?"

"Only you," she whispered.

His arms felt like bonds, holding her close where she didn't belong. Catrin tried to wrench away, but Nicholas wouldn't let her, instead wrapping her tightly in his embrace, one hand pressing her head against his chest.

His heart beat beneath her ear, the steady pounding

chipping away at her resolve until all she had left was a pulsating sense of loss where her own heart should be.

God, how the emptiness hurt!

Turning in Nicholas's clasp, Catrin slipped her arms around his waist. "When he raped me," she sobbed, "he didn't just destroy my innocence, he violated my whole life."

Nicholas held Catrin in silence, attempting to rein in the fury burning in his blood when he considered all she hadn't said. He couldn't believe that the loss of her maidenhead, as terrible as it must have been for her, would have been enough to reduce her to this state. The Catrin he knew would have likely gelded the bastard and gone on with her life.

This had to be something more, something far worse than losing her virginity, he thought. He glanced down at her as she sobbed in his arms. She was a strong woman; whatever had been done to her must be correspondingly vile.

Eventually her tears ceased, and she rested unsteadily in his embrace. She didn't remain that way for long. Shoving her hair aside and swiping at her cheeks with her sleeve, Catrin sat up.

He could see that she intended to pretend nothing had happened. But he had no intention of permitting such folly. Catrin had held this pain within her too long, allowing it to fester. Whether she knew it or not, she needed someone to listen. He was willing—nay, more than that—driven to hear what had befallen her.

Besides, if he didn't learn the rest, wondering about it would drive him mad.

"We should eat before the food grows cold," Catrin said, shifting her weight from his legs. She trembled as she rose to her knees, giving the lie to her indifferent tone.

Nicholas caught her by the arm and pulled her back onto his lap. "To hell with food," he snarled. "We've gone this long without it, a little longer won't matter." Ignoring her resistance, he settled her astride his lap, his hands on her waist holding her still. "*You* need to talk, Catrin."

She raised her chin in the stubborn fashion he'd come to know well, meeting his stare. He caught his breath; her tears had lent a luminosity to her eyes, enhancing her beauty. By God, but she was lovely—the arrogant tilt of her head, the way her hair curled wildly, framing the delicate loveliness of her face.

But Catrin was no dainty flower, frail and weak. Her beauty lay in her strength, her ability to survive with courage in a brutal world. In his eyes she defined the very essence of womanhood.

She was magnificent.

Nicholas directed his body to ignore the surge of longing rolling through him as he stared in frank appreciation of the challenging, delectable woman seated on his lap. 'Twas lust, nothing more, an appetite unlikely to ever be appeased.

Especially in light of what Catrin had told him.

He knew she'd suffered at the hands of a man. Even if she were willing to disregard all the other reasons she should not entangle herself with him, Catrin likely had no desire to involve herself with any man.

She tossed her head and flipped her hair back from her face, some of the ebony strands grazing Nicholas's cheek. He sucked in his breath, battering down the ache arising from the inadvertent caress, and directed his attention to her words.

"I don't wish to talk. Release me, if you please." The haughty lady had returned with a vengeance, he thought, amused by the contrast between Catrin's tattered clothing and the air of command she wore like a mantle. "All I need is food and rest."

"Well then, perhaps I need to hear you talk."

"I don't care what you want, milord."

"At least tell me who did this to you so I—"

"He is dead," Catrin said flatly. "He cannot harm me further."

But what of the harm he continues to do you? Nicholas asked himself.

She looked at him curiously—perhaps his thoughts showed on his face. Reining in his frustration, he schooled his features to a bland expression. He'd find another opportunity to explore this further.

"You needn't concern yourself with this." She wriggled as she attempted to slide off his legs.

"Sit still, Catrin," Nicholas said sharply, clamping his hands about her waist. He squeezed his eyes shut and urged calm on his rampaging manhood. Didn't she realize what she did to him when she moved like that? A sigh escaped his lips; perhaps she didn't know. "When you squirm it only makes things worse."

Opening his eyes, Nicholas saw that the lofty dame had disappeared, leaving in her place a curious wood sprite.

"Makes what worse?" She reached out and stroked her hand along the place where a muscle twitched in his cheek—only one of the visible signs of his tension, he thought, his mouth curving into a smile. Surprisingly her touch soothed him, and her answering smile eased some of the strain coursing through him. She didn't realize the reactions she prompted by the most innocent touch of her hand, he reminded himself. It was up to him to resist the temptation she so unwittingly presented.

Perhaps this wasn't the best time to try to wrest the

details from her. She didn't want to talk about it. How could he blame her? He knew what it was to live a lie, to hide the essence of his being. The Nicholas Talbot most people knew was naught but a lie, a creation designed to hide his true nature from those who would scorn him if they knew what he truly was like. Try though he might, his noble blood could not completely erase a man who was the product of his origins, a mercenary.

And if he thought about facing the place of his remembered fears and humiliation, his heart began to pound wildly in his chest.

He'd rather face an army of infidels than consider returning to Ashby.

But he had no choice in the matter. Catrin needed care he didn't know how to give. And if they didn't surround themselves with other people, he didn't know if he could defy the longing to make Catrin his. The yearning had grown so strong, so quickly, he feared he'd awaken some night and discover he'd already done the deed—or tried to. And given Catrin's experiences, and her temperament, that could cost him his manhood, at the very least.

And well it should.

Reaching up, Nicholas placed his hand over Catrin's, savoring the softness of her palm against his cheek for a moment before lifting her hand away. "I'm sorry," he said, his smile turning rueful, then disappearing altogether. "You're right, I shouldn't press you. I'm sorry for what happened to you, Catrin. But you shouldn't think it reflects on you—or makes you less appealing as a woman. I thought you were tempting before. I still do." His hands still clasped about her waist, he lifted her off his legs. "So I think I'd better remove the temptation before my body overrules my mind and does something we'll both regret."

Catrin couldn't prevent the slight lift her heart gave in her chest at his words. Though she knew it was wrong, she allowed herself to enjoy them for the nonce; it felt so good to believe that a man, a good man, desired her. Nothing could ever come of it, of course. Despite what he'd said, Nicholas couldn't possibly have a place in his life for someone like her.

But just for a moment, she told herself—for now it would do no harm to believe him. To trust him.

And surprisingly, she did trust him. A large part of her hesitancy around men came from the fact that she no longer believed she could discern a man's motive. After all, she'd made it easy enough for Madog to abduct her by her own naïveté. And since then, she couldn't help but suspect every man of evil intentions.

She knew it was foolish, but she simply couldn't help herself.

She'd always reacted too strongly to Nicholas Talbot for that very reason. As she'd told him, she found him attractive—more than attractive, now that she knew him better.

She watched in silence as he cut a slice off the piece of meat and handed it to her skewered on her knife. "Eat it slowly," he warned, taking a portion for himself. "Your stomach might rebel, otherwise."

Despite her growling stomach she did as he instructed, nibbling at the succulent meat. To distract herself from asking for more, as well as to satisfy the vague, odd feeling she'd gotten when Nicholas mentioned Ashby, she asked the first thing that came to mind. "Is Ashby a large keep? I've not heard much about it except that it commands a fine view of the river Dee." She licked some grease from her fingers. "The king's affairs must be important to drag you from your home. At least this sorry business gives you an opportunity to return sooner than you expected."

"Ashby isn't my home," he replied, all his attention seemingly centered on pulling at a loose thread on the knee of his chausses. "It's a possession, nothing more."

"All the same, I imagine you'll be glad to return." Nicholas looked up, his expression nearly startling a gasp from her. She hadn't seen this much pain in his eyes when he'd pushed the arrow though his arm. "We don't need to go there if you'd rather not." She placed her hand over his restless fingers.

His hand turned beneath hers, capturing her fingers in a tight clasp. Just as suddenly the tormented look left his face, replaced by a self-mocking air. "'Tis foolish, is it not, for a grown man to fear a place? But Ashby holds only bad memories for me, and I've not set foot there for twenty years," he said with a twist of his lips. "I didn't even go back once I inherited it."

"Surely you grew up there. Didn't you at least visit over the years?" Granted, her knowledge of Norman ways was limited, but what he said sounded unusual.

His jaw tightening, Nicholas leaned closer to her, his face nearly touching hers. Catrin almost pulled away from him when she noticed the odd gleam in his eyes.

"Visit?" he scoffed. "My uncle wouldn't have permitted us through the gates. My family wasn't welcome at Ashby, milady, or in any other noble household. But then, mercenaries seldom are."

Chapter Fourteen

Ian's journey to l'Eau Clair was wretched. The roads—
poor to begin with had become impassable in places.
They'd wasted hours traveling around the worst spots.

He wouldn't have been surprised if they'd discovered
Catrin bogged down along the way, but they saw no sign
of her.

Exhausted, mud-spattered and furious with his sister,
Ian led his men through the well-fortified gates of l'Eau
Clair with far less enthusiasm than he'd entered Gwal
Draig two days earlier.

Only the thought that soon he could vent his anger upon
Catrin herself made the journey bearable.

Gillian's husband, Rannulf, met him in the courtyard,
hand outstretched in greeting. "Ian, 'tis good to see you.
Gillian will be thrilled."

Ian removed his filthy glove and shook Rannulf's hand.
"How fares my cousin?" he asked as he dismounted and
handed the reins to a waiting servant.

Rannulf signaled to one of his men. "Owen, take Lord
Ian's men to the barracks and see to their comfort."

Ian nodded his approval. "You must have been expecting me." They headed for the stairs leading into the keep.

Rannulf's eyebrows rose. "Nay, though you're always welcome here."

"Catrin didn't warn you I'd be following on her heels?" He felt his anger build anew.

Rannulf stopped. "Catrin isn't here, Ian. We haven't heard from her in nearly a month. She sent word that you would escort her here once you'd finished some business for Llywelyn."

Ian pressed his fingers against the bridge of his nose, but it didn't subdue the pounding behind his eyes. He met Rannulf's worried gaze. "She and Padrig—the boy I offered you as a squire—left Gwal Draig four days ago with an armed guard."

"You saw no sign of them along the way?"

"'Twas all we could do to make it here. We had to leave the trail several times, since the path was blocked. I would guess they had the same trouble—it's been wet for weeks. Truth to tell, I expected—nay, I hoped—she was here." He fought to rein in his frustration. "We found no sign of a fight or struggle. They could be lost, but I doubt it. Catrin has traveled that route often enough to know the way."

Rannulf took his arm in a firm grip, pulling him to a halt outside the door to the great hall. "I'd rather you didn't tell Gillian, not yet," he said with surprising urgency. "She's not been well. If Catrin is missing, I don't know what effect it might have on her. She's gotten it into her head that no one but Catrin can deliver our child."

"Ian!"

Rannulf shook his head in warning, then ran down the stairs to meet his wife. Her movements cautious, Gillian crossed the muddy bailey to the foot of the stairs, an enormous basket held in her arms.

Ian waited, wondering how he could explain his presence.

The truth would not do.

Rannulf snatched the basket away from Gillian, scolding her all the while. Ian tried not to gawk once he had a clear look at her. She must be carrying twins, her stomach had grown so huge!

Rannulf had reason to worry. Childbirth was always dangerous, but if the babe were large, or if there were two...

Clearly Gillian needed Catrin's expertise as a midwife.

Catrin must be safe. But he couldn't avoid the suspicion that she was in danger, a feeling he'd had since he spoke with Father Marc.

They had to find her.

Gillian scolded Rannulf for his foolishness as he swept her into his arms and ran up the steep flight of stairs.

By the time Rannulf lowered Gillian to her feet on the landing, Ian had thought of a lie and, he hoped, erased the worry from his face.

Never one to stand on ceremony, Gillian ignored Ian's filthy clothes and moved into his open arms. "I'm so glad you're here, Ian." She kissed his cheek. "Where's Catrin?"

He returned her embrace and forced a smile. "I haven't been home yet. But since I was in the area, I decided to stop here and dry out. I may need to borrow your husband for a few days, if you'll let him out of your sight."

Gillian's green eyes, so like his own, narrowed. "Don't lie to me, cousin." Ian backed away, but he'd waited too long. She reached up, grabbed a handful of his hair and pulled.

"Let go, you little she-devil." She laughed at him and gave a final tug before she released him. "How do you stand her, Rannulf?" he asked as he rubbed his scalp.

"You should know better than to lie to me, Ian. I catch you at it every time." She linked her arm with his. "Come inside and take your ease."

He held his tongue until they had settled in an anteroom off the hall. He sprawled back against the padded bench and held the silver chalice he'd been drinking from against his aching head.

Gillian took the cup and refilled it. "Would you care to tell me why you're really here?" She joined Rannulf on another bench. "In spite of the way my husband tries to shield me—" she drew her hand along Rannulf's cheek "—I am not a dainty little flower, unable to bear the realities of life. You lie to protect me, and I'll not have it."

"You resemble Catrin when you take a man to task." Ian smiled at the flush that stained her ivory skin. "You don't look much alike," he reflected. "Perhaps it's your tone."

"Enough, Ian. Where is Catrin?"

Rannulf took her hand and kissed her palm, then laced his fingers with hers. "Why don't you believe him, love?"

The glare she sent him would have scorched a lesser man, but Rannulf remained unmoved.

"I'm not a fool." She jerked her hand free. "I want the truth, Ian. 'Twill harm me more to wonder what you're hiding. You might as well tell me." She sat back, folded her hands over the mound of her stomach and stared at him.

As he sought to avoid the accusation in her eyes, Ian's gaze came to rest upon her stomach. He'd swear it moved. How could she sit there and ignore it? Should he add to her misery?

He didn't want to distress her further.

"You might as well give in," Rannulf told him, his voice tinged with resignation. "We'll be here all night, otherwise."

Ian slammed his goblet down and leapt to his feet. "You win, cousin. But you're as stubborn as a damned ox." He knelt beside her. "'Tis because I care for you that I didn't want to say anything." He took her hands in his. "Catrin did not wait for me, Gillian. She left without me, days ago."

"Then where is she?" Gillian asked, her voice rising.

"I don't know." Ian stood. "You know as well as I that there's no stopping her once she decides to do something. These past few years—" he shook his head "—it's been worse. 'Tis as though she has no concern for her own safety...nor that of others, I'm afraid."

"Perhaps the poor weather kept her away," Gillian said hopefully. Her gaze shifted from Ian to Rannulf. "What danger could there be in traveling here?"

Ian sighed. "I've heard rumors of late, threats to me and mine. I don't know yet who is responsible, but when I find them... When I think of the work I've done for Llywelyn, plenty of possibilities spring to mind."

"You didn't tell Catrin about these threats, did you?" Accusation lent fire to Gillian's voice. "She's a woman grown, Ian, with a fine mind." Her eyes fairly shot daggers at both men. "You expect us to obey your dictates without ever giving a reason why we should."

"Enough, wife," Rannulf said sharply. "Don't blame Ian for what Catrin has done."

"Nay, Rannulf. She's right," Ian conceded wearily. "I should have warned her. I didn't want her to worry when I'm away. Nor listen to her concerns, either."

Rannulf stood, resting his hand on his wife's shoulder. "When do we leave?"

Gillian tugged him down beside her. After a whispered consultation, he nodded and straightened. "We'll find her, Ian. And if I know Catrin, once we do, she'll tear a strip off our hides for believing she could be in danger."

Although Rannulf appeared calm, Ian could see that worry shadowed his eyes. Unwilling to see his own fears reflected there, he nodded his thanks and turned away.

Gillian sighed. "As much as I want you to go, 'tis too late to set out now." After Rannulf helped her to her feet, she came to Ian and wrapped her arms about him. He returned the awkward embrace, resting his head against hers for a moment. "Rest awhile and take your ease," she added. "We'll have a search party ready to leave by first light."

Bryn Du

Steffan dug his spurs hard into the stallion's sides, pushing the beast to even greater speed. Nothing compared with this! The heady sense of strength, the mighty thrust of the animal beneath him—though the steed was powerful, he held dominion over it.

His mastery was complete.

If only he could say the same about the rest of his life. In the months since the debacle with Gillian, Llywelyn had begun to question everything Steffan did.

He gnashed his teeth. Not so long ago the mighty prince Llywelyn had depended on him for counsel. His opinion had worth, his word carried power. Now his visits to his kinsman were filled with sidelong glances, sly references to courage—or lack of it.

They were insults he didn't intend to bear for much longer.

He'd show them they were wrong.

Once he got his hands on Catrin he could manipulate

Ian any way he wished; 'twas well-known that the Dragon was a fool where his bitch of a sister was concerned. None would dare call him coward with Llywelyn's Dragon under this thumb!

And he might even get l'Eau Clair yet.

He'd waited for several days for the man Huw sent after Ralph and his bumbling pack of idiots to return, or to send word about where they'd taken Catrin.

He could not believe she was dead.

He hoped she wasn't. After his plans and schemes, his anticipation at finally getting his hands on his cousin, it couldn't all be for naught. He rammed his heels even harder into the stallion's sides as he considered the failure of his dreams.

At this point he didn't much care which woman he got. Gillian or Catrin, it didn't matter. Either of the wily bitches could provide him with entertainment—and the chance to gain more power than he'd ever have with only the puny estate of Bryn Du in his grasp.

Ah, the possibilities. Merely considering them sent a surge of power bursting through him, settling into an overwhelming ache in his loins. He squeezed his thighs more tightly around the barrel of the stallion, savoring the pounding rhythm between his legs. To gain dominion over either woman—or both—

He closed his eyes. 'Twould be the greatest pleasure he'd ever experienced. Pulling back on the reins, he jerked the stallion to a halt.

Women were mere vessels, receptacles for a man's lust. Power—and the anticipation of that power—was the true aphrodisiac. Emptying himself into a woman's body held little meaning to him beyond a temporary relief of tension.

Of course, if he could manage to get his hands on Gillian again once she'd rid herself of her Norman brat, she could be the means to greater power for him. She'd married that bastard FitzClifford, but there were ways to be rid of him, as well. Steffan felt his body spring to life at the thought of spilling his seed within the lush confines of Gillian's body.

That act would have meaning; impregnating Gillian with *his* child would ensure him possession of l'Eau Clair. The fickle hangers-on of Llywelyn's household would respect him as they ought to then.

Pounding hooves sounded along the trail behind him. His troops had finally caught up to him.

Smiling to himself, he watched in silence as Huw and his guard of four men brought their inferior nags to a shambling halt. "What took you so long?" he asked Huw, enjoying Huw's envious glare at his own magnificent steed.

"We were exploring, milord," he replied, his lips curled into a sneer. "We discovered something you might be interested in, if you've the time."

"What did you find?"

"It's better if you come see for yourself," Huw said. "'Tisn't far."

"Very well. Lead on." Steffan shifted in the saddle, falling into line behind Huw's rangy bay. He hoped 'twas something interesting. He was game for a bit of adventure. This was the first fine day they'd had for more than a week; he was sick of being caged up inside.

Huw led them through the rain-soaked trees to a copse not far from the walls of Bryn Du. Steffan recognized the place; he'd been there many times before. To his surprise a man-at-arms stepped out from the sheltering brush as they approached, running over to take the reins of his mount.

Motioning the others to remain on their horses, Huw dismounted and led Steffan across the clearing. "This way, milord," he said, pointing to a faint trail in the underbrush.

He followed Huw to a decaying tree lying alongside the path. Huw reached into the tall grass behind the tree, stirring up a cloud of flies and the stench of death, and dragged out a blood-smeared corpse. "Your spy didn't get very far," Huw said, rolling the body over to reveal the young soldier he'd sent to follow Ralph.

"Damnation! I knew there was more to those idiots than there appeared to be." Steffan kicked at the log, sending pieces of rotten wood flying. "I should have realized that no one could be that inept."

He whirled and grabbed Huw by the tunic. "Couldn't you at least have chosen someone who knew enough to stay alive?" he snarled, leaning toward the other man and flinging the words into his face. He tightened his fingers in the coarse fabric, fighting the temptation to close them around Huw's throat instead. "I need to know where they went."

Cursing under his breath, he thrust Huw away, backhanding him across the face and knocking him onto his backside. "Find yourself another spy—one who knows his business this time—and discover where Ralph went."

Huw rose slowly to his feet, wiping his bloody lip on his sleeve. Steffan noted Huw's glare with a smile of satisfaction. He didn't care if the man loathed him, so long as he did his duty. And it never hurt to knock some deference into servants, lest they forget their place.

Huw sketched a mocking bow. "As you wish, milord. Who would you suggest?"

"Must I do your job for you? How the hell should I know? Just choose someone capable of finding them." Steffan poked at the body with his toe, wrinkling his nose at the noisome stench. "Have you anyone with a brain?

Look at this—stabbed in the chest. Did he walk up to them and ask their plans?''

He leaned back against a tree and folded his arms. ''I need to know what they're doing. Catrin must be hidden somewhere close by. They didn't have enough time to go far. I don't know why Ralph would bother to hold her, but he must have her, the sneaky bastard.''

''Possibly they think to gain a greater bounty for her from someone else.'' Huw dragged the body into the middle of the trail. ''Her brother, perhaps.''

Pushing away from the tree, Steffan paced, his boots beating down the dry grass as he considered this development. ''Nay, you idiot.... Go to the Dragon to ransom his sister? They haven't the balls for that! Besides, they'd have to explain how they came to have her.'' He shook his head and stared off into the trees. ''No, they must have some other scheme in mind.''

''What should I do with him?'' Huw gestured toward the corpse.

''Toss him on the midden, for all I care.'' Steffan turned his back on the body. The man had failed him; he deserved no special consideration.

Steffan headed down the path toward his horse, leaving Huw to follow after him. Leaping into the saddle, he spurred the stallion toward the keep.

He had plans to make. He would find Catrin. And once he did, he'd use her to take Gillian, as well.

Power.

Soon the power would be his, Steffan vowed. Fire swept through his blood as he considered how best to shape his fate.

Chapter Fifteen

Catrin grabbed at the mare's bony withers and tried to hold herself upright. The movement sent pain radiating across her shoulders and neck. Wincing, she stifled a moan, not wishing to draw Nicholas's attention. But the terrain rose and fell so sharply, it took all her strength to remain atop the horse.

Her eyelids drooped with weariness. They'd waited one more day before they left the cave, a day filled with tension as she and Nicholas remained quiet and wary of each other. After another restless night they'd set out at dawn.

Nicholas must be tired, as well, leading the way on foot. He hadn't slept any more than she had. But he plodded on in silence, slashing a path through the bushes with a viciousness she would have expected of herself, not him.

Ever since his startling revelation the other night he'd been strangely silent, but his eyes reminded her of a cornered animal's. He refused to meet her gaze, and every time she'd opened her mouth to speak, the look he sent her froze the words before they left her lips.

By her estimation they'd been traveling for at least three or four hours. If Nicholas didn't call a halt soon, she'd have to ask him to.

Idris bounded back down the trail toward them. His injuries appeared to have done him little harm, she was happy to note. She seemed to be the only one still suffering the effects of the attack, if she discounted any misfortune Nicholas felt at being saddled with her. Considering the grief she'd given him, she couldn't blame him if he wished to leave her to her own devices.

But as she'd known all along, though only now would she admit it to herself, Nicholas Talbot was a decent man. Why else would he go to Ashby when it so clearly caused him pain?

He did it for her.

The mare stopped, jarring her from her thoughts. After looping the reins around a branch, Nicholas came to help her down. Though it galled her to confess it, she needed his help. She accepted his assistance without giving him her usual argument. He still looked greatly troubled.

Nicholas lowered Catrin to the ground, grabbing her about the waist again when her legs wouldn't hold her. He swung her into his arms and carried her to a grassy knoll alongside the path, uneasy with the way she trembled. "Rest here while I find some water."

She smiled as though to reassure him, but her face was very pale. Perhaps he could convince her to take some of the painkilling potion.

"I need to—" She tilted her head toward the trees. Nodding his understanding, he helped her stumble into the bushes. He stood waiting with his back to her, trying not to laugh at her sudden shyness. Evidently she didn't remember the things he'd done for her the past few days.

Or she chose not to.

When she rejoined him, he could see that it was an effort for her to manage the short distance. Sweeping her into his arms again, he carried her back to the knoll and wrapped her in the extra cloak.

He tried to check her for fever without being obvious about it, pulling the cloak up around her throat, but Catrin realized what he was doing. "Yes, I still have a fever," she said, burrowing deeper into the fabric. She grabbed his arm when he would have stood. "We don't have to go to Ashby, Nicholas. Not on my account."

The sympathy shining in her eyes shamed him. "Save your pity for someone who needs it, milady." He infused his voice with ice. Shaking off her hand, he rose to his feet. "I don't want it."

"But I'm feeling much better. If we wait a few more days I could go on to l'Eau Clair. You needn't do more than take me there, and then you'd be free to travel on to Llywelyn's keep to take care of your king's business. We need not go to Ashby at all."

Nicholas dropped wearily to the ground beside her. "Aye, 'tis necessary." Leaning against a tree, he tilted his head back and closed his eyes. "King John's business be damned! It can wait, for I doubt its importance. My liege enjoys making me jump to his commands. Indeed he has used the spur of my former life to goad me on." He opened his eyes. "But no more. I cannot hide my past—nor avoid Ashby—forever. I've taken the coward's way for too long already."

"You are no coward." She placed a hand on his arm, then removed it when he remained silent. "In spite of the things I said in the past, I never truly believed that of you. 'Twas only another insult to throw your way."

He scanned her face for a moment, then looked away. She meant the words, he was certain of it.

And glad.

But it changed nothing. He knew what he must do. "I

sent a man to Ashby to command it in my stead, but I've balked too long at going there myself and making it mine." He shook his head. "Besides, we're much closer to the place than to l'Eau Clair. If I brought you to Gillian in your present condition, 'twould shock her into giving birth on the spot—if she didn't kill me first."

"If you're sure." He nodded. "Then I'll gladly be your first guest, milord. Thank you for your kind invitation."

Hearing the smile in Catrin's voice, he could no longer ignore the temptation to look at her. Nicholas reached out to toy with the strands of hair curling about her face. "One of the things I've always admired about you—when I wasn't cursing you for it—is the way you meet every challenge headfirst. No hesitation, no equivocation, just an immediate response."

"Is that how you see me?" He couldn't be sure, but he thought 'twas pleasure softening her eyes to the pearly gray of dawn's first light. "I'm not like that at all. I'm never certain what to say or do. More often than not I'm wrong. You must have noticed."

"What I notice is that you always act. If you're afraid it never shows. Mastering one's fear is one of the first things a warrior learns, but of late I've allowed my fear to rule me. 'Tis a craven way to live."

"I'm sure you have reasons for avoiding Ashby," Catrin said. "I know what it is to dread something so much that I'll try to evade it at all cost."

"If you knew what my life was like before I inherited the honors of Ashby, you'd truly think me mad to have stayed away. There were times I would have given up the promise of heaven merely to have a roof over my head and enough food to fill my belly." He kept his features set in a smooth expression, but inside Nicholas shuddered as he remembered those days. "Of course, now I have the wealth of my holdings to provide me with a comfortable life. But I have other worries instead.'' *Such as what the king will do to me if I spoil his plans again,* he thought, giving a fatalistic shrug. "I wonder what it takes to be happy.''

He wondered if Catrin had heard him, not that it mattered. But her attention seemed to focus on something within, something humorous, judging by her expression. "Is what I said so funny?''

Eyes alight, she met his gaze, sending a jolt of pure appreciation through his overeager body. *Calm yourself,* he ordered. He stared at the trees, the sky—anything but Catrin. However, the full, rich—rare—sound of her laughter nearly destroyed all his efforts within the space of a breath.

"No, no, it's not that. I beg your pardon for laughing, but what you said reminded me of Gillian as a child.''

He was confused by the change of subject. What did Gillian's childhood matter when he couldn't think beyond fighting the insistent demands of his body?

"Clearly you've not heard what my beautiful, charming cousin was like as a child,'' Catrin said, one eyebrow raised questioningly.

"No, never.''

"Gillian's childhood was unusual by most standards. Her mother was dead, and Lord Simon, God rest his soul, knew nothing about raising a daughter. Gillian ran wild at l'Eau Clair, roaming the countryside dressed as a lad. The first time I saw her—she must have been ten or so— she was rolling about in the bailey wrestling with a pack of boys, as filthy as any villein.''

That was a sight he couldn't imagine! He couldn't contain a snort of laughter.

"Do you doubt me?" Catrin asked indignantly. "Ask your friend Rannulf about the first time he met his wife."

"I was there for that. I recall nothing unusual about it."

"I don't mean last year when you came to command l'Eau Clair. I'm talking about six or seven years ago. Rannulf didn't realize Gillian was a girl until she'd nearly bested him at swordplay. I hear she pinned him to the ground before he realized the truth." She laughed in remembrance.

"I wish I'd seen it," he said, chuckling so hard he could barely speak. "Rannulf is so proper, so noble. He took it hard, I'd imagine. But how did what I said remind you of this?"

"'Twas what you said about being happy. Before the confines of the outside world intruded on Gillian's life, she was probably the happiest person I've ever met. She gained so much joy from life. 'Twas beautiful to witness such innocence. But I think her happiness stemmed from the fact that she didn't know any better."

Wrapping his arms around his upraised knees, Nicholas considered her words. "Like Adam and Eve in the garden?"

Catrin nodded. "Few people ever have the opportunity to remain so unaware. And by our very natures, we always seem to want whatever we do not—or cannot—have, once we realize it exists."

"That's more true than you know," Nicholas muttered under his breath. In a louder voice he said, "Enough of such profound thoughts. Will you accept that I wish to go to Ashby?"

"I yield, milord. I'll badger you no further." Catrin's lips curved into an enchanting smile, her tongue darting out to moisten them.

He yearned for another taste of her mouth. Before he realized it, he'd brought his finger up and dragged it along her lower lip. When he pressed lightly, she opened her mouth enough to allow him access and he slipped his fingertip in, smoothing it along the damp, petal softness. The delicate brush of her tongue over his rough skin sent a trail of fire running directly to his loins.

Cupping her chin in the palm of his hand, Nicholas bent his head and trailed his tongue over the same path his finger had followed. He took her lips in the most delicate of abductions, scarcely dipping his tongue within the warmth of her mouth, enticing her to echo the caress.

Catrin sighed as she felt her breasts brush against his chest. Nicholas moaned, the sound vibrating from deep within him.

It acted as an alarm, cooling her ardor as swiftly as Nicholas had aroused it. Jerking her mouth from his, she stared at his lips, wanting nothing more than to kiss him again. "No, no, no. Why do I let you do this to me?" she groaned. She buried her face in her hands. "Why do I do this to myself?"

Nicholas slipped his hand beneath hers and gently forced her to raise her head. "Is it so wrong to kiss me? Or for me to kiss you?" He brushed his thumb along her lip.

"Stop that!" she demanded, pulling his hands away. "'Tis what started this in the first place. No more, do you understand?" She hated the quaver in her voice, for it showed Nicholas the reaction she couldn't hide.

"As you wish, Catrin," he said, bringing her hand to his lips. His eyes sending her some indecipherable message, he kissed her fingers, then placed a lingering caress on the inside of her wrist.

"You're right, 'tis time to go." When she would have

stood, her legs refused to hold her, so she allowed him to scoop her up off the ground and set her atop the mare.

Whistling Idris to his side, Nicholas took up the reins and set off.

His feet so cold and wet they felt like blocks of ice, Padrig stumbled and pitched forward, rolling headlong down the steep embankment. Experience had taught him to curl into a tight ball, though he already bore so many bruises, he couldn't imagine he'd ever look normal again. He made no effort to stop himself; 'twas futile. At least this was faster than trying to walk down the slippery slope.

He hit the bottom with a thud, then lay there, struggling to get his breath back. He didn't fight for air, as he'd done the first few times this happened, for all that did was close his lungs up more.

Despite his many aches and the fact that his stomach cried out for food, he couldn't help grinning.

He was alive!

Three days ago, he wouldn't have believed he could survive this long.

He'd been afraid—especially at night, when the clouds hid the moon and he could do little more than huddle under a pile of wet leaves until it was light enough to see. Sounds he'd never heard from within the confines of Gwal Draig sent shivers of foreboding rippling along his spine.

But as soon as he could see to travel, night or day, he set off once again. He had a mission, a duty.

He would save Lady Catrin, or die trying.

Padrig filled his lungs with air and rose to his feet. The only trouble with falling down a hill was that he still had to climb up the other side. He cast a glance at the pink-streaked sky. He hoped there would be sun today, instead of the unceasing rain, for it had been a struggle to get his bearings.

If he were correct, he should be near l'Eau Clair by now—or a town, a keep. Surely there must be people living here.

Somewhere.

These past few days, he'd felt as though he were the only person left in the entire world. Trudging through the forest, running when he could—he refused to give in to the fear that Lady Catrin might perish because he had failed her. But he found no signs of civilization, not so much as a shepherd's hut.

He paused to catch his breath when he reached the crest of the hill. After the first day, he'd learned to pace himself, to rest when he needed to. He made better progress.

The rhythmic sound echoing eerily through the trees was so faint, he almost didn't notice it over the noise of his ragged breathing. But the sound lingered, slowly grew louder, until he could place its direction.

Was it real, or a figment of his weariness?

Voices joined with hoofbeats, drawing ever nearer.

Padrig jumped up and headed toward the sounds. "Hello! Over here!" He raced through the trees onto a rough trail. Boots slipping in the mud, he climbed another rise and stood, panting, on the crest.

"Lord Ian!" he shouted as the riders came into view. Grinning, he waved his arms, then swiped at a tear with his sleeve as the men spurred their mounts up the road.

"Padrig—it's good to see you, lad!" Ian left the saddle before his stallion had come to a stop. He'd recognized that orange cloak immediately, despite the muck and leaves clinging to it. The boy looked frozen and ill, face pale but for the bright slashes of color high along each cheek.

He whipped off his cloak and swung it about Padrig's bony shoulders.

"Milord," Padrig said, his voice raspy. He attempted a bow and nearly fell over. Ian grasped his arm and steadied him. "We were set upon by bandits days ago—four days, I think. They took us by surprise, and the guards—"

Ian ignored the tears washing over Padrig's dirt-smeared cheeks and urged him toward a large rock alongside the trail.

"Sit, lad, and catch your breath." Dai handed Ian a flask; he uncorked it and held it to the boy's lips. "Rest a moment. You can tell us when you're ready."

Rannulf joined them, wrapping a blanket about Padrig. He crouched next to him and offered him food. Padrig refused with a shake of his head. "Later, milord," he said. "I can wait a while longer."

The boy huddled into the blanket, still shaking like a leaf in the wind. But he looked determined.

"I fear for Lady Catrin, milord." He swallowed, fighting back tears. "She took my sword, ordered me to go for help, then ran after the bandits. I heard sounds of battle, but she made me swear to leave at once." He tugged the blanket high about his throat. "It's been so long, sir. I came as fast as I could."

Ian patted him on the shoulder. "You've done well, lad. You'll make Lord Rannulf a fine squire." He turned to Rannulf. "Would we be better served to make camp here, or to take him back to l'Eau Clair?"

Rannulf led Ian away from Padrig. "From the look of the boy, we'd best get him inside the keep. L'Eau Clair is near enough as to make no difference." Ian nodded. "Do you think he can tell us where they were?"

"I hope so," Ian said. "At least we'll know where to start looking."

He turned back to Padrig. "Think you can sit a horse?" he asked.

Padrig nodded, then crumpled over in a faint.

Chapter Sixteen

Late afternoon found Nicholas and Catrin plodding wearily along the rutted track leading to the gates of Ashby. Surprisingly, they met no one approaching or leaving the keep. The unnatural silence and the absence of people sent a chill down Catrin's back.

"Nicholas, there's no one working the land." The fields surrounding the road were devoid of laborers and lay untended—nay, abandoned—for as far as she could see. It looked as though they'd seen neither scythe nor plow in many years, far too long for them to be left fallow.

"I know." He led the mare to the side of the road. "'Tis eerie to see no one. These fields should have been plowed and planted, and we ought to have met someone on this road—it leads to the main gate of the castle." His hand lowered to his waist, meeting the emptiness where his sword should be. "Damnation. I don't like the feel of this at all. And to enter a strange stronghold unarmed—"

"But 'tis *your* keep. Surely there's no danger to you."

He tugged his hauberk off the mare's back and unfolded it, spreading it over her rump. "At least I have this." He wriggled into the armor. His head popped out of the neckline, the sight of his disheveled curls making Catrin's fingers itch to smooth them.

She laughed. "You don't quite have the look of an invincible warrior, I must admit." But no one would ever mistake you for anything else, she thought as her gaze roamed over his powerful body and took note of the air of command that was so much a part of him.

"I doubt anyone here would recognize me under any circumstances. Who knows what they might do before they discover who we are?" He bent and slipped the small dirk into his boot, then buckled his belt and settled it about his waist. Checking the dagger and sharpened stick, he tucked them into the belt. "Although I must admit, the men they've sent me to train up as men-at-arms were singularly ill-prepared. There's probably little threat. But I'd rather not take any chances with your safety. I brought you here to get well, not to harm you further."

Catrin felt more secure simply knowing that Nicholas was prepared for adversity. He'd gone to so much trouble for her already. "A moment, Nicholas," she said before he had a chance to walk away. He turned back to face her, his expression questioning. "Wear my favor, milord. For luck."

"You honor me, milady," he said formally, coming to stand before her. She reached down and tied one of the laces from her gown around his upper arm.

'Twas a Norman custom, one she'd only heard of. Catrin couldn't have said why she'd had the sudden impulse, or why she'd given in to it. It appeared she'd done it properly. But now she felt a fool, until she chanced to look into Nicholas's eyes.

He seemed pleased by the gesture. Capturing her hand in his, he raised it to his lips. "Are you ready?" He turned her hand over and kissed her palm, then closed her fingers over it. "For luck," he repeated, before he turned and took up the reins.

The warmth engendered by Nicholas's touch lasted until they crested the last rise and Ashby came into view. Outlined against the orange and pink of the setting sun, it looked harsh and forbidding, a typical fortress. A fortress under siege, she thought. The drawbridge was up and, as in the fields along the way, she didn't see anyone outside the walls—or on them, for that matter.

Nicholas led the mare to the very brink of the moat, practically gagging at the noisome stench rising from the murky water. Perhaps it wasn't too late to turn back after all, he thought as he surveyed the crumbling walls of his ancestral home.

This was the specter that haunted his worst nightmares, the embodiment of all he'd never be because of his father's shame? His boyhood memory was of an awe-inspiring citadel, standing so high above him he was unworthy to set foot within its gates. The image faded away like a morning mist, leaving only a curious sadness in its place. Ashby had gone the way of the family honor, it seemed, becoming tarnished and shabby around the edges.

But like his honor, Ashby hadn't disappeared completely. With luck, there was enough left of it to restore it to its former glory.

Heartened, he raised his head proudly and scanned the empty battlements. "Open the gates for Lord Nicholas Talbot," he bellowed.

And waited.

The mare shifted restlessly behind him. He turned to see how Catrin fared and discovered that somehow, despite her pain and weariness, she held herself straight and tall. She was a vision of queenly grace. Only someone standing as close as he would notice the strain in her eyes, and the way her nose twitched as she inhaled the foul air. He watched her proudly. She was a true lady.

Was there no one alive within the shabby walls? Impatient, Nicholas watched Idris frisk about as if he were a pup, darting around them, then veering away to race over the open land surrounding the keep.

If only I could run off my frustrations so easily, Nicholas thought.

The sound of steel scraping against stone brought Nicholas whipping around. Tilting his head back, he saw a man move into view between two battered crenels above the portcullis.

"What do you want?" the man snarled. "Best to go away—we got no use for the likes of you." He leaned forward and spit over the wall.

"I am Lord Nicholas Talbot, the master of this godforsaken place. Lower the drawbridge that I might enter."

"Get ye gone. You ain't Lord Nicholas," he scoffed. "That misbegotten whelp'd never dare show his face here."

Nicholas had heard enough. He drew himself up to his full height, pulling the aura of command about him like a cloak. "If you don't open the gate—and soon—I will find some other way to get inside. And when I do—" his fingers caressed the hilt of his knife "—I will show you what this 'misbegotten whelp' learned from mercenaries and infidels."

"Ye don't scare me—ain't no way you're Lord Nicholas, ye scabby oaf." More scraping heralded the arrival of another man. "What do ye want, Clarence?" the guard asked impatiently. He looked back over his shoulder.

"Clarence, show yourself," Nicholas ordered. Clarence was the man he'd sent to Ashby in his stead. Perhaps now they'd make more progress.

Clarence ignored the summons. "Go on," the guard said. He swung at the unseen man. Clarence suddenly appeared, the guard jerking him closer to the edge of the wall by the tunic. "Tell him he ain't who he says, so's we can get back to rollin' the bones."

If he weren't already so aggravated by his reception, Nicholas might have done violence when he saw Clarence. The man had hidden his weakness well in London, it seemed, but now his round face was ruddy with drink.

Clarence lurched forward until he appeared in imminent danger of falling over the wall. His eyes widened suddenly when he saw Nicholas, and he grabbed wildly at the crumbling stone to keep from tumbling forward. "Shit." His face turned an odd shade of green. "We're all dead men now." He leaned his head over the wall and disgorged the contents of his stomach, then disappeared from view behind the crenel.

Although they weren't in his path, Nicholas leapt back, pressing the mare back with him. "Christ," he growled. "Damned drunken sot."

He turned and glared at Catrin when he heard her stifled giggle. "I—I'm sorry," she stammered, her gray eyes dancing. "'Tis just that it's so ridiculous." She drew a deep breath and straightened her shoulders, enticing his gaze to the movement of her unbound breasts beneath the thin material of her gown.

Reluctantly dragging his gaze away, Nicholas picked up the reins and spun to face the castle. "Lower the drawbridge and open the gates," he bellowed. A ponderous creaking signaled that this time his orders had been obeyed. The drawbridge thudded into place amid the ear-splitting squeal of rusty chains. Beyond it, the portcullis rose jerkily into the gatehouse.

About to set foot on the bridge, Nicholas looked down

at the splintering wood and nearly balked. They'd be fortunate if they weren't forced to swim across the moat after all, he thought, grimacing at the notion of falling into the putrid swill below.

But they had little choice. So far as he knew, this was the only way into Ashby. "Best say a prayer," he told Catrin. Setting his shoulders, he led the mare onto the planks.

Moving swiftly—he didn't intend to remain on the span any longer than necessary—they made it across without mishap just as the portcullis ceased its noisy ascent. Nicholas felt an uncomfortable itch between his shoulder blades as they passed through the dim passageway, the mare's hoofbeats echoing hollowly on the cobblestones. He almost expected to see his uncle, the former master of Ashby, awaiting him in the bailey, ready to boot him out the gate again.

But the spectacle that met them when they emerged from the long corridor into the sunlight bore no resemblance to the scene from the past etched upon Nicholas's memory.

It was far, far worse.

Ian sent up a prayer of thanksgiving as he rode into the clearing surrounding l'Eau Clair. Padrig was still alive, though Ian feared the boy clung to life by a thread.

Shifting in the saddle, he sought once again to move the lad into a more comfortable position. He'd carried Padrig in his arms on the brief journey back to l'Eau Clair, listening to his raspy breathing, feeling the fiery heat of his feverish body even through the layers of fabric that separated them.

Padrig had yet to regain his senses, a fact that concerned Ian. Had he lasted till l'Eau Clair, only to lose the battle now? He prayed the lad would improve, would awaken and survive.

And not just for Catrin's sake, although that was of prime importance to him. Padrig was a brave lad, with a bright future ahead of him, should he live.

Ian cursed his sister's impulsiveness, even as he prayed for her safety. She had endangered more lives than her own, and for what reason? Boredom? The chance to show him that she would do as she pleased? Disappointment weighed heavily upon him; Catrin had been raised to protect those within her charge, not to be capricious with their well-being.

The lad's safety had been in his keeping, and he'd failed in his duty to protect him.

Gillian and a slew of servants hurried into the bailey.

"Wait, Gillian," Ian snapped when she reached up to examine the blanket-wrapped bundle he held. Rannulf dismounted and caught his wife up in his arms, setting her on her feet a short distance from Ian's mount.

"Let me bring him into the keep first," Rannulf said. Suiting action to words, he lifted Padrig from Ian's grasp.

Ian slipped from the saddle and, placing an arm about Gillian's waist to help her, followed Rannulf up the stairs into the keep.

"Bring him into the anteroom behind the hall," Gillian directed, shrugging out of Ian's grasp as they entered the huge room. Clapping her hands, she directed the maids to bring hot water to the chamber, then set off after her husband, moving swiftly and with a surprising grace, considering her burden.

"Come along, Ian," she called over her shoulder. "I'm sure I'll need your help before I'm through."

Ian sprawled in a chair by the fire, a goblet of his favorite spiced mead clasped loosely in his hands. Gillian had treated Padrig's injuries and dosed him for the fever several hours earlier. They could do little now but wait, and hope the lad came to his senses soon.

Considering that he'd been awake and able to speak when they found him, Gillian didn't believe his swoon was so deep that he'd sleep much longer now that he was in out of the cold and damp. Although he hadn't yet awakened, several times he'd come close, and his breathing seemed much better. As for the fever, it had already eased. He should recover, with time and care.

But time was a commodity they did not have. Days had passed since the attack, plenty of time for the bandits to have spirited Catrin away—or done worse. Ian chafed at the inactivity of waiting for Padrig to awaken.

If it didn't happen soon, he'd strike out on his own.

Rannulf slipped into the room and closed the door. Motioning for Ian to remain seated, he moved to stand beside the bed. "He hasn't stirred?" he asked, staring down at Padrig consideringly.

"Nay. Nothing more than a few moans," Ian said. He poured mead into another goblet. "If he doesn't wake soon, we'll have to go back out and continue looking. I'm not certain he'll be able to tell us anything useful, but..."

Rannulf tucked the blankets beneath Padrig's chin, then dropped into the other chair by the fire, accepting the mead with a nod of thanks.

"I sent Dai back out to look," Ian told him. "He'll keep searching for Catrin and the others. I'll wait a bit longer for Padrig—then I plan to go out looking, as well. The chance we'll find them unharmed is slim, I'm afraid."

"Gillian found blood on Padrig's tunic," Rannulf said. "Not his, but it looks as though someone was badly injured." He sipped his mead. "We'll find her, Ian, I promise you."

"How is Gillian?"

"She's anxious about Catrin. Her concern for your sister has completely outweighed her fear of giving birth." Rannulf shook his head. "I'd heard that pregnant women have strange ideas. Gillian has believed all along that she could not deliver this child without Catrin. Now her main concern is that we find Catrin and that she is well, but I swear she's determined not to give birth until we find your sister."

Ian rose and replenished his drink, then wandered to the unshuttered window. "It's nearly midday." He stared out at the sky. "'Tis in God's hands whether the lad recovers or not, though with Gillian caring for him, he's luckier than most. But there's nothing we can do for him now." He set his goblet on the table with a thump. "I'm going back out to look for them. If you'd rather not come with me—"

"Are you mad? If I don't go, you're apt to find my wife trailing along behind you," Rannulf said with a wry laugh. "Wouldn't that be a sight?" He continued more soberly, "Of course I'm coming. I'll do everything within my power to find them." He stood. "No sense in waiting any longer. If we leave now, we can cover a wide area before dark."

Ian turned to look down at Padrig. The boy's breathing and color seemed more normal.

Rannulf joined him. "He's a tough lad to withstand so much. He'll make a fine squire."

"I hope you're right." Ian took one last look at Padrig before he left the chamber.

But he couldn't escape his fears so easily. He knew the memory of that pale, battered face would haunt him until he found Catrin.

Chapter Seventeen

Catrin sat atop the mare, stunned by the filthy, ramshackle scene before her. The outside of Ashby had been shocking. But this—this looked like the portal of hell.

Not ready to sort out the chaos, she focused her attention on Nicholas. Watching him now, she was sorry she'd laughed at Clarence's crude reaction. Nicholas had enough to deal with at the moment without that.

All she could see of Nicholas was his back, but even that limited view told its own tale. The shoulders beneath his grimy mail were taut with tension, his spine so straight she wondered it didn't snap.

She doubted his response had any connection with the reasons he'd stayed away from Ashby the past four years and everything to do with the filth and depravity littering his keep.

Groups of people—servants by the look of them, both men and women—clustered about the bailey in various stages of dress and cleanliness. One quick glance at the raucous frolicking revealed drinking, dicing and wenching. Did no one do an honest day's labor here? And how did they happen to arrive in the midst of this? Perhaps 'twas a feast day she didn't know about, or a special celebration of some kind.

But she couldn't believe either reason was true, and a moment's thought didn't reveal any other excuse for the neglect and debauchery surrounding them. No explanation could defend this state of affairs. 'Twas past time someone exerted control over these people. Since Nicholas hadn't done anything yet, she would have to take up the reins of responsibility.

As Nicholas continued to stand there, Catrin noticed the sheer volume of noise seemed to ebb. People were becoming aware of him, ceasing their revelry to turn and stare. But despite their attention, no one came forward to take the horse or greet them in any way.

She'd seen enough of their disregard for their master's presence. Granted, she and Nicholas didn't appear overly impressive at the moment, but he had stated his name, and the man on the walls had confirmed his identity. Furthermore, anyone with eyes to see couldn't fail to notice Nicholas's air of command.

Even chance strangers seeking shelter for the night should have received more attention than this.

But hospitality appeared to be in short supply at Ashby. If none was offered, Catrin decided they would go after it themselves.

Disregarding the throbbing ache in her back and the trembling weakness pervading her entire body, Catrin summoned all the arrogance at her command—no small amount, she thought with a wry twist of her lips—and leapt into action.

"You there," she said, her voice loud in the growing silence. Biting her lower lip against the pain, she slid down from the mare with as much grace as she could muster, then stood tall and straight. She pointed to a shabby youth hovering nearby. "Yes, you. Come here and take your master's horse to the stables."

Mouth agape, the boy stared at her for a moment, then limped toward them. Nicholas's expression was not welcoming; the youth hung back, looking as if he'd bolt at any moment. "Go on," she urged, making it clear with her voice and demeanor that she'd brook no disobedience.

He looked at her again, taking her measure. "Aye, milady," he mumbled, bobbing his head awkwardly in acknowledgment. He cast a defiant glare at the others still gathered about. Then, hand outstretched, he moved a step closer to Nicholas. "Take yer horse, milord?" he asked, his voice more steady. Nicholas gave him the reins and he led the mare away, his mouth curved in a gap-toothed smile.

Catrin ignored Nicholas's scowl, sending him a challenging look and silently daring him to interfere. Since he responded by folding his arms and gazing at her expectantly, she felt free to proceed.

"Where is the seneschal?" she asked, speaking loudly enough to be heard by all. When no one replied she scrutinized the crowd, one eyebrow raised in question. She paused on a face every so often, simply to underscore her power.

Just as she was ready to scan the throng again, one of a bevy of unkempt women lounging near the gatehouse stairs stepped forward, dragging a groaning man with her. "This be Clarence, milady, but he ain't much good to ye now, is he?"

"Ain't much good, period," another woman said, inspiring a burst of laughter from the others.

The woman holding up Clarence released her grasp on the front of his tunic. He crumpled into a heap at her feet, belching loudly as his head hit the muddy ground. Moaning, he closed his eyes and lay unmoving.

Catrin motioned the woman closer. At this point, she didn't dare ask more of her legs than to hold her upright. "What is your name?"

"I'm called Tildy, milady." Smiling ruefully, she tugged her loosened bodice into place. "Beg pardon, milady."

"You seem a strong woman, Tildy. I'd wager you're capable of a hard day's work."

"Hard night's work, more like," a male voice called out from the midst of a large group to Catrin's left. The laughter that greeted his remark faded quickly when Catrin turned and glared.

Tildy scowled at the man, then gave Catrin a grateful look before answering. "Aye, milady. Used to work in the laundry, I did, carryin' and scrubbin'."

"Good. You're just the person I need," Catrin said. "I want you to find two or three others who don't mind working—if that's possible in this place," she added with a scornful glance about her. "Lord Nicholas and I each require a chamber, and we also need a decent meal as soon as one can be prepared." Her gaze was drawn back to Clarence, still sprawled on the ground. "And find someone to take care of this offal."

Two men immediately hauled the seneschal up and carted him away. Perhaps there was hope for Ashby yet, with a bit of guidance. She raised her voice. "I'm sure everyone else can find something useful to do until Lord Nicholas has refreshed himself. You may wait in the hall after the evening meal for your orders," she said, dismissal in her tone as well as her words. Amid a buzz of mumbling, the groups began to disperse.

She didn't dare permit her shoulders to droop until she

was safe from curious eyes, but, oh, how tempted she was to slump into a heap where she stood. She looked down. On second thought, she had no desire whatsoever to touch that muck with anything beyond the soles of her boots.

Nicholas noted the iron control Catrin exerted over her weariness. While he admired her strong will, he couldn't believe she'd lasted so long without wilting. When she looked up, he unfolded his arms and stepped closer. "Are you through ordering my household, madam?"

"Someone had to do it," she snapped. The fire in her eyes dared him to disagree.

"Aye." He stifled his amusement as he met her glare. "And you're far better at it than I would be. My usual method is to flay about me with a sword. Since I've lost mine, I believe I'll leave such things to you."

He could see she'd spent her burst of strength. Scooping her into his arms, he headed for the stairs to the keep. Other than a little squeak, she didn't make a sound, but the tension on her face eased immediately. She closed her eyes and laid her head on his shoulder, apparently comfortable even though she rested against the rough weave of his hauberk.

"How long will it take those sluts to clean a room?" he asked. He paused at the top of the stairs and opened the warped door. As pleasant as it was to hold her, he couldn't continue to do so. He had much work to do before nightfall.

"I couldn't say," she murmured against his neck, her lips on the skin of his throat sending a jolt of fire through his veins. "Depends on how filthy it is."

"Then it might take days." He laid his palm on her forehead and frowned. The fever, though less intense, still burned within her. Catrin needed comfort, care and good food, but he had doubts about whether she could get them here.

Perhaps she'd been better off in the cave than in this sty.

He hoped that after Catrin regained her strength, he could take her to l'Eau Clair and then be on his way to Llywelyn. It had been nearly a week since the attack. Surely Catrin's absence had been noted by now.

Her family would be worried; he had no wish to cause them further pain. Messengers would set out for Gwal Draig and l'Eau Clair at first light.

He should not wait long before continuing on his journey, either. 'Twould take very little to push him out of the king's favor altogether, especially since last year's debacle. King John still hadn't forgiven him for losing l'Eau Clair to the Earl of Pembroke's foster son—Rannulf FitzClifford. The king had wanted a man in control of the Marcher Keep whose first allegiance was to him—not to a man whose power nearly rivalled his own. Although Nicholas knew he'd done the right thing by encouraging Rannulf and Gillian to wed, he also realized—now—that the king had planned for _him_ to marry Gillian.

That would have been a mistake for all of them. Though he loved Gillian well, he thanked God she belonged to Rannulf, not to him.

But for the moment, Catrin was his concern. She'd begun to worry about Gillian once she began to feel better. He wasn't sure that Catrin's health would improve completely while she continued to brood about her cousin. But the journey to l'Eau Clair would have been too much for her, he was convinced of it. Despite the conditions at Ashby, coming here had been the right decision.

He stood in the doorway of the hall, squinting into the gloom. Shouldering aside the door, he carried Catrin into the room. "Kindle some lights here," he shouted. Not waiting to see if his order was obeyed, he crossed the chamber to a group of benches and chairs in front of a shadowy area he took to be the fireplace.

He stepped carefully through the debris that littered the floor, glad he couldn't see what it was. Judging by the stench, he'd rather not know.

As he lowered Catrin into a chair, a maid brought several lighted tallow candles and placed them on a table. The smoky flames provided the perfect illumination for the shabby furnishings.

"Perhaps the candles were a mistake," Catrin said as she surveyed the room. "It looked better before."

He took up a candle, intending to start a fire, but the hearth was piled high with ashes and he didn't see a stick of wood nearby. "I wonder how long it's been since the place was clean?" He kicked at a large bone lying among the tattered rushes. "Likely not since my uncle died." He slouched onto a bench and plucked the dagger from his belt, studying the edge of the blade, avoiding the curiosity in Catrin's eyes. He sighed. "I think Clarence managed well at first. I received an adequate income from Ashby. The past two years the amount had dwindled, but Clarence wrote that they had trouble with the crops."

"You should have come to see for yourself," Catrin said quietly. "'Tis too much of a temptation for a weak man, to allow him free rein over your affairs."

He forced himself to meet her steady gaze. "And thus I pay for my ignorance." He indicated the disorder around them with a sweep of his hand.

Shoving the knife back into its sheath, he stood and paced the expanse of the hearth. "I'm almost too weary to care. I tell myself it doesn't matter—I never had anything of value before. But I owe my people better than this. It's past time I attended to my duties.''

He looked beyond Catrin to see Tildy descend the spiral stair to his left. "Beg pardon, milord," she said, bobbing a curtsy. "We've cleaned a chamber, leastways enough so yer lady can rest. Couldn't help but notice ye're ill, milady," she added with a nod toward Catrin. "And I told them lazy knaves in the scullery to haul up water so ye can bathe, if ye like."

Nicholas found Tildy's assumption that Catrin was his wife amusing. Doubtless Catrin hadn't noticed, else she'd have flown into a temper by now. But he said nothing to correct the woman's mistake; surprisingly, the notion didn't bother him as it once would have. "That's fine. See that food is brought for her." Once Tildy left, he picked up Catrin again.

"You did that very well," Catrin said as he carried her up the winding stair. "You see, you do know how to give orders. A little courtesy wouldn't be amiss, but that will come with practice."

At her teasing tone, he responded in kind. "Your flattery will turn my head, milady. If you persist, I'll become as arrogant as the king himself."

"I look forward to seeing you deal with the entire household." She giggled.

The sound startled him. "You won't be there to see it," he told her, infusing his voice with mock severity. "You will stay in your chamber and rest."

"Aye, milord," she murmured so softly he could scarcely hear her.

Suddenly he wished he could see her face, but the stairwell was dim and Catrin had nuzzled her face into the hair at his nape. As it was, her breath on the back of his neck was enough to drive him mad. Wanting her had made him crazy; knowing she'd been raped, he should consider her beyond his reach, unattainable, a nun.

He certainly shouldn't be imagining what it would be like to run his hands over her until she giggled again.

"I could grow accustomed to being carried about," Catrin whispered, her lips tickling his ear.

"Stop that," he growled as his loins tightened in response.

"Stop what?"

Nicholas didn't know if he should trust that innocent tone. She couldn't possibly be trying to provoke him...

Could she?

Whether it was intentional or not, Catrin had succeeded in heating his blood.

He hurried up the last few steps, slipping past the goggling maid in the doorway and nearly dumping Catrin onto the bed. "I have to leave now," he said, his breath coming much too fast. *Before I make a complete fool of myself*, he added silently, staring down at her as she sprawled across the mattress. "Enjoy your bath."

He sped out the door.

Wrapped in a length of linen fragrant with the scent of roses, Catrin drowsed in a cushioned chair by the fire. The bath had been sheer luxury, a true surprise, given the state of the keep. She'd soaked in the perfumed water until her skin was wrinkled and all the warmth had vanished. Tildy took away the tattered remains of her clothes, promising to find her something to wear by the time her hair dried.

Clean and fed, she waited.

For Nicholas to return?

After days in his company she should be heartily sick of him, but she missed him. Life seemed flat without him there. He provided the spark to her temper, intensifying her reactions, her emotions, bringing to life feelings she'd believed long dead.

His touch didn't bring Madog's mauling to mind, but she had no idea how far she could go without rekindling the horrible memories.

Yet Nicholas had already carried her deeper into passion than she'd ever believed it possible for her to go. In the past, she'd found the mere thought of a man's touch repugnant.

Nicholas did not repulse her...in any way.

Perhaps he could erase the memories of the past, replace the shadows with the bright glow of passion. Not that it could ever lead to anything, she reminded herself.

A knock on the door jolted her. "Come," she called, staring into the fire.

The solid tread of boots on the floor told her this wasn't Tildy bringing her clothes. Tugging the linen towel higher over her breasts, Catrin shifted in the chair until she could see the door.

Nicholas closed the door quietly and crossed the room. He, too, had bathed; the shirt and chausses he wore, while threadbare, were clean. His hair was combed away from his face, but a damp curl drooped over his brow. Her fingers itched to smooth it back.

His violet eyes skimmed over her, hesitating a moment where the damp linen clung to her bosom before coming to rest on her face. She'd been idly brushing her hair when he came in. Kneeling beside the chair, he took the brush from her unresisting fingers and drew it through her hair.

She felt as though she were caught in a dream, held there by the passion burning in Nicholas's eyes. Each leisurely stroke of the brush sent a ripple of sensation from her scalp to the soles of her feet. He touched her so gently she scarcely noticed when he began to trace the fingers of his other hand over her neck and shoulders.

All she noticed was the sensations he aroused.

Laying the hairbrush aside, he gathered her hair in one hand and draped it over her shoulder, allowing the long tresses to pool in her lap. His hands gentle, he turned her slightly in the chair so that he was behind her. He skimmed his lips over the back of her neck, carefully avoiding the bandage, then nipped lightly on her earlobe.

Shivers coursed over her skin, sensitizing her flesh. Closing her eyes, Catrin let herself wallow in Nicholas's touch.

"You are so beautiful," he whispered, his voice causing an insidious warmth to grow within her. He continued to stroke her neck, his fingers dipping lower with each caress until they slipped beneath the edge of the linen.

I should tell him to stop, she thought, but it felt so wonderful she couldn't force the words past her throat. Her breasts seemed swollen; she wished his hand would dip lower still and ease the throbbing ache.

"Nicholas," she murmured, reaching behind her to sink her fingers into his hair.

He slipped around the chair to face her. "What do you want? Shall I kiss you?" Bending his head, he glided his tongue along the seam of her lips, nudging them open to allow him entrance.

His kiss was an act of possession, his tongue enticing her to follow his lead. All the while his hands maintained their teasing caresses, until she yearned for more.

She moaned when he released her lips, blindly reaching out for him. "Open your eyes, Catrin." She obeyed his low-voiced command, staring in wonder at his flushed face and the intensity of his gaze. He took her hand and placed it atop his. "Show me what you want. Shall I do this?'' He drew his fingertips over her collarbone until they came to rest in the shadowed cleft between her breasts. "Or this?''

Catrin moaned as he dragged his lips over her aching nipples, nibbling at them through the cloth. "You taste so sweet," he said, reaching for the top of the material. "Let me—"

The sudden pounding at the door was like an icy torrent of water pouring over their heads.

Chapter Eighteen

"Christ's bones!" Nicholas rested his head on Catrin's shoulder. Heaving a weary sigh, he looked up and shouted, "Go away."

The pounding continued. Cursing beneath his breath, he disengaged himself from Catrin's arms and stomped across the room.

He wrenched the door open, causing the birdlike old crone hammering away on the splintering panels to tumble into the room. He caught her before she fell, the deed earning him a glare as he set her back on her feet.

He hadn't seen her among the motley band of servants and retainers assembled in the hall earlier.

Reaching up—she stood no higher than the middle of his chest—she grabbed his ears in a surprisingly hard grip and tugged. "Lean down here, you fool, where I can see you," she said, her voice squeaking like a rusty hinge.

With a frown, he obliged. She made him feel like a child about to receive a scold. But perhaps if he did as she demanded she'd release him.

As soon as he stooped nearer her level she let go of his ears, giving a hard tug on the hair at his nape before she moved her gnarled fingers away. Rheumy blue eyes examined him, her gaze coming to rest on his face. "Aye, you've the look of him," she said, nodding once. "Have you his disposition, too?"

"Who are you talking about, old woman?" he asked, in no mood to be poked at and badgered. He straightened and glared down at her.

"Don't you remember me, milord?" She shook her finger at him. "I remember you. Pretty little lordling you were, trailing along after that slut your father ran off with. 'Twas a wonder your uncle didn't die on the spot from the hate-filled looks you gave him."

Nicholas felt all the old anger resurface at her words, kindling the white-hot rage that tainted his memories of his mother. He could hardly beat an old woman, no matter how much she irritated him.

But he didn't have to listen to her impudence, either. "Watch your tongue, you old besom. I'll not have my mother insulted. Especially under my own roof."

"It's no insult to speak the truth, boy. Didn't your father teach you that?" She bent to pick up the bundle she'd dropped when she fell into the room. "Like as not he didn't," she added, her voice muffled as she gathered the armful of material close to her chest. "Lord Robert wouldn't have recognized the truth if it came up and bit him on the backside."

Folding his arms, Nicholas leaned back against the door frame, scowling when he saw the look of interest on Catrin's face. But the sight of her in such delightful disarray swiftly distracted him. Although she'd tugged the linen high around her neck, hiding the glorious skin he'd caressed such a short time earlier, her hair flowed in a tousled ebony cascade over her shoulder, framing her beauty. And her lips were rosy and full, reminding him of how soft they'd been beneath his.

"State your business and begone," he growled without looking at the old woman. Instead he kept his gaze fixed on Catrin, enjoying the flush sweeping up her throat and over her face.

"Aye, you're like your father," the crone said, chuckling. She poked him in the gut with her elbow, drawing his attention from Catrin. "An eye for the ladies, and impatient with it."

That description fit his father, at least after his mother's death. "You knew my father well?" he asked, trying for a tone of casual interest.

"So you really don't remember me. Ah, well, you were a very angry little boy. Besides, too much happened when you came here for you to take any notice of me." She heaved a gusty sigh. "I was your father's nurse," she said with pride. "Anna's my name. I took care of Lord Robert from the moment the midwife swaddled him until he took up with that slut."

"You try my patience, woman," he snarled, thinking longingly of tossing her out of the room.

"Enough, milord. Peace," she said. She backed away, hands raised in supplication. "Old habits die hard."

"What the hell do you want from me?" he asked. He pushed off from the door frame and moved to stand by the fire. "I don't care to talk about the past. And I'm sure you could better occupy yourself elsewhere."

"Is this how you treat your elders, boy? I came here to care for your lady." She held her bundle in front of her like a shield. "I brought my balms and potions. Tildy said she carries some nasty wounds on her."

Scowling, Nicholas watched as Anna placed the parcel on the bed and spread open the fabric to reveal a variety of smaller bundles and packets. Squinting mightily, her faded eyes nearly lost within her wrinkled face, she turned to scrutinize Catrin as thoroughly as she'd examined him, though he'd wager she found Catrin more to her liking.

Her sunken mouth twisted into a smile of sorts as she shuffled over to Catrin's chair. "You're a pretty one," she said. "By your leave, milady." She brushed Catrin's hair aside and pushed the linen towel down to expose the wounds.

Humming absently, Anna unwrapped the bandages, her hands far gentler than when she'd touched him. "Bring the candles closer," she ordered, her attention on Catrin's back.

Nicholas positioned the candles beside Catrin, as Anna directed. She inspected the wounds thoroughly, frowning as she traced her fingertip along several faint, reddish streaks. She prodded gently at the stitches. "Who set these?"

"I did," Nicholas said, nearly shuddering in remembrance. It wasn't an experience he'd care to repeat—ever. "There were three arrows. I cut them out. One was embedded to the barbs. But I didn't have much to work with, and the wounds mortified."

Catrin winced when Anna continued to probe the area. Her face had paled considerably by the time Anna stopped and touched her soothingly on the shoulder.

Turning to Nicholas, she said, "You did well, boy. The fact that she's still alive attests to that." Brushing past him, Anna went to the bed and picked through her supplies.

"What about the fever?" Nicholas asked. He placed the branch of candles on a table near Catrin's chair. The woman seemed to know what she was doing. Perhaps she had a tonic for the sickness in her assortment of cures. "It comes and goes."

Picking up a packet, Anna crumbled the contents into

a goblet and poured wine from the ewer beside the bed. "There's infection inside the wound. Likely that's the cause of the fever. I'll have to drain it. I'll heal your lady in no time, milord."

"I'm not his lady," Catrin said. "I'm only—" She looked over her shoulder at him, confusion shadowing her eyes. "I don't know."

Anna snorted. "You seemed well acquainted when I came in here."

"We know each other only because I'm kin to Lord Nicholas's ward, Gillian," Catrin said, raising her chin. He recognized her stubborn, combative expression—and waited for the next volley. "In truth, we loathe each other."

Anna hooted at that, pounding her fist on the mattress. Catrin undoubtedly possessed a gift for understatement. He wouldn't call what they'd been doing before Anna interrupted them loathing, he thought, suppressing the remembered pleasure before his body could react.

Far from it.

A few moments more and Catrin would have been stretched out naked beside him on the bed, if he'd had his way.

"It's true," Catrin said. "Ask him how he got that bruise on his face." Her gaze darted toward Nicholas, then away when a chuckle, swiftly suppressed, escaped his lips.

Catrin glanced at him again and scowled when he shrugged and remained silent. "I punched him in the face."

Anna looked at him. He nodded, touching the faint bruise beneath his eye. "Aye, she did." His voice shook with laughter. "But she didn't stay angry long," he added.

Anna squinted at Catrin, then seemed to come to a decision. "Whether ye be enemies or lovers, it matters not to me. 'Tis something you must sort out yourselves. But you can trust me to heal your hurts." She handed Catrin the goblet. "Drink this, milady. 'Tis a mixture to cure your fever and ease your pain." She searched through her belongings until she found a tiny pot. "Shall I lance the wound now, or come back later?"

Catrin swallowed and closed her eyes briefly before she answered. "You might as well do it now. Waiting will only make it worse. I'd rather get it over with than worry about it."

Anna nodded. "'Tis a wise decision, milady. Better to face the pain now than let it fester and grow."

She slipped a tiny, needle-sharp knife from her belt and thrust it into the coals. "Care to help, milord?" she asked, her gaze resting on his face.

He would swear she knew how much the idea disturbed him. "Why not?" he replied, taking up the candles again and moving closer to Catrin.

"I'll not lie to you, milady. 'Twill hurt like the very devil. But mind you sit very still. I don't wish to cause you more harm, nor to mar your pretty skin. Lord Nicholas could hold your arms, if you wish."

Catrin's head snapped up, her eyes wary, reminding him of a cornered animal. He banged the candles down so hard that several blew out. "She doesn't need me to hold her."

He didn't want to remind her of how he'd bound her the last time.

Or remind her of when she was raped. There was still much about the incident that he didn't know. Once this ordeal was over, he intended to talk to her again.

He had no desire to distress her by doing anything that might bring back memories of the assault.

"As you wish," Anna said.

Willing his hands to steadiness, he lit the candles he'd extinguished. Anna brushed by him and retrieved her dagger from the fireplace.

Squinting at the glowing tip, she nodded her satisfaction. "You'd best put your knife in the coals, too, milord. I might need it to seal the wound once I'm done."

Nicholas did as she asked, hoping as he buried the blade in the embers that they wouldn't have to use it. He'd borne worse himself without a qualm, but the thought of pressing the heated metal against Catrin's soft ivory flesh sickened him.

Catrin shifted in the chair, turning to give Anna better access to her back. Anna busied herself setting out her supplies on the table, humming a sprightly air as she worked.

"Stop that infernal noise," he snarled. How could the old woman go so blithely about her business, knowing she would cause pain?

Anna stopped humming and turned toward him. "Hold the candles steady, milord." Taking up her knife, she asked, "Are you ready?"

Nodding once, Catrin tightened both hands about the arm of the chair and Anna began her task.

Nicholas forced himself to watch as Anna lanced the abscesses and allowed them to drain. If Catrin could endure it, he could do no less. Though she couldn't hide her pain, she made no sound, simply closed her eyes and tightened her grip on the chair until her nails bit into the wood.

Although it seemed to take forever before Anna finished, the candles had scarcely burned down. "I won't need your knife," she told him as she smeared salve from the clay pot over the wounds.

He set the candles down more gently this time. Snatching up a cloth, he knelt beside Catrin and dabbed at the sweat beaded upon her face. She sat slumped over the arm of the chair, resting her forehead on her arms for a moment, then straightened as Anna wound fresh bandages around the cuts.

"How do you feel?" he asked.

"I'll be fine." Her voice shook slightly, but already the color had begun to return to her cheeks. He handed her the goblet, watching as she drained it.

Anna bustled about, gathering her belongings together. "You'll do fine now, milady." She paused to pat Catrin's arm. "I'll return in the morning to have a look at you. Mind you let her rest, milord," she added as she limped out of the room.

"What an odd woman," Catrin said after he closed the door behind Anna. "She's blunt, but very kind."

"Are you certain you're well?"

"Yes. The salve is very soothing. It's dulled the pain so I scarcely feel it. Or perhaps 'tis the herbs she put in the wine. I feel surprisingly well."

Nicholas tended the fire, pulling his dagger from the coals with a brief prayer of thanks that they hadn't needed it. Leaning his forearm on the mantel, he stared down into the flames.

What did he find there, she wondered. The past? It wasn't something pleasant, for she could see the hurt etched on his face, the shadows emphasized by the flickering firelight. "Are you sorry we came here?"

So much time passed, she wondered whether he'd heard her. Finally he raised his head and pushed away from the mantel. "No, I'm not sorry." He dragged a stool beside her chair and sat down.

"It's a shame Ashby fell into such disrepair." She tugged the linen higher about her throat when she felt Nicholas's gaze settle there. "But you'll make it right again. I'm sure of it."

He stared down at his hands, clasped loosely about one upraised knee, then looked up suddenly. "Do you know what troubles me the most?" he asked. She shook her head. "'Tis the fact that I permitted Ashby to get this way. It's just a place, a building, a thing—and I feared it. It has no life, no power. It cannot harm me unless I allow it. Yet for all these years Ashby has personified my deepest fears."

"I don't understand." She leaned forward and placed a hand on his arm.

He laid his hand atop hers, his fingers tightening almost to the point of pain. She grimaced, and he eased his grip, threading his fingers with hers. "My father was the second-born, and to his father and his older brother, Gerald, he was nothing. So one day he ran off with the castle whore."

Although Catrin tried to hide her shock, he must have noticed it. "Aye, what Anna said was true. My mother was a Welshwoman who came to Ashby looking for work when most of her village was lost to sickness. Because she was Welsh, she was distrusted by most. The only work she found was on her back." He closed his eyes briefly, and when he opened them they were filled with pain. "But my father loved her until the day she died. They ran off to France and he joined a band of mercenaries."

"Then how did you come to inherit Ashby?" Catrin asked, confused. That wasn't precisely what she wanted to know, but she couldn't think of a delicate way to phrase the question.

She needn't have worried; Nicholas understood. "Oh, I'm the legitimate issue of a proper marriage, I assure you," he said with a mirthless laugh. "My parents wed as soon as they were beyond my grandfather's reach. And my father made certain his father knew it. But Uncle Gerald never managed to produce a child that lived past its first year. Though God knows, he tried. It became an obsession with him." His grip on her fingers relaxed. "How he must have hated knowing everything he had would go to me."

"Were you a mercenary, too?" She couldn't imagine the Norman king permitting a mercenary to inherit a powerful estate, although she'd heard that King John had no qualms about rewarding his hirelings with land and property.

"For a time. My father had some standards. I became the squire of one of his more proper friends." His gaze held hers. "And later, I did hire out my sword. Honor is a strange concept to me, at least the way most noblemen understand it. I swear I found more honorable men among the mercenaries I lived and fought with than among the nobles I've met since I became lord of Ashby. But a hired sword is considered beyond the pale, no matter his reasons for what he does."

Releasing her hand, he stood. "I should leave so you may rest."

She held out her hand. "Stay—please. You listened to my dismal grumbling, and it eased my mind. Please allow me to return the favor." She smiled. "Besides, you cannot pique my curiosity and then leave me unsatisfied."

At that, he returned her smile, but whereas hers had been meant to soothe, his was teasing, devilish. "Never let it be said that Nicholas Talbot left you unsatisfied, milady." He dropped down beside her chair and, lifting her hand to his lips, placed a lingering kiss on her palm.

But as he rested his head against Catrin's knee, he continued his tale in a flat, impersonal voice, his flirtatious manner dropping away as swiftly as it had arisen. "When I was ten my mother became very ill. We had little money, and it became too difficult for her to follow the troop from skirmish to skirmish. So Father collected me from my foster family and came home to throw himself on my grandfather's mercy."

Catrin stroked Nicholas's hair away from his brow with a soothing touch, waiting.

"Mercy was beyond my grandfather's ken. At first he wouldn't even permit us to enter Ashby, but my uncle convinced him to allow us in. Despite how he lived, my father was very proud. That he swallowed his pride long enough to listen to his family's abuse is a measure of how dear my mother was to him."

His father wasn't the only one with pride, Catrin thought, running her fingers through his disordered curls.

"But they refused to let him stay." He raised his head. She met his eyes steadily, her own filled with tears. "That selfish, unyielding old man wouldn't even give her a place to die in peace."

He sat back on his heels. "Since then, every time I think of Ashby I remember how my mother comforted my father as we rode away. She didn't last a week. She died in a broken-down hovel we found in the woods. I'm not even certain where it is."

Catrin reached out to him, but he shrugged away from her comforting hands. "I hated them. They took away everything I had—my mother, my father's pride, my innocence. And now that I've finally come here I see that

I've feared a phantom all these years. It wasn't Ashby I hated—it was them."

Catrin shivered, as much from his words as from the lack of warmth without him pressed close beside her. She held out her hands to him again. "Let it go, Nicholas. 'Tis in the past. It cannot harm you further unless you permit it."

He stood and bent to lift her out of the chair. Enveloping her in his arms, he carried her to the bed.

Catrin knew a momentary alarm when she noticed their destination, but she soon realized she'd misjudged him yet again. Nicholas desired comfort from her now, not lust. He sat on the mattress and held her cradled in his arms, his face buried against her throat.

At last his muscles relaxed beneath her and they slumped over on the bed, still clasped together.

Peaceful at last, he slept.

Chapter Nineteen

'Twas the most wonderful dream, Nicholas thought as he nuzzled his lips along Catrin's collarbone and up over her shoulder. He stopped in the hollow of her throat, savoring the scent of roses blended with Catrin's own sweet essence rising from her warm, supple skin.

When she moved against him, drawing her hand down his chest and stopping just above his throbbing manhood, his eyes snapped open.

This was no dream.

Catrin lay curled about him, her towel twisted until it revealed more than it covered.

The past night's surgery appeared to have done her no harm. The skin beneath his lips felt pleasantly warm from sleep. No dew of fever-induced sweat dampened her smooth flesh. And she'd slept peacefully in his arms the entire night, apparently undisturbed by nightmares or troubling memories.

At times during the night he had hovered on the edge of sleep, aware of Catrin nestled in his arms. He had no intention of seeking his own bed, when he could savor the pleasure of holding her.

Too soon, the night had ended. But while Catrin slept on, he had no plans to leave.

Instead, he intended to enjoy his good fortune. The woman curled up beside him was warm, soft, beautiful. He'd be a fool to let her go.

His movements leisurely, Nicholas caught the edge of the towel between his fingers and eased the fabric away.

The faint light of dawn creeping through the shuttered windows lent a rosy glow to her ivory flesh. Nicholas caught his breath at his first complete glimpse of Catrin's beauty. Her breasts were full and well formed, and her tiny waist flared into gently rounded hips perfect to cradle a man—or a child. Closing his eyes, Nicholas permitted himself to consider the idea instead of shoving it aside as he had in the past.

He'd never wanted a child, never wanted any woman enough to share that intimacy. If he intended to have Catrin—to make love with Catrin, he corrected himself—the possibility that they might create a child was something he should consider. He no longer believed this passion between them could be ignored...nor satisfied with a hurried coupling.

A lifetime with Catrin might not be enough.

The image of Catrin, belly rounded with his child, was frightening—and arousing. A renewed surge of desire swept through his manhood.

It was all well and good for him to make plans, but 'twas unlikely he'd find Catrin as eager as he. Although she hadn't seemed disgusted or scandalized by his past, it didn't necessarily follow that she'd be willing to consider a future with him.

He didn't even know if she truly wanted him as her lover. Granted, each time they touched was more explosive than the last. But given the things he suspected had happened to her, she might not want a physical relationship with him.

Or any other man.

In the days when he was with the mercenaries, and even when he was part of the king's army, he'd seen too many women who'd been assaulted.

Rape happened all the time, when men traveled far from home, when the blood lust was upon them, at times simply because some men were no better than rutting beasts when they encountered a defenseless woman. He'd witnessed the blank stares, the trembling, cringing victims flinching from everyone, the bloodied, broken bodies sprawled on the ground, dignity denied them even in death.

Nicholas had never permitted his men to rape. The idea of forcing himself on a woman revolted him, although he'd met plenty of men, of high degree and low, who saw it as their right.

It was a tribute to Catrin's strength, her will, that she hadn't become a cringing victim. Although he didn't know what she'd been like before, Nicholas had no doubt the ordeal had made her tougher, tempered her as a steel blade thrust into fire was made stronger.

Her strength was part of her appeal. He feasted his eyes on her beauty once more, his gaze lingering on all the places his hands ached to touch, before reluctantly tucking the towel around her. When had he become so noble?

Or was he simply being foolish not to grab what he wanted?

His hands lingering on her shoulders, he gently kissed her lips. He had intended to leave her then, but her eyelids fluttered open.

Her sleepy gray eyes focused on his and the corners of

her mouth curved up in a smile. "Nicholas?" she murmured, snuggling closer to him.

"You'd better hope so," he said, chuckling. "I trust you realize who you've cuddled up to." Brushing aside a cluster of ebony curls, he grazed his lips along her cheek. "Good morrow, milady."

He drew her closer still and nibbled at her lips, taking advantage of her acquiescence to ease his tongue into her mouth. Her movements languid, Catrin took up his challenge, her tongue mating with his in a seductive thrust and parry.

Groaning deep in his throat, Nicholas gradually shifted more of his weight atop her while continuing to kiss her. He didn't want to do anything to shock her. Uncertain whether she would accept the intimacy he wanted, he proceeded slowly, allowing her to grow accustomed to him.

Though his body nearly rebelled at the thought, his mind found the notion intriguing.

Surely he could survive such sweet torment!

Catrin burrowed her fingers into his hair, her fingertips kneading his scalp in a surprisingly sensuous caress. He felt the sensation all the way to the soles of his feet.

In the meantime, her other hand had been busy untying the neckline of his shirt. Reaching down to the hem, she began tugging and pushing at the material, trying to shove the shirt up over his head.

"Wait," he whispered, stilling her hand. His gaze met hers, searching. He wasn't sure what he expected to find—excitement, or perhaps a measure of fear?

But 'twas passion shining in her eyes, and something else he couldn't put a name to. While he'd never seen such an expression turned his way, Nicholas knew that whatever that soft, delicate thing was, it was good.

And he wanted it just as much as he wanted the delectable woman sprawled so trustingly beneath him.

He brushed his lips gently over her eyelids, sealing her expression forever in his heart. "Are you certain 'tis what you want?"

Catrin nodded and found her voice with difficulty. "Yes," she murmured, overcoming the urge to turn her eyes away from his, to hide from Nicholas and what he made her feel.

But cowardice had never been her way. "Yes," she repeated with more determination. "I want to touch you, Nicholas. And more." Her bravado faltering beneath the questions in his eyes, she slipped her hands under his shirt and smoothed them over his back and shoulders.

He closed his eyes and arched into her stroking hands like a cat, a low moan rising from his throat. "Be very sure, Catrin." Grasping the neckline of his shirt, he hesitated before drawing the fabric over his head. "'Tis not my intention to frighten you. But I want you very much."

He pulled the shirt off and tossed it aside. Leaning his weight on his elbows, he framed her face in his hands, his fingers stroking lightly along her temples. "If I do anything you don't like, or that disturbs you, tell me. I'll stop."

A flush of embarrassment crept up her neck. "I want you, Nicholas. Truly." She ruthlessly curbed the urge to cry. "But I don't know if I'll be able to do this."

He brushed kisses over her forehead, her eyes, her lips. "Whatever you can give me, I'll take gladly. But my pleasure comes from giving pleasure to you. I just don't want to do anything to remind you of—" He broke off, his eyes intense.

"Nothing you do will be what he did." She stroked his shoulders. He looked unconvinced; she wanted to erase the worry from his smoky violet eyes. "I know you would never harm me, Nicholas. I trust you."

Wrapping her arms around his muscular chest, she whispered, "Show me how it should be."

He shifted his weight and drew her over to lie beside him. "We'll learn together. This sharing is new to me, as well."

His eyes asking her permission, he outlined the edge of the towel with one questing fingertip, pausing in the shadowed cleft between her breasts. Raising her hand, she guided his, and together they separated the fabric.

The linen fell away, exposing her to his gaze. He lay there so long, simply looking, that Catrin began to wonder if he'd changed his mind. "Is something wrong?" she asked, her confidence, fragile to begin with, starting to ebb.

Placing his hands on her stomach, he slowly inched them up her ribs, not stopping until the backs of his fingers were nestled against her breasts. "Nay, not a thing." His mouth curved into a sweet, devilish smile. "I only wish to savor my good fortune. I've never beheld a woman so lovely as you." He began to gently massage her ribs with his fingers, every stroke pressing his knuckles nearer to her aching nipples.

Catrin drew in a slow breath, battling the urge to grab his hands and raise them the slight distance. But she could see the enjoyment in his face, a glow of anticipation she understood. After all, she'd found herself staring at Nicholas's magnificent body more than once while they were in the cave.

She knew of no reason why she shouldn't make him ache, as well. The mere thought stoked the fire in her blood. Her eyes teasing, Catrin raised her hand and wove her fingers in the mat of dark blond curls spread across his chest.

Scraping her fingernails lightly against his skin, she toyed with the wiry hair, drawing ever closer to a coppery nipple nestled in the curls. She was vaguely aware that the motion of Nicholas's hands on her flesh had intensified, the fire caused by his touch spreading to a place deep within her. Her legs moved restlessly until he wedged his thigh between hers. It seemed he knew what she needed, even if she didn't.

He flexed his leg, pressing the rippling muscles against her womanhood at the same time he bent his head and took her nipple into his mouth. 'Twas a miracle she didn't fly straight off the bed from the sensations simmering through her.

Her hand stilled against his chest, all her attention centered on her response to him. He dragged his mouth from her breast, tracing his tongue lingeringly up the column of her throat to her mouth. "Don't stop now," he said. He lifted her hand from his chest and nuzzled her palm.

She tried to speak twice before her voice would work, and even then it was faint and husky. "What should I do?" She'd never had—nor desired—the opportunity to give her imagination full rein. As she ran her gaze over Nicholas, garbed only in clinging chausses, the possibilities seemed endless. "I don't know where to begin."

"Whatever pleases you," he murmured, "will certainly please me. Do whatever you wish." He sucked her finger into his mouth, swirling his tongue around it before nipping lightly at the fleshy tip. All the while he stared into her eyes, his gaze holding her captive and heating her blood. His eyes darkened until they appeared nearly black.

He made promises with that look, promises of pleasure and more.

Catrin tore her own gaze away, not certain what he meant. She'd give him what she could, and take the delight he offered.

Beyond that she refused to think.

Smiling, she leaned toward him, glad to hide her face against his chest so he couldn't see how flushed she'd become at her boldness. She rubbed her cheek against the soft curls spread across his chest, then nuzzled her way to his nipple.

His body tensed beneath her hand when she closed her teeth delicately over the tiny nub. Pulling her with him, he fell back on the mattress, his fingers threaded through her hair as he urged her to repeat the caress.

She sat back on her heels and rubbed her palms over his torso, moving lower across his stomach with each sweep. She watched his face as she traced the thin line of darker hair bisecting his stomach, savoring the pleasure tautening his features. His eyes were closed and a flush rode high along his cheekbones.

Dear God, but he was handsome!

Growing daring, she leaned over Nicholas and trailed her fingers just inside the waistband of his chausses. His eyes flew open suddenly and, grabbing her about the waist, he lifted her over to straddle him. "You are so beautiful," he growled, pulling her head toward him and taking her mouth in a consuming kiss.

Their naked flesh pressed together from neck to waist. The soft curls covering his chest rubbed against her already sensitized nipples, sending a rush of heat to pool between her legs.

Nicholas reached down and clasped her tight against his loins. 'Twas enough to make her melt into a puddle of sensation.

All the while he continued to kiss her, his body taking

up the same thrusting rhythm as his tongue. He beset her senses on all fronts—her mouth, her breasts, her entire body felt enveloped in Nicholas's touch, seared by the heat of his passion.

She was vaguely aware of him moving them across the bed. His lips still clinging to hers, he sat up, bringing her with him.

He eased his mouth from hers, nibbling at her lips, then soothing them with his tongue. Finally he sighed and abandoned her mouth. "You're so sweet," he said, devouring her with his eyes. He gathered her tousled hair together and nudged it over her shoulder. "So very lovely." His lingering gaze made her breasts feel heavy, aching for his touch.

He must have seen the yearning in her eyes, for he brought his hand up and caressed her cheek. "Show me what you want. I'm yours to command, but you must tell me."

Emboldened by his words and the desire etched across his face, Catrin asked, "And what do you want, Nicholas?"

A wry smile on his lips, he shook his head and laughed, the sound more like a groan. "You'll not elude me so easily. If I told you everything I want of you, I'd frighten you away. I want to bring you more pleasure than you've ever imagined."

He drew up his knees, causing her to slide forward until she straddled him. Her cheeks flushed. "How can you be shy?" he teased. "Look at you—you're sitting naked on a hungry man." He thrust his hips gently beneath her. "And you've got him completely in your power." Leaning forward until his lips were near her ear, he whispered, "I'll do whatever you like. Tell me."

He was right. Considering her position, 'twas foolish to be timid.

And she did find the idea of having this handsome, strong, very desirable man at her beck and call extremely appealing.

Tossing back her head, she told him, "Kiss me."

"I did that already. Surely there's something else you'd like."

"I liked it when you kissed me," she said, staring at his mouth. "Perhaps you could kiss me—elsewhere." Slipping her hands into his rumpled curls, she drew his head to her breasts.

She felt his lips curve into a smile against her flesh before he captured her nipple in his mouth. He suckled her greedily, caressing her other breast with his fingers. Catrin gave herself over to the sensations, arching her back and pressing him tightly to her.

Nicholas dropped his hands to her waist and lifted her, moving her to fit more closely against his thrusting manhood. He released her nipple, gasping for breath.

His loins were afire, and only Catrin could ease the ache.

God help him if she stopped him now.

He'd likely die of it.

She grasped him by the shoulders, stilling him. He watched in amazement as once again a wave of color washed over her face.

How could she blush now?

Her tongue darted out to moisten her lips, tempting him to take her mouth again. But he waited, eager to discover what had caused the pretty flush still staining her cheeks. "Would you mind—" Her fingers plucked at the drawstring of his chausses. She cleared her throat and began again. "Would you take these off?"

Mind? Was she mad? If he hadn't been concerned about offending her or frightening her, he'd have removed them long ago, just for the pleasure of feeling her against him from head to toe.

"You do it," he said, hoping to see that wave of color wash over her again.

He wasn't disappointed.

She didn't refuse. She didn't say anything at all. She answered by lowering her hands to his waist, her trembling fingers plucking at the drawstring.

Impatient now, Nicholas picked her up and sat her next to him, rolling onto his side to give her better access. Her bottom lip caught between her teeth, she worked at the knot, every movement nudging her fingers against his aching flesh.

If she didn't finish soon, *he'd* be finished; he'd spill his seed half-dressed, like an inexperienced boy.

He sighed with relief when she finally untied the string, but the torment hadn't ended yet. Her eyes wide, she began to ease the material down.

Nicholas knew the precise moment Catrin saw his engorged manhood; her swiftly indrawn breath wasn't quite a gasp, but it came close. Placing his hand beneath her chin, he made her meet his gaze. "I would never hurt you, Catrin."

"I know that," she whispered. It wasn't fear he saw in her eyes, but trust.

He drew her down beside him. "Will it bother you to feel me over you? Or would you rather lie atop me?" He slowly stroked her from neck to waist.

"Nothing you've done has frightened me," she said. She nuzzled at the hair on his chest, then looked up and stared into his eyes. "I know 'tis you, Nicholas. I'll know it when you're deep inside me, no matter how we make love. I could never mistake you for anyone else."

A shudder passed through him. Easing her back against the pillows, he nudged her thighs apart with his, kneeling there so she could become accustomed to him.

His gaze holding hers, he captured her lips, stroking them with his tongue while he slipped his hand between her legs to test her readiness. "Gently, love," he whispered against her mouth when she started to clamp her legs together. "Do you want me to stop?"

She shook her head and relaxed her legs, allowing him access. Plunging his tongue deep within her mouth, at the same time he slipped his finger into the waiting folds of her womanhood.

Her flesh tightened around him, clasping him gently as slight ripples coursed through her. Reluctantly withdrawing from her warmth, he brushed his damp finger over the tiny nub hidden within the petals of her femininity.

Catrin quivered against his hands, a soft, keening moan rising from her throat. Nicholas lowered his weight, spread her folds slightly with shaking fingers and slid his aching flesh deep.

Raising her knees, Catrin arched into him, accepting him fully. The soft, gasping sounds she made nearly sent him over the edge, and he paused, still buried within her, waiting for the urge to spill his seed to pass.

"Nicholas?" she whispered against his cheek, her eyes questioning. "What's wrong?"

"Nothing," he gasped. "I just want to make this last." Catrin stared up at him, her eyes a smoky gray, a look of wonder lending her features an ethereal beauty. "How do you feel?"

"Just fine," she said. She raked her fingernails over his back, nearly undoing his attempt to slow down.

If all she felt was "just fine," she wasn't ready yet. He devoted himself to making her feel so wonderful she wouldn't be able to imagine the words to describe it.

Lowering one hand to toy with her breasts, he began to rock his hips, pressing himself deep within her, then withdrawing slightly. He concentrated on her pleasure, ignoring the scorching heat boiling through his veins to pool in his loins. As her body began to pulse around him he altered the primal drive for completion to a slow, deep quest for mutual fulfillment. He wouldn't permit himself to reach that pinnacle without her. With lips, hands, body, he drove her toward it, savoring her response and allowing it to carry him along with her.

She was so close. He could hear it in the sounds she made, feel it in the press of her hands, her nails into his flesh. "Look at me, Catrin," he said urgently, continuing to press deeply into her quivering body. He wanted to watch her when it happened.

He wanted her to watch him.

Her eyelids fluttered open. She gazed at him intently, her body arching to meet his thrusts. Slipping his arm beneath her, he lifted her, holding her more tightly to him.

Nicholas knew the moment it happened, would have known even if he hadn't felt her body spasm around his own pulsing flesh. Catrin held his gaze, the look in her wide gray eyes touching him to his very soul.

Chapter Twenty

Nicholas's cry of release still echoing in her ears, Catrin blinked until the room came back into focus. Tears puddled in the corners of her eyes, soaking her eyelashes and running down her temples to soak into her hair. She hated to cry, and the fact that these were tears of pleasure made no difference.

What had she just done? Had she gone mad, to make love with Nicholas Talbot?

She'd realized how wrong she was for him days ago. That hadn't changed. And doubtless he'd expect certain things of her now, things she couldn't give.

But dear God, how she wished she could!

She didn't regret making love with him. How could she be sorry she'd sampled such joy?

She hadn't known it was possible to feel so intensely.

Although she lay quietly beneath him, inside she fought against a swirl of panic. More than anything, she wanted to push him aside and run—away from her fears, her worries—away from Nicholas.

She didn't want to be on this bed with him when he opened his eyes.

She didn't want to hurt him.

It was bound to happen, sooner or later. Catrin knew she'd never be docile, meek, submissive—all the qualities noblemen looked for in their ladies. She might as well get out of this now, before she hurt them both.

Shoving at his broad shoulders, she tried to wriggle out from beneath him. But he raised himself up on his elbows, his mouth seeking hers before he even opened his eyes.

She turned her face away; his lips brushed against her cheek. "Catrin?" Opening his eyes, he held her trapped with his gaze, as well as his body.

"I'd like to get up now, please," she said, voice flat. She stared past his shoulder at the moth-eaten tapestry on the wall.

If she met his eyes, she'd be lost.

"What's wrong, love? Tell me." Grasping her chin in a gentle grip, he tried to turn her to face him.

But Catrin resisted, firming her resolve when her eyes filled with tears again. "If you please, milord."

"As you wish," he said shortly, rolling onto his side. After staring at her for a moment, his expression revealing his confusion, he pivoted to sit on the side of the bed.

She scrambled across the mattress and snatched up the coverlet, winding it about her body like a shroud. Her eyes wouldn't cease their infernal watering. She dashed the moisture away, angry at her lack of control.

Nicholas slipped on his chausses and stood, his eyes on her as he absently tied the drawstring. "Tell me what's wrong." He held out his hand, reaching across the mattress. The bed had seemed so small when they were in it, but it loomed large now, when she considered what bridging that distance might mean.

Better to leave while she could, before Nicholas battered down her feeble defenses and she found herself in that bed with him again. It would take very little effort for him to lure her back where she truly wished to be.

She hoped he didn't realize that.

But she couldn't go just yet, she realized with dismay. Tildy had never brought her clothes. She scanned the chamber for something—anything—she could put on besides the bedcover she wore now. She settled on a mass of white linen at the foot of the bed.

It was Nicholas's shirt. Her feet hampered by the heavy fabric wrapped about her, she shuffled over to the shirt, snatching it up just before Nicholas could.

She dropped the garment over her head and wriggled her arms into the overlong sleeves. "I haven't any clothes," she mumbled, settling the soft material around her with a final shimmy and letting the blanket fall. The shirt hung to below her knees. Although not what she'd prefer, at least she was decently covered.

Stepping over the rumpled blanket, she headed for the door.

"Where are you going?" He grabbed her by the arm and spun her around to face him. "You're not leaving this room with only my shirt to cover you."

Catrin wrenched free and stepped back. "I'll do as I please." Giving him a wide berth, she again headed for the door.

She managed to unlatch the door before he caught her again. This time he wrapped his arms around her middle and lifted her off the floor. "Put me down, you idiot!" He slung her over his shoulder. "Damn you, Nicholas!"

In two strides he'd made it back to the bed. "Don't tempt me," he said, his hand hovering over her backside threateningly. Draped over his shoulder, her head hanging upside down in a tangled web of hair, she could do little to fight him, although that didn't stop her from trying.

Her hands slid over the tight musculature of his back and waist as she attempted to pinch him. But since she couldn't find a bit of loose flesh to grab, she poked him in the ribs instead. "Release me now, or else I'll—"

"You little hellcat," Nicholas growled. His flesh twitched beneath her meager assault. He must be ticklish. She redoubled her efforts, fully expecting him to slap her on the rump—he couldn't miss it, sticking up next to his face. But instead he swung her around in his grasp and fell across the mattress with her cradled in his arms.

Before she could scramble away he pinned her to the bed with his body, her wrists held above her head on the pillows, shackled by his hands. Shifting until he lay atop her, he stared down into her face.

"What is wrong?" he asked sharply. She squirmed, trying to break free, so he settled his weight more fully over her, his legs holding hers so she couldn't kick at him. "Stop it."

She was no match for his strength, so she ceased her struggles and lay motionless, though it galled her to obey him.

He hadn't expected her to do as he'd ordered. Her sudden compliance took him by surprise. He bent to kiss her cheek, but the pain he saw in her eyes stopped him.

Why this complete change? A short while ago she had appeared happy in his arms, and he knew he'd given her pleasure. "Is it something I did?" he murmured. "I would never harm you. I thought you enjoyed what we shared."

From the stubborn set of her chin, he knew he'd gain no answers now. And he didn't want to add to the distress he saw in her eyes. Perhaps once she'd dressed, after some time had passed, she'd be more willing to tell him what was wrong.

He rolled away and got to his feet, offering his hand to

help her up off the bed. She refused, moving to the other side of the mattress.

"You needn't get up," he told her. "'Tis your chamber, after all. I'll leave."

Catrin nodded. She looked so small and frail lying there, her face drained of color and her eyes huge. He felt like a brute, hefting her about like a side of meat—especially so soon after her injuries.

He refused to berate himself for making love with her, however; she'd been as active a participant as he, no matter what qualms she might have now.

If, indeed, 'twas their lovemaking that accounted for the return of Catrin's sullen behavior.

Perhaps he overrated his own importance.

But he hated to leave her like this. Gathering the coverlet from the floor, Nicholas spread it over her. "I'll send Tildy in with some clothes for you. Once you've rested, would you meet with me in the hall? We've plans to make."

He fought the urge to smooth the tangled curls back from her face, but he couldn't walk out the door without saying something.

Taking her unresisting hand in his, he raised it to his lips. "Thank you for the joy you gave me," he murmured, staring into her eyes. He turned her hand and placed a kiss on the inside of her wrist. "Until later." Releasing her, he bowed and left.

The thump of the door clicking shut echoed loudly in Catrin's ears. She felt beyond thought, beyond caring. But deep inside she knew that wasn't true. If she allowed herself to ponder everything roiling within her heart and mind she'd go mad.

Too drained to confront her worries, she burrowed her face into the pillow and let the tears flow.

* * *

Ian and Rannulf followed Padrig's trail through the forest, covering a good distance before darkness forced them to halt. After a cold, miserable night, they set out again as soon as dawn brightened the sky.

Ian led Rannulf along a barely noticeable path through the woods. He'd traveled many of the trails before, though he wasn't as familiar with this one. But he knew that the trail should merge with one of the many routes between Gwal Draig and l'Eau Clair. If necessary, he'd follow them all. It was a matter of time until they found the place where Catrin's party had been attacked. They couldn't have simply disappeared.

However long it took, they'd find her.

As the day wore on, his eyes burned from the strain of searching; once they left the trees and picked up the road, Rannulf took the lead. The faint warmth of the midday sun, combined with too many sleepless days, weighted him down with weariness.

"Let's stop," he called. He estimated they'd been on the road for an hour without a sign that anyone had passed this way. "Perhaps after we rest and eat, we'll be more alert." He dismounted and led his horse down the trail. "I believe there's a clearing up ahead. 'Tis a good place to stop."

Rannulf dismounted, as well, and they walked along in companionable silence.

Suddenly Rannulf halted in the middle of the trail and bent to examine the ground. "This hoofprint—" Rannulf traced the rain-worn mark with his fingertip. "It looks familiar." Sitting back on his heels, he drew his finger around the print again. "'Tis Nick Talbot's stallion. He might have passed this way after he left l'Eau Clair." He stood and scanned their surroundings. "The king sent him to see Llywelyn. He visited with us—left about a week ago." He met Ian's gaze. "Around the same time Catrin left for l'Eau Clair."

"Just because Talbot passed this way doesn't mean he saw Catrin," Ian protested. "It would be too much of a coincidence. Besides, if either of them saw the other coming, they'd head in the opposite direction. There's no love lost between those two."

Rannulf laughed. "Perhaps. But you haven't seen how they look at each other when they think no one is watching. If they're ever in the same place for any length of time they might discover they're kindred spirits—if they don't kill each other first."

Though it was an amusing thought, Ian wasn't sure he could imagine his sister paired with a Norman. 'Twas a trifling thought, at any rate. His sister was missing.

Finding her was all that mattered.

Taking up the reins, Ian again headed down the road.

He noticed the smell first, near where the road ended and the clearing began. Moving silently, he looped the reins around a sturdy branch; Rannulf did the same. He slid his dagger from its sheath with one hand and closed the other about the hilt of his sword, then slipped into the trees surrounding the copse.

The clearing held no threat. He let the sword slide back into the scabbard, but kept his dagger in hand when he entered the field.

'Twas butchery. Although animals—both wild and human, from the look of it—had been at the bodies, they'd left enough behind for Ian to recognize them as human.

His heart in his throat, he moved from body to body, each time fearing the next would be Catrin's. Rannulf watched in silence as he walked about the clearing.

Finally, knees weak and heart heavy, he leaned against a tree and closed his eyes.

The corpses were all men. Catrin's remains did not lie here, ravaged by beasts, thieves and the elements. Even as he mourned his men, however, he thanked God that his sister appeared to have escaped their fate. "When I find whoever did this, they'll rue the day they meddled with my family."

Had Catrin witnessed the slaughter?

"They're your men?" Rannulf asked.

"I knew three of them. The others—" He shrugged. "But mine were good men, though not the best of fighters, alas." He shook his head. "When I get my hands on my sister, I'll blister her backside for this." Hands clenched, he pounded his fists against a tree. "And I'll never let her out of my sight again. She knew, damn her—she knew they weren't soldiers. Yet she brought them out here anyway." He kicked at a pile of wet leaves. "When will she learn to think? I've given her the chance to prove she can be reasonable, over and over. Every time she disappoints me. Once I find her, she'll not leave Gwal Draig again. I swear it."

"Hold, Ian." Rannulf picked up a scrap of parchment Ian had sent fluttering across the ground. "There's writing on this." Squinting, he read the untidy scrawl. "It looks like the directions for some medicinal compound. Gillian has a bundle of these, bound together into a book. Could this belong to Catrin?"

Ian snatched the parchment from Rannulf's hand and examined it. "Aye, 'tis her writing." Crumpling the scrap in his hand, he closed his eyes and tilted his head back, expelling a harsh breath.

Rannulf laid a hand on Ian's shoulder. "Let's see if there are any clues to tell us who did this."

Rannulf was right. He'd gain nothing by ranting about things he could not change. But how his palms itched to give Catrin the beating she deserved!

Even as the thought entered his mind, Ian knew he'd never do it.

Damned woman!

Sighing, he joined Rannulf as he searched the clearing, poking and prodding.

When they finished, by unspoken agreement they began scraping out two shallow graves—one for Ian's men, another for the rest—while they discussed what they'd found.

"It looks as if they were attacked as they approached the clearing." Ian gouged at the wet soil with a stout branch. "It's the perfect place for an ambush. While I'm not sure who did it, several possibilities come to mind."

"You don't believe that robbery was the motive?"

"Nay, though that didn't stop them from stripping the dead," Ian said with disgust. "Catrin didn't bring much with her, certainly not enough to tempt any but the most desperate bandit. I think the trap was in place before she got here. Someone planned on taking her."

"Nicholas must have come through here around the same time as Catrin." Rannulf paused in his labors to strip off his shirt. "My only question is who left with whom." Ian looked at him curiously. "The signs are faded from the rain, but I think they left in two groups. A small one, and a larger one. I'm just not certain what that means."

Arms folded, Ian leaned back against a tree. "Even if Talbot interfered somehow, they might have taken him, as well. Perhaps they left here in two groups and met up later."

"Or headed for two different places," Rannulf added. "We've no way to tell. But if you have any idea who was behind this—"

"Believe me, I do," Ian growled. "Let's finish here. After this, I'll be in the perfect mood to visit Steffan."

Lips quirked into a mirthless smile, Ian watched as rage transformed Rannulf's pleasant expression into that of an avenging warrior. "You'd better wait for me outside Bryn Du, Rannulf," he said. "I doubt Steffan will permit you within the gates anyway."

Rannulf remained silent, but his eyes were cold and deadly. Ian shrugged away from the tree and stood facing him. "I realize that the thought of killing Steffan is appealing, but we cannot simply ride in and do it. For some reason Llywelyn likes him. There'll be time enough to go after Steffan once we discover if he's the one we seek."

Rannulf took up the makeshift shovel he'd been using and attacked the hard-packed soil.

At this rate, they'd be on their way to Bryn Du in no time.

Ian and Rannulf parted company in the forest, taking no chances that Rannulf might be seen by anyone on the walls of Bryn Du. It made no sense to risk Steffan learning of Rannulf's presence. Ian wouldn't put it past his cousin to entertain him royally while sending a troop out to seize—or murder—Rannulf.

He knew how ruthless and amoral Steffan could be, one of the many reasons he suspected he was behind the attack. It bore the telltale mark of Steffan's sly ways. Ian sighed. At the moment, his brain was so weary, 'twas a miracle he could think at all.

Rannulf made himself comfortable alongside a pleasant stream, stretching out on the mossy ground. "Do you really believe Steffan will admit it if he had anything to do with this?"

Ian shook his head. "No. But he's such an arrogant bastard, perhaps he'll make a mistake and let slip some tidbit of information. He's capable of anything, so long as he can find someone to do his dirty work for him." He checked his weapons. "That's the key to discovering what Steffan's been doing—find the scum he hired to carry out his schemes. Perhaps I'll be lucky enough to do that." He climbed into the saddle. "Don't get too comfortable," he warned, then nudged his stallion into motion.

No sense putting it off any longer. He wouldn't be satisfied until he looked Steffan in the eye and asked what he knew about Catrin's disappearance.

With luck he'd be done and back outside the walls before sunset. They could spend the night at Gwal Draig and set out again in the morning. Squaring his shoulders for the unpleasant task ahead, he spurred his horse onto the road to Bryn Du.

"Welcome, cousin." Steffan motioned Ian to a cushioned bench near the central fire pit, then took a seat. With a clap of his hands he summoned a servant to bring them wine, then lounged back into his chair.

"It's always a pleasure to see you, Ian. It's been too long since you honored us with a visit." Steffan smiled, but his eyes remained cold.

It amused Ian to imagine the thoughts going on behind Steffan's urbane expression. There had never been any love lost between them, though Steffan preferred to shroud his dislike in fulsome posturing. He had the manners of the courtly knights of French legend, and the soul—if he even *had* a soul—of Satan himself.

It was one of the greatest frustrations of Ian's life that he'd never been able to prove his suspicions.

He knew Steffan had always hated him, but that hatred must surely have deepened since Catrin had helped Gillian escape Bryn Du. Steffan likely wished him dead, yet being Steffan, he wrapped his loathing in flowery courtesies.

Nothing could have irritated Ian more.

A slatternly maid brought them wine. She glanced at Ian from beneath her eyelashes when she handed him the goblet, her expression curious, then crept away at Steffan's growled dismissal. Evidently his manners didn't extend to his servants.

"What brings you here?" Steffan asked, his eyes alert.

Ian drained his goblet before answering. The wine was fine, and he doubted he'd have the chance to finish it once he stated his business. "I'd like to hear what you know about my sister's disappearance," he said, casually moving one hand to his sword.

"Catrin is missing? How distressing. I do hope she hasn't come to harm." Although his tone conveyed concern, Steffan's dark eyes glowed with a strange, avid light. He leaned forward in his chair. "Such a terrible situation, cousin. But then, Catrin is so very—" his lips twisted into a patently false smile "—independent."

Ian reined in the urge to clout that smile away. "It appears she was attacked while traveling to l'Eau Clair. Not far from here, actually. I wondered if you had heard anything about it," he added, observing Steffan closely.

"No. No, this is the first I've heard of it." Steffan sat back and spread his hand wide. "I would have notified you at once if I'd heard the slightest bit of news. Such a terrible thing."

Though Steffan mouthed all the right words, Ian noticed the glimmer of pleasure, of anticipation shimmering in his eyes. The bastard was enjoying this—far too much.

Ian had seen enough to convince him that Steffan was involved, somehow. How he wished he could wrap his hands about Steffan's neck!

But there were guards everywhere; he'd never leave Bryn Du alive if he tried anything.

However, he'd set some men to spying on the place as soon as he returned to Gwal Draig.

This battle would be won another day.

Ian rose. "Send word if you hear anything."

"You may depend upon it." Steffan ushered him toward the door. "If you let me know how the search progresses I may be able to discover something." He backed away. "Huw will show you out." Motioning to the burly soldier, Steffan strode away.

So much for asking if anyone else knew anything, Ian thought, ignoring Huw and heading straight for his horse. He should have realized Steffan wouldn't allow him a chance to question anybody.

Likely his people were so cowed they wouldn't dare answer, anyway.

Ian found Rannulf waiting where he'd left him.

"Learn anything?" he asked, rising stiffly to his feet and stretching.

"Aye. I think he's the one."

"Then why is he still in there?" Rannulf cocked his head toward Bryn Du.

"I can't just drag him out of his own keep. Llywelyn has warned me away from Steffan more than once." Ian slapped the reins against his leg. "Llywelyn's Dragon, impotent by Llywelyn's own command. I don't know what hold Steffan has over our illustrious cousin, but once this is done I'll discover what it is, I swear." He closed his eyes wearily. "We need to find the men Steffan hired to carry out his dirty work. If we find them, likely we'll find her, as well."

Opening his eyes, he gestured toward Rannulf's horse. "Let's go. We can plan while we ride. Gwal Draig awaits."

Chapter Twenty-One

Several hours after Nicholas left Catrin to her solitary slumber, she went in search of him. She slept after he left, and awakened in a more calm frame of mind. But she still felt too susceptible, too weak to think clearly. With rest, good food and time, she didn't doubt she'd regain her usual spirits. Until then, she wished she could avoid Nicholas, but that wasn't her way.

Nor was it possible while she remained at Ashby.

With Tildy's help she dressed, each garment she donned another layer of armor to protect her from Nicholas—and from herself. Earlier she'd forgotten how to be strong.

Permitting herself to care about Nicholas, to grow close to him, had made her far too vulnerable. She needed to leave, now. If he didn't arrange for her to go to l'Eau Clair, she'd take care of it herself, a course of action she'd rather avoid. Her impatience had gotten her into this situation in the first place.

After sending a servant to look for Nicholas, she settled into the hall in a chair near the fire. Some effort had been made to clean the chamber. While she couldn't say the room met her standards, she could see an improvement.

She heard Nicholas's footsteps as he crossed the large room, but she continued to stare into the fire until he sat down on a bench near her chair.

"So obedient, Catrin," he said, his voice tinged with weariness. Turning, she saw how he slumped on the bench, his whisker-stubbled face exhausted. "I expected you to have run off by now."

Shame broke over her like a wave. While she sulked in her chamber, concerned only with *her* worries and fears, evidently he had toiled like a slave. She could have helped him, if she hadn't been behaving like a spoiled child.

She could help him now. She rose and poured a mug of ale from the pitcher on the table. "When did you last eat?" she asked, handing him the cup.

"This morning after I left you." He drank down the ale in one long swallow, then held out the mug for more. "'Tis dusty work, shoveling out this midden."

After refilling the mug, she went to the door leading out to the scullery. She gave orders for food to be brought, then returned to Nicholas.

"I never asked last night if you met with everyone after supper, as I told them you would." She toyed with the stack of wooden trenchers on the table, unwilling to meet his eyes.

"We didn't discuss that, did we? I think perhaps we were too busy." She looked up at his teasing tone. The veil of weariness had lifted from his eyes, leaving them a beautiful dark violet. A wry smile lifted one corner of his mouth and his expression taunted her, challenged her, dared her to come closer.

When he held out his hand, she couldn't resist.

No sooner did she step closer than he stood and swept her into his arms. Lifting her until her feet left the floor and her eyes were level with his, he took her mouth in a demanding kiss.

By the time his lips abandoned hers they were both short of breath. "I've hungered for you all day," he whispered. He slid her down his body, nudging her gently with the proof of his desire before her feet touched the floor. "But it seems I'll be satisfying a different hunger for the moment," he said with a nod toward the servant placing a tray of food on the table.

His attention on them instead of his task, the man bumped the pitcher of ale and set it wobbling. And she didn't care for the smirk on his face.

Evidently Nicholas didn't, either. "You'd do well to attend to your duties," he snarled. He grabbed the pitcher before it could topple over. "And you'll show respect to the lady, else you'll be dredging out the garderobe pits."

Face pale, the servant bowed low. "Aye, milord. Beg pardon, milady." Snatching up the tray, he hurried back to the kitchen.

"Insolent knave," Nicholas growled, pulling the bench up to the table. He met her gaze before he sat down. "I apologize for his discourtesy. They know little of manners here, but it won't happen again, I promise you."

Perhaps the servants knew now that she wasn't his wife—and where he'd spent the night.

Or mayhap they simply had no idea how to comport themselves in a noble household.

Whatever the reason, she was grateful for his consideration. She nodded, then silently prepared a plate of food for him before joining him on the bench. "The fare is simple, but tasty." She poured him more ale. "Tildy said they've depended upon the siege stores the last few months. Scarcely any land has been readied for crops."

She let him eat, saving her questions until he pushed the remains of the meal away.

"In case you were wondering, Idris is in the stables," he said, smiling. "He reduced the maids—and at least half the men—to hysterics in no time. I judged it best to keep him out of their sight for the moment. Of course, you may bring him to your chamber, if you wish."

"He'll be fine in the stables. Besides, we'll be leaving for l'Eau Clair soon. No sense in upsetting your servants."

Nicholas sent her a quizzical smile. "Leaving so soon?"

She frowned at his tone. "You know I must get to l'Eau Clair as soon as I can. And you have business with Llywelyn, do you not?" She pushed at her end of the bench, but Nicholas braced his feet and held the seat—and her—in place.

"Calm down. I vow I've never met a woman as easy to provoke as you."

The look Catrin sent him would have brought most men to their knees, begging for mercy.

But not Nicholas. "Messengers went out to Gwal Draig and l'Eau Clair at first light." He picked up her hand and toyed with her fingers. "Once you've had another day or so to rest, I'll take you to your cousin. We'll go well guarded, since we still don't know who attacked you."

"Whoever it was likely believes I'm dead. I'll be perfectly safe," she said, regarding it as the truth. "Surely you've more important duties to attend to. You needn't escort me."

"I cannot send you off without seeing to your safety myself. I'll do what I can to set things right here before we leave, and I'll return once my business with Llywelyn is complete. In truth, 'twill be a relief to stay here, instead of trailing along after the king. And I look forward to the challenge of rebuilding Ashby.''

"I'll do what I can to direct the household servants, if you like.'' The rest of what she planned to say flew out of her brain when he stroked his fingertip along the sensitive flesh of her wrist, sending a shiver of reaction down her spine. An intimate, knowing smile and the warm glow in his eyes were his only response.

"I can travel into Wales just as easily from there as here. 'Twill take no time at all, so long as I don't encounter another damsel in distress." He raised her hand to his lips and kissed her fingertips one by one. "Although there's no one I'd rather rescue than you."

She hadn't objected to his affectionate display; in truth, she had no wish to stop him. He made her feel as if she were the focus of his attention, her opinions and her person valued and desired. It was easy to forget the realities of life, away from the rest of the world.

Would it be wrong to enjoy this, if only for a little while longer? The admiration in his eyes cast a powerful lure. Throwing caution to the wind, she made her decision.

For as long as it lasted, she would savor—cherish—his attentions. She felt like a rose, unfurling petal by petal.

Surely something so rare, so wonderful should be treasured.

She twined her fingers with his and pulled his hand toward her. Her gaze holding his, she drew his thumb into her mouth, gently biting it, then soothing his flesh with her tongue. His indrawn breath told her of his pleasure; abandoning his thumb, she moved on, slipping her tongue along the sensitive skin between his fingers.

Her attention focused on Nicholas, Catrin wasn't aware anyone had approached them until his hand jerked. "What is it?'' he asked, his voice hoarse. He clasped Catrin's hand when she would have pulled it away.

She lowered her gaze, refusing to look at the man. Doubtless her desire for Nicholas was written on her face.

And right now, her face felt as hot as her blood.

"Beg pardon, milord, but you're needed in the bailey," the servant mumbled, bowing slightly. Some of the people here knew their place.

Perhaps there was hope for Ashby yet.

"I'll be along directly," he said, dismissing the man. Nicholas waited until the servant reached the door before he stood. "You have a powerful effect on me, love." He cast a rueful glance at his body.

Her flush deepened when she followed his gaze. "I'm sorry."

"Don't be—I'm not." He captured her chin in his hand, bent and brushed his lips across hers. "I'm only sorry we weren't alone."

He released her. "You should have Anna take a look at your back, then get some rest. If she says you're well enough, we'll leave for l'Eau Clair the day after tomorrow." He grasped her about the waist and lifted her from the bench. "Likely I'll be too busy to see you until we leave, so this will have to last us." Clasping her tightly to his still-aroused body, Nicholas ravished her mouth with his. When he'd reduced her to mindless confusion, he set her back on the bench and hastened from the room.

Steffan clutched a goblet of unwatered wine in his hand and paced the confines of his private quarters. Plots and plans whirled through his brain, fueled by anger at remembered slights to form a roiling stew of rage.

He paused by the window, but the cessation of movement did nothing to halt the frantic activity in his head.

Would he ever know quiet—peace—again? The buzz of disembodied voices gave him no respite. Even in sleep the confusing babble droned on, barely audible snippets of command and demand jostling to be heard.

What did he have to do to silence them? Slamming the goblet onto the stone window ledge, Steffan stared as the dregs of his wine flew up, spattering the wall and his hand. The liquid dripped slowly down his fingers, deep red and viscous, like blood.

A throbbing grew in the palm of his hand, beating in rhythm with the pounding in his head. He released the battered remains of the goblet from his grip, then turned his hand over and watched as blood crept with a dreamlike indolence from the cut across his palm to mingle with the wine.

Surprisingly it didn't hurt, he noted, tilting his hand this way and that. How odd.

Hammering at the door drew his attention. "Come."

Huw slipped into the room. "There's a man here from Gwal Draig, milord. He says he's got news about your cousin."

A surge of excitement pulsed through Steffan's body. "Catrin?"

Huw nodded.

"Send him in."

He flopped into his favorite chair, sprawling there while he pondered what the information could be. His lips twisted in a smile.

Huw ushered the man in, then left them, closing the door behind him. "Your name?" Steffan asked, resting his elbows on the carved arms of the chair and steepling his fingers in front of his face.

"Owen, milord." He snatched off his cap and crumpled it in his hands, bobbing his head in a belated show of respect. "I live in the village 'tween here and Gwal Draig."

He scrutinized the man in a leisurely fashion, enjoying his obvious discomfort and waiting until the filthy, scrawny varlet began to shift his feet and squirm. "Huw said you've news of Lady Catrin."

"I might know somethin'," Owen said. "I heard ye'd pay well to learn what happened to her."

"I'm sure something can be arranged," he said with a languid wave of his hand. "Please, tell me what you heard."

"A messenger rode into Gwal Draig yestereve, late. Came from someplace on the border called Ashby. The man told Lord Ian that his master had found Lady Catrin in the forest and brought her to his keep. Lord Ian and Lord Rannulf left for l'Eau Clair at first light, so that must be where she's headed."

Steffan leaned forward, the man standing before him fading away in the red-tinged mist of anger clouding his vision. "I knew it," he muttered, pounding his fist on the arm of the chair. He stopped when blood seeped from between his fingers; no sense in getting bloodstains on the cushions. "I knew the bitch wasn't dead."

"What's that, milord?"

"I wasn't talking to you, fool," he snarled. "Be silent. I need to think."

Why did Ashby sound familiar? He couldn't recall—

It didn't matter. 'Twould come to him in time.

He never should have permitted Ralph to leave. The lying bastard had to have known Catrin still lived. And he'd had the gall to ask to be paid! Steffan complimented himself on having the sense to send the greedy son of a bitch away empty-handed.

But he shouldn't have left Bryn Du at all, he thought,

pounding his fist against the chair once more. To hell with the upholstery—

What did a few stains matter when all his plans had come to naught?

He struggled to separate his thoughts from the rising cacophony in his head. At least the crimson mists had cleared from his vision. His eyes darting about, he noticed the man Huw had brought in—Owen. Aye, that was his name. Owen still stood before him, looking ready to jump out of his skin, he noted with satisfaction.

"Huw," he bellowed, knowing the soldier would be waiting just outside the door.

Huw stepped into the room. "Aye, milord?"

He gestured toward Owen. "Take him out and lock him in the cellars until I decide what to do with him."

Owen immediately began to back away. "B-but you said you'd pay me, milord," he sputtered. "I've done ye no harm—"

Huw grabbed Owen's arms from behind. "Come along, now," he said, nearly dragging the smaller man across the floor and hustling him out the door.

"Huw," Steffan called after him, "come back after you tend to him. There are some things I want you to do."

The moment the door closed behind Huw, Steffan bounded out of his chair and began to pace the confines of the chamber. He needed an outlet for his burst of energy, else his mind would race away from him.

He stopped in the middle of the room. He couldn't think; he had to do something to clear his mind. Hands fisted and jaw clenched with frustration, Steffan tilted back his head and groaned.

His revenge could be so close now, if he made the right move. Returning to the chair, he made himself comfortable while he waited for Huw to return. They'd have to come up with a foolproof way to get Catrin. And this time he'd do it himself, so there'd be no mistakes.

He wanted Catrin, and this time he would have her. Listening to the thoughts rolling round his mind, Steffan began to shape his plan.

Chapter Twenty-Two

Nicholas glanced thankfully at the midday sun high overhead and brought his ragged troop to a halt near a stream along the boundary of l'Eau Clair lands. During his brief tenure as Gillian's guardian last spring, he'd patrolled these woods often, seeking out the brigands who wreaked havoc on the outlying farms. Another league and they would reach the castle itself.

And none too soon. Catrin needed to rest.

Although she protested each time he asked if she wished to stop, he knew she kept going on willpower alone. And their guard... He shook his head.

Judging by the way they drooped and moaned, they needed the respite more than she did.

He rode to the rear of the straggling column and smacked the last man across the buttocks with the flat of his sword to hurry him along. "Come on, you laggards. If the Welsh come upon us now, they'll be all over you like a pack of wolves on a lamb. Keep dawdling and you'll be dead."

Idris trotted out of the woods, tongue lolling from the side of his mouth in a canine smile. Nicholas joined in

the dog's amusement when he noticed how his men tried
to edge away from Idris without appearing craven.

He could scarcely wait until he had the time to whip
these lazy oafs into a respectable troop of fighting men.
He'd do it, just as he'd shape Ashby into the fine keep it
had been in his grandfather's day. Anticipation lent a keen
edge to his appreciation of life: not since his childhood
had he looked forward to each day with such eagerness.

Turning his mount, he jogged toward the front of the
line, slowing when he reached Catrin's side. She rode the
mare they'd found after they were attacked. A fine animal,
possessed of an even temperament, the mare had already
begun to fill out. Catrin had named her Rhosyn. When he
protested that no one named a horse after a rose, she
laughed and told him she never did anything the same as
other people.

He found that easy to believe!

He rode so close to Catrin, his knee nudged against
hers. "Your rose doesn't smell too sweet," he teased.

She smiled and met his gaze. "You'll not convince me
to change her name." She patted the mare's neck. "Besides, roses are beautiful, and so is Rhosyn."

"My miserable troop needs to rest again, milady."
He'd noticed how her shoulders sagged with weariness
despite her brave front. At least the men had served one
purpose; their lack of stamina provided ample excuse for
them to stop, to Catrin's benefit.

If she hadn't been along, Nicholas would have harried
them unmercifully until they developed some backbone.
As it was, he thanked God they hadn't met up with any
type of threat. Even a rampaging wild boar would likely
have panicked them into a hasty retreat. He and Catrin
would probably have been trampled to death in the pro-

cess, too, he thought wryly. Still, they presented the appearance of a guard, if he didn't look at them very closely.

"Nicholas, we're almost there. Surely they're capable of walking the rest of the way without stopping again."

He shrugged. "You've seen Ashby, Catrin. There wasn't a person there who'd done an honest day's work in months, ever since Clarence heard I was dead. I still don't understand where that rumor came from. But if I'd paid more attention to Ashby, things never would have gotten so bad—and Clarence would have known the rumor was untrue."

"'Tis no wonder he reacted so violently when he saw you standing outside the keep," she said with a laugh. "He must have thought you were a ghost come to haunt him."

"At least he could have tried to discover if I had actually died. Instead the fool began a celebration that lasted far too long."

She reached over and took his hand, her lips curved into a grin. "Isn't it touching to realize how they mourned you?"

He grimaced. "They'll wish *they'd* died before I'm through with them," he vowed. "And I'm certain Clarence is grieving the loss of an extremely profitable position—for him. The bastard bled me white this past year and more. I could see that much just from the cursory glance I took at the accounts before we left."

"I doubt you've anything to worry about on that score now." Catrin squirmed in the saddle. "Clarence is long gone, and you put the fear of God in everyone else before we left."

He chuckled in remembrance. "I think some of the women had the impression that I took their men with me as hostages for their good behavior." He sent her a questioning glance. She refused to meet his eyes, but she looked very pleased with herself. "I don't know where they got the idea, but I'll be very happy if it works. Thank you."

"Can't we move on yet?" she asked. "I know what you're doing. I'm fine. I don't want—or need—to stop again."

He should have realized she'd see through his pretense. His concern was genuine; he hadn't even been sure they should make the journey so soon. But he feared that if he didn't bring her to l'Eau Clair himself, she'd find some other way to get there.

And he didn't want to chase through the marches after her.

"We're still going to rest," he told her firmly. "It matters not whether 'tis for your benefit or for theirs. 'Twill only be for a little while, then we'll be on our way."

Despite Nicholas's enforced stop, it took all Catrin's remaining energy to stay upright in the saddle. And he noticed it, too, damn him. Not half a league left, and he halted the troop again.

Hungry, filthy and tired, she glared at him when he brought his horse right up beside Rhosyn, but before she had a chance to open her mouth he reached over and scooped her from the saddle and onto his lap.

He covered her mouth with his hand. "Not a word." After settling her more comfortably, he leaned over her shoulder and looked her in the eyes. "And don't even think of biting me," he warned before he moved his hand away.

As if she'd consider putting that glove in her mouth ever again!

This really wasn't so terrible, to feel Nicholas's warmth

and strength surrounding her. They had spent no time alone together since the morning they'd made love, and much to her surprise, she missed him. Closing her eyes, Catrin snuggled into his embrace, resolved to enjoy her good fortune for the brief remainder of the journey.

Nearly a fortnight after she left Gwal Draig, Catrin finally reached l'Eau Clair. Although she wasn't pleased to enter the keep draped over Nicholas's saddlebow like a war prize, it was far better than the alternative. If not for his bravery, they'd be carrying in her lifeless body on a hurdle.

Assuming her body had ever been found at all.

Her pride would permit this. After all, how many women were fortunate enough to make an entrance cradled in the arms of a gallant, handsome man? 'Twas the stuff of girlish dreams—even hers. Smiling to herself, she nestled back into his arms.

Their approach had been sighted, and they rode over the drawbridge and through the gates straightaway. Once they passed into the bailey they were engulfed by a cheering crowd. People waved, braving the horse's hooves to reach toward them as they crept through the throng.

As she looked out over the sea of faces, Catrin was stunned by the expressions of goodwill. She blinked furiously and turned in Nicholas's arms to see his face.

He looked overwhelmed. When he met her gaze his lips twisted into a grin, lighting his expression from within. He responded to a saucy comment with a laugh and a wave, appearing happier than she'd ever seen him.

These people respected Nicholas, and it seemed they liked him, as well.

This was how his return to Ashby should have been, she thought sadly. But his people didn't know him as these people did. Once they saw what a good leader—a good man—he was, his homecomings to Ashby would likely reflect this same joy.

For his sake, she hoped so.

As she scanned the crowd for a sign of Gillian or Rannulf, she noticed that some of the voices and comments were directed at her, asking after her well-being or simply calling her name. Their concern touched her, and a smile rose to her lips even as tears threatened once again.

Though Nicholas's mount was enveloped in the crowd, they'd been swept along on the swarming tide until they were nearly across the bailey. Her gaze was drawn to the stairs along the outside of the keep, and she saw her family waiting there.

Framed by Ian and Rannulf, Gillian leaned against her husband's side, her face ecstatic as she called their names. She'd grown so huge, Catrin noted with concern. How did she manage to stand there without toppling over?

Nicholas halted his horse at the foot of the steps. Ian bounded down to meet them, scooping Catrin into his arms and wrapping her in a tight embrace.

"Have a care," Nicholas said sharply as Catrin winced.

Ian eased his grip, but he didn't let her go. "I should warm your backside so hard you won't sit for a week," he growled, raising his head. "But since I'm so happy to see you, I won't…this time." He squeezed her again, more gently. Green eyes dark and solemn, he looked her over carefully before kissing her cheek. "I thought I'd lost you."

Catrin raised her hand and touched his face, meeting his eyes for a moment. She couldn't recall when she'd last seen Ian express so much emotion. But she didn't want to wallow in solemnity now; they had plenty of serious matters to discuss soon enough. But if she didn't laugh, she'd cry, and she didn't want to do that. Once she started, she wasn't sure she'd be able to stop.

She forced her lips into a grin and poked him in the stomach. "You should know by now, you can't be rid of me so easily."

Ian's face twisted into a grimace, although Catrin knew she hadn't hurt him. But there was an unexpected joy in the familiar things she'd taken for granted before. She hugged him again, completely losing the forced sense of lightness she'd tried to project. "'Tis so good to see you." She stifled a sob. "Ian, what of Padrig? Did you find any sign of him?" she whispered. The lad had never been far from her thoughts, although she held little hope for his safety.

"He found us."

"Thank God," she murmured, losing her battle against her tears.

"He'll survive, although at first we weren't certain he would. But he's a tough lad—there's no doubt he's related to you. Come inside and see for yourself," he said, hoisting her into his arms and turning to mount the stairs.

"Ian, put me down!" She clung to his tunic. "I'm perfectly capable of walking. At least let me greet Gillian and Rannulf." Blowing her disheveled hair from her face, she wriggled in his grasp until she could see them.

Nicholas had joined them on the stairs; Catrin had been vaguely aware that they, too, were exchanging greetings. "Would you please tell him to set me down?"

Gillian's eyes merry, she solemnly shook her head, Rannulf and Nicholas following her lead. It looked to her as though they were all trying not to laugh, damn them!

"Fine. Carry me to Padrig's chamber, you overgrown idiot. I hope 'tis a good, long distance away." She glared at them, one by one, before she let her head droop against the comfort of Ian's chest.

No sense in letting them know she'd reached the end of her strength.

Ian dipped his arms threateningly in response to her demand, forcing her to cling more tightly to him.

Rannulf scooped Gillian off her feet and started up the stairs. "Come along, you lazy wench," he said, his voice shaking with laughter. "We'll all be more comfortable inside."

Nicholas let them pass, then fell into step with Ian. Catrin met his eyes briefly before Ian swung her about, making the bailey spin wildly before her. "Tell me, Talbot," Ian said, pausing on the step and ignoring Catrin's squirming. "How did you happen to find my sister?"

Catrin poked Ian in the ribs. "You may ask him all the questions you like—once you put me down." Freeing one hand from Ian's clothes, Catrin shoved her hair back and stared meaningfully at Nicholas. He only laughed.

"Could you get him to put me down?" she asked dryly. Ian started up the stairs. "Nicholas—"

Coming to a halt, Ian shifted her in his arms and brought his hand across her buttocks in a gentle swat. "Silence, wench." His body shook with suppressed laughter.

He glanced at Nicholas, who continued to chuckle. "Come along, Talbot. If I don't get her up there soon, Gillian will come down after us."

"We don't need that. Between the two of them—" Nicholas's eyes teased her "—they'll likely jaw us to death as it is. We don't want them angry, too."

Frustrated by her inability to break free and give both men the kicks they so richly deserved, Catrin contented herself with growling low in her throat. Padrig must be well, else they'd not have seemed so happy.

But she refused to let Ian off the hook so easily. "I wish to see Padrig now!"

He must have realized she'd reached the limit of her patience. Clamping his arms more securely about her, he ran lightly up the rest of the steps, Nicholas dogging his heels.

Finally!

She closed her eyes, uncertain, now that she was safe in the midst of her family, whether she could bear any more without breaking down completely.

Chapter Twenty-Three

Nicholas trailed along behind Ian as he carried Catrin to Gillian's solar. In spite of Ian's teasing, Nicholas suspected the real reason he'd picked Catrin up was that he realized she'd reached the end of her endurance.

Though she'd never admit it, the signs were clear enough to him.

And now that Catrin had finally arrived at l'Eau Clair, Nicholas doubted she'd rest until Gillian gave birth. He knew already how it would be, for Catrin could not stay still when she thought she might be needed. There had been ample evidence of that before they left Ashby.

Though she should have been mustering her strength for their journey, he'd encountered her handiwork everywhere. She seldom left her chamber, but she'd discovered a willing and able emissary in Tildy. The maid had a knack for harrying the most idle servants, bullying and cajoling until they gave in and got to work. Perhaps 'twas simply self-defense, he thought with a chuckle.

Whatever the reason, Catrin and Tildy proved an invincible combination. In only two days they made a number of improvements in the way things were done.

"I'll take you to see Padrig in a bit," Ian said. "He's

not going anywhere for a while, and neither are you." He set Catrin on her feet by Gillian's chair. She knelt beside her at once and carefully slipped her arms around her cousin.

"You look better than I imagined after receiving Nicholas's message," Gillian said, wiping a tear from her cheek. "But I can see you've been ill."

Rising, Catrin accepted the chair Rannulf pulled forward for her and settled onto the cushioned seat with a sigh. "You needn't mince words. I'm sure I look a fright. I've had little opportunity to beautify myself of late."

"I see nothing wrong with your looks." Nicholas moved behind her chair. It bothered him when she belittled herself; she did it more frequently than he'd first realized. She surrounded herself with an aura of self-assurance, of arrogance, but now that he knew her better, he recognized that she wasn't like that at all.

"I feel much better, thanks to Nicholas," she said, not responding to his comment. But she reached up and touched his hand where it lay on the back of her chair, sending a tingle up his arm. "He'd make an excellent healer, Gillian. Wait until you see the stitches he put in my back. I hear they're very fine."

"Perhaps you could help Catrin while you're here," Gillian said with a teasing look. "I'll need her services as a midwife very soon."

Although he knew she didn't mean it, Nicholas couldn't disguise his horror at the thought. "'Twas sheer luck Catrin got better. It's a wonder I didn't kill her with my ignorance."

Reaching up, Catrin linked her fingers with his. "You did very well, and I'm more grateful than I can say."

He felt his face redden at the look in her eyes. Glancing away, he saw that the others watched them with a variety of expressions, from Gillian's blatant curiosity to Ian's frown.

And was that amusement in Rannulf's eyes? "How did it seem, returning to Ashby?"

Nicholas sent him a grateful look. "The place is a midden, a veritable sty. Knowing how I've come to enjoy the comforts of noble life, can you imagine how I'd fare in such surroundings?"

"Actually, I imagine you'd manage just fine," Rannulf said, surprising him. "Before you returned to court last year I realized you were not quite the man you appeared."

"There's more to you than you allow others to see," Gillian added.

Nicholas felt his flush deepen at their words. "Enough! Next you'll try to convince everyone I'm a saint, when nothing could be further from the truth."

He moved around to the front of Catrin's chair. "I realize we all have plenty to discuss, but I can see that both these lovely ladies need their rest."

"Nicholas, never tell a woman she looks tired," Gillian scolded. "Though you've become quite the gallant of late, you've still a ways to go."

"I'm not trying to impress you, I'm being honest. After all my efforts to nurse Catrin back to health, I have no intention of allowing her to become ill again." He bent and lifted Catrin out of her chair. "And don't you dare to give birth until Catrin has rested, understand?" he said, leaning down to kiss Gillian's cheek.

"I don't believe there's much she can do about that," Catrin said. She shoved at his shoulders. "Would you put me down? At this rate I won't remember how to walk."

Heedless of their audience, Nicholas raised her higher in his arms and pressed his lips against hers, cutting off the flow of words. This had to be the most effective way he'd ever found to silence her, he thought, fighting the urge to deepen the kiss.

He tore his mouth free, looked up at their stunned companions and grinned. "It works, doesn't it?" he asked of no one in particular. He carried her out the door quickly, before she had a chance to say anything more.

Laughter followed them down the corridor. "I've never been so embarrassed," she said, her voice faint. Burrowing her face against him, she didn't say another word.

Now what? Catrin groaned, slowly rolling over and pulling a pillow over her head. Running feet thundered past her door, and faint shouts rose from the bailey.

Judging from the fading daylight still visible through the shutters, she couldn't have slept more than a few hours. Despite Nicholas's efforts to see that she rested, soon after he placed her on her bed and left her with another soul-stirring kiss, Gillian slipped into her chamber.

Moving quietly so the men wouldn't discover them, Gillian and Catrin had gone to see Padrig. Although she would always carry responsibility for the guards' deaths on her soul, at least by sending Padrig away she'd managed to do something right. From what Gillian had recounted of his travail, 'twas only by God's grace that the boy had found his way here. Still, he'd survived, and she was thankful for it.

Surprisingly, Padrig didn't seem to blame her for his suffering. He'd made tremendous improvement since they'd carried him into l'Eau Clair, and he sounded more eager than before to begin training for the knighthood.

Once Padrig settled into sleep, Gillian hastened Catrin back to her chamber and began to interrogate her about Nicholas. Giggling like a young girl, Gillian taunted and teased, but in the end she told Catrin she couldn't have chosen a better man for her herself.

And who'd ever have believed he could be so gallant? Gillian had asked saucily.

Catrin's face grew hot whenever she thought of Nicholas's bold caresses—within sight of her family and his friends! By the Virgin, they'd all be expecting a betrothal soon if he didn't stop. She had an incredibly difficult time trying to convince Gillian there was nothing between them.

And Gillian hadn't believed a word she'd said.

But so far as she knew, there was nothing between them but one morning of passion. Although Nicholas had become affectionate toward her, he'd mentioned nothing of feelings.

It was probably just lust on his part. She yanked the pillow off her head and wrapped her arms around it. If she had any sense, she'd make certain lust was all she felt for him.

But she couldn't delude herself. Her feelings for Nicholas had always been strong, if a bit misguided at first. They couldn't be summed up as something so simple as lust.

She sat up as more footsteps pounded along the corridor. This time they stopped outside her door.

"Lady Catrin, you must come quickly."

Catrin recognized the voice of Emma, Gillian's maid. Slipping from the bed, she tugged her bliaut into place and opened the door.

The old woman looked frantic. "'Tis time, milady. Her water's broke, and Lord Rannulf's fit to tear the walls down," she said, clutching at Catrin's arms.

All thoughts of exhaustion forgotten, Catrin tugged Emma's fingers from her arms. "Tell Lord Nicholas to keep Lord Rannulf away from Gillian's chamber. We don't need a wild man getting in our way. I'll be along directly.''

Although Emma's face remained creased with concern, she appeared less distracted now that she'd been given something to do. Nodding, she moved down the passageway with determination in her shuffling step.

Catrin paused only to weave her hair into a single braid before she headed for Gillian's chamber. Likely she had no need to hurry; doubtless it would be a long while before the child finally made an appearance.

''I don't want to do this anymore!'' Gillian shrieked, her fingers grasping clawlike at Catrin's gown. Culling strength from some hidden reserve, she hoisted herself upright on the bed. Her eyes darted frantically from Catrin to the maid standing beside the bed, but she maintained her hold. ''No more, Catrin,'' she whimpered, her tongue darting out to moisten her lips. ''Make it stop.''

Catrin fought the drag of Gillian's weight on the front of her bliaut, struggling to remain upright as she sought to release her white-knuckled grip. ''Enough of this,'' she said, infusing her voice with a stern tone as she pried Gillian's fingers from her bodice one by one. ''The babe must be born, and you must work to help. You know I cannot make it stop.''

Free at last, she straightened. She held one of Gillian's hands clasped firmly in her own as she eased her down onto the bolsters. Her back sent up a sharp twinge of protest, but she forced the pain aside. Gillian needed her now. Her own discomfort could wait. But she couldn't stop her hand from trembling when she reached out to smooth the sweat-soaked hair away from her cousin's face.

Catrin noted the pallor and strain on that face with an inward wince of alarm. This birthing was taking much too long. A full day and night had passed since Emma fetched her from her chamber, an eternity of pain and exhaustion for Gillian—and herself. Under normal circumstances she'd have been better prepared to face this, but now...

Her scant hoard of strength was nearly gone. She had to deliver this baby now.

Gillian hovered on the edge of hysteria. Catrin knew it would take strength to pull her back from the precipice, a strength she wasn't sure she possessed.

Her love for her cousin spurred her on, reviving her flagging spirits. Gillian depended on her; she could not fail her now.

She sat on the edge of the bed. "You must help us, Gillian. Come now, you must push." She smoothed a wet cloth over her face.

Gillian's fingers crushed her own as another contraction racked her. Murmuring encouragement, Catrin tried to calm her, but it was clear her efforts were for naught. Gillian's moans rose to a pitiful cry before subsiding to whimpers when the spasm eased.

She had to do something now, before Gillian became too muddled to be of any help.

At this point, she'd try practically anything to jolt Gillian into action.

She motioned Emma to her side. The maid's careworn face was tense, her lips held in a firm line as though to still their shaking. "What are we to do, milady?" Her faded blue eyes gleamed with unshed tears. "My poor lamb—I've never seen her like this. I don't think she even knows what's happening."

"Bring Lord Rannulf here. Mayhap he can lend her the

strength she'll need." Surprisingly, Emma didn't question her suggestion as she hurried away.

Catrin paced beside the bed until the next contraction seized Gillian in its grip. Coaxing and cajoling, she bullied her cousin through the paroxysm, so completely involved she didn't hear anyone enter the room.

But when she looked up during the brief interim between pains, she discovered Nicholas standing next to her, staring at her with a strange intensity. Raising her finger to her lips, she motioned him away from the bed.

Once they reached the door he took her in his arms, cradling her gently. "How long has she been like this?" he asked, brushing his lips comfortingly over her forehead.

She rested against him, briefly savoring his strength. "Hours, I think. Too long." She looked about the room. "Where's Rannulf?"

"I wanted to hear for myself that you asked for him. Emma's practically incoherent, and I didn't know if you truly wanted him here. He's like a caged beast, Catrin. I'm not sure his presence will help her. He's more likely to terrify her." He glanced at the woman on the bed. "Or become completely mad with worry."

"Perhaps they can help each other." Catrin sighed and stepped back from Nicholas's comforting arms. "I cannot make her try anymore, and if she doesn't we could lose both her and the child." Recognizing from Gillian's whimpers that another pain had started, Catrin hurried to her side. "Warn him what she's like before you bring him in," she added, sitting beside Gillian and taking her hand. "But get him in here now."

Nicholas brought Rannulf into the chamber as the next contraction eased, not a moment too soon. Catrin mo-

tioned him over, tiredly noting that he looked nearly as
bad as his wife. At least he was sober, thank God.

"You must talk to her, Rannulf," she said softly. She
placed a hand on his arm. "Gillian is too exhausted to
heed me any longer, but perhaps she'll listen to you. It's
not too late, but I'll not lie to you—she needs your
strength to carry her through this."

He nodded, his gaze never leaving Gillian. "What must
I do?"

"Argue with her, threaten her—it matters not how you
do it, but you must rouse her enough to help herself. She's
so weary, I think she's fighting against her body. She's
very close to delivering the babe," Catrin reassured him.
"But you must make her try."

Catrin was aware that Nicholas stood on the other side
of the bed, but she didn't send him away. She—or Rannulf—might need him before this was over, and she found
his presence comforting. She summoned up the energy to
give him a faint smile, the look he sent her in return washing over her like a balm and lending her the spirit to see
this through.

"Rannulf, sit on the bed behind Gillian. You must hold
her up and support her when she pushes."

Rannulf swiftly obeyed her directions, then spoke
sharply to Gillian before leaning down to whisper something in her ear. Whatever he said caught her attention,
her eyes darting about groggily before settling on Catrin
where she stood near the foot of the bed.

She thought Gillian still had the look of a cornered
animal, but she also saw a growing awareness in her cousin's weary green eyes. "I'm going to see how far you've
come, Gillian," she said, raising the sheet draped over
Gillian's legs and suiting action to words. Another contraction struck while Catrin examined her; she could tell

that this time Gillian concentrated on riding the spasm through, panting as she'd taught her. Rannulf encouraged her.

Another paroxysm arrived nearly atop the first, and she judged it time for the real work to begin. "The next time you must bear down and push hard," she told Gillian. "Lean back against Rannulf and let him hold you up."

Folding back the sheet, Catrin positioned Gillian's legs wider and helped her brace her feet. Between them, she and Rannulf coaxed Gillian through the contractions. She marveled at Gillian's returning vitality; with each push she seemed to gain the strength and the will to bring her ordeal to an end.

Finally it was time. "I see the babe's head," Catrin cried, willing herself to patience. "Push again."

Gillian's voice broke as she concentrated all her energy on this last, powerful thrust. Catrin reached out and caught the child as it began to slide from Gillian's body.

Blinking away tears of joy, Catrin turned the babe and eased it the rest of the way. "You have a daughter," she said, grinning at Gillian and Rannulf.

"Aren't you a beauty?" she crooned as the child screwed up her face and began to wail. She needed to free her hands to cut the cord. "Here, Nicholas," she said, placing a tiny blanket beneath the babe and holding her out to him. He looked at her as though she'd gone mad. "Take her—'tis only for a moment."

Nicholas moved closer and held his hands out awkwardly. "Like this." She placed the child in his arms and showed him how to support her. Satisfied he'd manage, Catrin turned her attention to her remaining tasks.

Swiftly averting his eyes while Catrin attended to her business, Nicholas gazed down at the slippery, squalling infant. Skin bright pink, her face looking slightly squashed, she couldn't be called beautiful, Nicholas thought, but there was something compelling about the tiny scrap of humanity he held in his hands.

Not ready to identify the foreign emotion, he looked up and saw that Catrin had cut the cord. Wrapping the blanket more securely about the child, he brought her to her parents.

Gillian lifted her daughter from his hands with a cry of happiness, immediately moving the cloth aside to inspect the babe from head to toe. Smiling, his eyes suspiciously wet, Rannulf enclosed his family in his arms.

Seeing their joy made Nicholas aware of an ache of loneliness somewhere in the region of his heart. Not wishing to intrude upon their privacy, he turned to go.

"Nicholas," Catrin called when he'd nearly reached the door. Halting, he turned to face her. "I'm almost through here." She crossed the room to where he stood. "Will you wait for me?"

"I've intruded long enough. I thought I'd leave so they can be alone. Once Gillian realizes I was here, she'll never look me in the eye again," he said with a wry smile.

"Perhaps. But you might be surprised." She placed her hand on his arm. "If you don't wish to stay here, will you wait for me in my chamber? I don't want to be alone."

A strange lightness flowed through Nicholas's blood. Would he await her in her chamber?

He'd be mad to refuse.

"Neither do I," he said softly. He bent to whisper in her ear. "Take your time. I'll wait however long it takes you. Some things are worth waiting for," he said, taking a last look at the joyful parents before closing the door behind him.

Chapter Twenty-Four

Nicholas settled into a chair by the small fireplace and, pushing off his boots, warmed his feet by the hearth. This had been his chamber when he was Gillian's guardian, and he felt very comfortable here.

He poured a goblet of mead from the flagon on the table. Smiling, he raised the drink high to toast the newest FitzClifford. He hadn't noticed whether she favored one of her parents over the other. But she was bound to be pretty; both Gillian and Rannulf were attractive.

If he and Catrin had a child, what would it look like? He knew he was considered handsome, although he took no particular pleasure in it, and he found Catrin's dainty face and form exquisite. But perhaps any offspring of theirs would be no more than passing fair.

It wouldn't matter. Considering the surge of emotion he'd felt from simply holding someone else's child, one of his own would be a treasure to cherish.

Especially if he'd created that child with Catrin.

Tilting back in the chair and closing his eyes, Nicholas settled into an almost dreamlike state. He'd not slept in several days, and the potent mead worked powerfully upon him, bringing to mind thoughts he'd never before considered.

What would it be like to have someone waiting for him when he came home from battle, someone to share the small, precious details of everyday life?

He started to push the idea away, but decided against it. Too many times in the past he'd buried thoughts of home and family, warmth and love, deep within where they couldn't hurt him. Those concepts did not fit in with the persona he'd created, of a noble knight who expressed few feelings—and indulged them even less.

But he'd not hide behind that mask any longer. He didn't care whether his background—who he was—offended anyone or made them think less of him. The time had come to allow his true feelings—his true self—free rein. The joy would outweigh any risk, any hurt he might suffer to gain happiness—

To earn Catrin's love.

He would take that gamble and win.

The creaking of the door halted his reflection. He rose to his feet as Catrin slipped into the room.

Her shoulders drooped with weariness and circles darkened the delicate flesh beneath her eyes, but she radiated an energy he noticed at once. He pulled another chair near the fire and she sank into it with a sigh.

"Mother and child are well, I trust?" he asked, moving behind her.

"Aye," she said. "Gillian seems quite lively for a woman who just labored to the point of exhaustion for nearly two days. But that isn't unusual." Careful of her healing injuries, he placed his hands on her shoulders and began to slowly stroke the tense muscles. She moaned. "'Tis a shame only the mother feels that surge of power. The midwife could use a bit of vigor now, as well," she added, her low laugh sending a flash of heat through his blood.

He leaned down and nuzzled her ear. "What would it take to renew your strength? A nap? A soak in the tub?" He nipped at her earlobe. "Or would you like me to continue what I'm doing?"

Catrin moaned.

He took that for assent.

Lifting her into his arms, Nicholas carried her to the bed and tugged down the covers. She nestled into him like a cat, her body soft and warm, enticing him to sink into her softness.

He sat down on the mattress and laid her full-length next to him. Her eyes opened slowly, her lips curling into a smile so seductive he couldn't resist.

His gaze holding hers, Nicholas smoothed the curling wisps of hair away from her face, his fingertips lingering on her cheek, then brushing over her mouth. His own mouth followed, tongue darting out to cajole a response from hers.

She met him touch for touch, taste for taste, until he would swear the room was afire. He drew back. "It's too warm in here for so many clothes, don't you think?" When he tugged at the laces of her gown, she smiled and turned to give him better access.

Together they removed her clothes, until she lay before him clad only in a silken shift. The rose-tinted fabric lent a warm glow to her skin, tempting him to touch. Fingers trembling slightly, Nicholas picked up her disheveled braid and unplaited it, then spread her hair over the pillows like an ebony veil. "How do you feel?" he asked as he combed his fingers through the wavy strands. "Shall I rub your back for you?"

She reached up and untied the neck of his shirt. "Aye—if you take this off first."

"Whatever you wish." He pulled the shirt over his head and tossed it aside, sucking in a breath when she smoothed her hands over his chest. "Wait, love—I said I'd rub your back..."

"And I'll rub your front," she said, gifting him with a winsome smile.

"Yes—but later." He covered her hands with his and slowly slid them to his shoulders. "Else our pleasure will be over too soon."

Though it was torture to do it, Nicholas urged Catrin over onto her stomach, closing his eyes for a moment and praying for control before he reached out and laid his hand on the strap of her shift.

Opening his eyes, he nudged the silk off her shoulder. Her skin was so smooth against his battle-hardened palm, the delicate ivory a stark contrast to his darkly tanned flesh. Slipping a finger beneath the other strap, he pushed it aside, then eased her shift down to her waist.

Careful to avoid her nearly healed wounds, he laid his palms over her back and ran them over her tense muscles in long, smooth strokes. Catrin arched beneath the caress, the sound she made reminding him of a contented kitten. He kept at it until she felt soft and relaxed beneath his hands.

She rolled over, her smile radiating contentment, and took his hands in hers. "So strong, yet so gentle," she murmured, nuzzling his palm. "So very talented—in so many ways."

Releasing him, she sat up, catching the front of her tunic just before it slipped over the tips of her breasts. She held the fabric up with one hand, and used the other to push him back against the pillows. "Your turn...or is it mine?" she mused. "I believe I'll enjoy this as much as you will."

She let the hand holding up her shift fall away, the slippery material following in its wake. She left it where it fell, pooled about her hips, and leaned over him.

"Don't move," she whispered against his lips. Her nipples brushed over his chest, making his fingers ache to caress them. But she pressed his hands into the mattress on either side of him and sat back on her heels.

"Temptress," he groaned.

"If you wish."

Nicholas fought the urge to close his eyes, fascinated by this new side of Catrin. He didn't want to miss a moment, a nuance of this.

Her hair brushed over his stomach when she leaned close, the feathery sensation sending a lightning bolt of fire straight to his loins. "Do you like that?" she asked, her voice little more than a purr. The sound spoke of pleasure—hers, as well as his—and conjured up an exciting array of erotic images.

They all centered around the woman he needed more than life itself.

"It feels wonderful." He moaned when she worked on the knot of his chausses, her fingers brushing against the flesh of his belly in a not-so-innocent caress.

Fingernails scraped along his thighs as she eased off his leggings. She sat back, her gaze sweeping over him from head to toe. "So I see."

"Come here," he demanded, burying his hand in her hair and drawing her down for a scorching kiss.

Though he initiated the kiss, she swiftly resumed her role as the aggressor. Catrin sprawled over him, surrounding him with her scent, the feel of her lips devouring his, the cascading caress of her hair slipping over his body.

She paid no heed to restraining his hands now—nor to any other restraint between them.

She met his passion with her own full measure.

Nicholas's hands closed about Catrin's waist, shifting her to sit astride him. She didn't want him that way, she decided suddenly. Though she knew he would give her pleasure—passion beyond her imagining—she wanted to feel him over her, around her.

Lips still meshed with his, she shifted off Nicholas and lay beside him on the soft mattress. "Come to me," she whispered, drawing him over her.

"Are you certain?" Concern darkened his eyes, and he refused to rest his weight upon her.

She nodded. "I need you—here, now. You'll not harm me," she added, once again urging him near. "You make me feel safe, protected within your arms. Please, Nicholas."

"As my lady wishes," he said with a crooked smile. "When the temptress demands, what can her lover do but obey?"

But he moved away, just far enough to lavish attention upon her aching breasts. He suckled hard, drawing an answering response from deep within her. Soon her legs entangled with his, and her hands moved lower to caress him.

"Do you want me now?" he asked, staring into her eyes. "Do you want what I can give you? Passion? Love? A child of our own?"

Her heart stilled for a moment, then picked up again at a frantic pace. Could it be that he offered her all, everything she thought she could never have?

"Yes, Nicholas," she whispered, welcoming him into her body. She had never felt such joy! "Yes."

He watched with heart-melting intensity as they moved

together, the look in his eyes, his expression making this act a promise, a solemn vow.

"You are mine, Catrin," he said as waves of passion broke over them. "And I am yours."

A wordless roar woke Nicholas. His mind still caught in Catrin's sensual spell, he shook his head to clear it and blinked the sleep from his eyes.

Ian crossed the room with murder in his eyes, jolting him awake. Nicholas jerked the coverlet up over Catrin's nakedness and scrambled from the bed, hands held before him. "Ian, it's not what you think."

"Do you think I'm blind, you Norman bastard? I'd say this looks clear enough." His sweeping glance took in the clothing scattered about, the disheveled bed and Nicholas standing nude beside it. "The question is, what do you intend to do about it?"

Before Nicholas could answer, Ian turned his back and crossed to the open door. "FitzClifford!" he bellowed down the passageway. "FitzClifford, get in here now."

A maid passed the doorway, pausing briefly to look inside the chamber. She stared past Ian to Nicholas, her eyes growing wide, then covered her mouth with her hands and scurried off down the hall.

Nicholas picked his chausses up off the floor and stepped into them. Evidently Ian didn't intend him harm, for the moment, at least. "Why don't you just invite everyone in while you're at it?" he asked dryly.

Cursing, Ian slammed the door shut and turned. "At least you've the decency to cover yourself now. Too bad you didn't think of it earlier—before my sister saw you."

Catrin stirred behind him. Ignoring Ian, he sat on the edge of the mattress and reached out to tug the blankets around her.

"A little late for modesty, don't you think?" Ian sauntered over to a chair by the cold fireplace and slumped into it.

"Shut up, Ian." Catrin pushed her hair back from her face and leaned against Nicholas. His heart warmed at the sign of trust. "I doubt anyone invited you in, so don't complain if you see something you don't like."

"You can't talk your way out of this," Ian snarled, his eyes flashing. "I've permitted you too much freedom. That much is clear. First you race off from home and get four of my men killed, and now this."

Nicholas didn't intend to sit idly by while Catrin's brother took her to task. "It's not her fault she was attacked—"

"Keep out of this," they both snapped. He might have found their expressions humorous in another situation, but not when he was on the receiving end of their matching glares. However, since Catrin obviously didn't want—and likely didn't need—his help, he folded his arms across his chest and resolved to hold his tongue, no matter the provocation.

Catrin snuggled closer to Nicholas's side and turned toward her brother. "Why do you have to be this way? Can't you allow me the first happiness I've had in years? What I do is none of your business."

"Do you think it doesn't matter to me that this Norman took your maidenhead?" Ian leaned forward in his chair and glowered at Nicholas. "I should take him out to the bailey and run him through."

"He didn't take anything from me that I didn't give willingly."

"Took, gave—the word doesn't matter. But the fact that you permitted him to take liberties—"

"Liberties! Listen to yourself, Ian," she said with a

mirthless laugh. "Do you mean to tell me you've never taken a woman to your bed?"

Nicholas missed Catrin's warmth next to him when she straightened and moved toward the side of the mattress. Once she was beside him again, he slipped his arm around her and held her close.

"What I've done is not the issue here," Ian said.

Catrin leaned against Nicholas's shoulder, grateful for his support. "I've tried to shield you, Ian. But I'll do it no more," she said, her voice quavering. "I won't let you ruin my happiness simply to protect you from my past. Not any longer."

"What are you talking about?"

"I wish I could have come to Nicholas untouched, but I didn't."

"That's impossible," Ian said flatly. "You've never allowed a man that close. I'm surprised you let him."

"You don't know everything." She felt like getting up and clouting him in the head, but it wouldn't have done any good. Why did he have to barge into her chamber and find them like this? Now she had no choice but to tell him—but she didn't have to like it. "Don't pretend you do. I was raped."

"What?" Ian sprang from the chair. "When did this happen? You never said a word." He paced before the fireplace. "Who was the bastard? He'll not live much longer, I promise you."

"Sit down," she said, weariness edging her voice. "It happened four years ago. And I never told you because there was nothing you could do about it."

"Who was it?" Ian repeated, his tone lethal.

"Madog ap Gerallt."

Ian looked at her as though she'd gone daft. "Madog is dead, Catrin. He died in a fire."

She swallowed the lump in her throat and looked down. She didn't dare meet either man's eyes. "I know he's dead. I killed him."

"Are you sure?"

She met Ian's gaze. "Oh, yes, I'm very sure. If a knife through the heart didn't kill him, the fire certainly did."

"That's not what I meant, Catrin. Are you sure 'twas he who raped you?"

"How dare you doubt me?" Anger burned through Catrin's veins, cleansing away the fear she'd felt about confessing to Ian—and Nicholas.

Now she'd truly like to smack her witless brother in the head!

"Don't tell me you were misled by his charming ways, as well," she said sweetly, then allowed her rage to show through. "Do you believe I'm stupid? Of course I know who raped me. I'm hardly likely to make a mistake about it. He held me captive for nigh a week."

Nicholas's arms closed about her, pulling her back against his chest. She burrowed into his embrace, but his solace didn't soften her toward her brother. "Shall I tell you how many different ways there are to take a woman? How many ways to bend her to your will? I know you've been to war, Ian. You've seen the horrors men can do. But I very much doubt—" Her voice broke. Dashing away tears, she cleared her throat. "I truly don't imagine you have any idea the evil some people are capable of."

Ian knelt before her and took her hand, his eyes moist. "I'm sorry. I wish he were still alive so I might kill him myself," he fumed, clasping her hand in both of his and raising it to his lips.

She felt a tremor run through Nicholas. "You'd need to wait your turn," he said, his voice deadly.

A surprising thread of humor wove its way through her

mind as she listened to Ian and Nicholas. What did they think to accomplish by this?

"I'm flattered to have two such notable champions, but the man is already dead. Be glad he is, for he'd surely have killed me once he tired of me. I used to wish I could kill him over and over, for everything he did to me, but such wishes are futile. I cannot change the past. But that does not matter anymore, because now I have a future."

She squeezed Ian's hand and slipped hers free. "I am a woman grown, Ian. I know I haven't always behaved that way, but 'tis the truth. Nicholas and I have harmed no one, so I'll thank you to mind your own business."

Although she didn't quite trust the look in Ian's eyes when they rested on Nicholas, there was little she could do beyond warning him off.

She turned toward Nicholas. "Did he knock before he barged in?" She wondered why Ian had come to her chamber.

"If he did, I didn't hear it. I was asleep."

"Did you come here for a reason, or were you spying on me?" It wouldn't be the first time her brother had snooped in her room—or her business, she thought, frowning.

"You may acquit me of that," Ian said, rising to his feet. "Before I got distracted by Talbot, I'd come to tell you I've news about the men who attacked you. I'm going to Chester to see what I can discover. And before you ask, Talbot—no, I don't need your help. Besides, I believe there's a messenger downstairs looking for you—from your king," he added with a grin.

He headed for the door, pausing with his hand on the latch. "At any rate, 'tis just as well you cannot come with me. I still don't like the idea of you sleeping with my sister. It's better you're not around to tempt me," he said, his hand going to the hilt of his sword. Catrin squirmed in Nicholas's clasp as Ian opened the door.

How dare he continue thus!

But she restrained herself when she saw Rannulf standing in the doorway, hair mussed and half-dressed, a sword in his hand. "One of the maids said there was rape and murder going on," he said, gasping for breath. He lowered the sword. "I'm relieved to see she was mistaken."

Nicholas moved his arms from around Catrin and stood. "'Tis a good thing she was," he said with a grin. "It took you so long to come to our rescue, we could have all been dead by the time you got here."

"Evidently Emma refused to wake me—an error she won't repeat, I assure you. And not only did the maid demand my presence, but a messenger from the king has, as well." He looked about the room. "I believe it's safe to leave. I've kept the man waiting long enough."

Hand on the door, Rannulf paused. "He wants to see you, too, Nicholas, and he sounds impatient. Perhaps you should come with me now."

Nicholas picked his shirt up off the floor and put it on. Catrin tried to smile when he looked up and sent her a steaming look, but she felt exhausted, drained by the past few days.

He was beside her in a moment, his hands cradling her face. "Go back to bed, love. We'll talk later. I won't be gone long."

He kissed her gently, then followed Ian and Rannulf out, closing the door firmly behind him. The warmth of his mouth lingering on her lips, Catrin slept.

Chapter Twenty-Five

Nicholas sat on the edge of Catrin's bed and watched her sleep. Her delicate beauty touched him, made him yearn for a life with her. He could face anything if he knew she'd be waiting for him, ready to flay him with her tongue. He smiled at the imagery that phrase called to mind.

She could flay him—in word or deed—anytime.

He hated to wake her, but he couldn't leave without saying goodbye. His duties for the king had been of little importance of late, but he could ignore them no longer. Damn the king, sending him to Llywelyn with "urgent business."

It seemed the messenger had left court with further information for him within days of his departure for Wales. More likely King John hoped to catch him in some misdeed. Who could fathom John's thoughts?

Any fool could have performed this chore. Indeed, he knew of no reason why the messenger couldn't simply climb back on his horse and continue on to Llywelyn's keep himself. Yet it was clear that King John derived great pleasure from dispatching Lord Nicholas Talbot to do it. Perhaps it gave the king a secret thrill to entrust these ridiculous diplomatic chores to a man of his background. Mayhap he believed Nicholas might throw in his lot with the mighty Welsh prince and leave his English possessions open to forfeiture to the Crown.

But though he didn't know his liege lord's reasoning, he wasn't fool enough to ignore a royal command.

The sooner he left, the quicker he could return to Catrin.

He smoothed the sleep-tangled curls away from her brow, his body quickening as he breathed in her scent. So sweet, yet seductive, a perfect complement to her tart tongue. He stretched out beside her on the mattress and kissed her brow.

"Time to awaken, my beauty," he whispered into her ear.

"Nicholas?" Eyes still closed, she cuddled against him through the blankets.

"Wake up, love. I need to speak with you before I go."

Her eyes snapped open and she lifted herself up, leaning her hand on his chest. "Go? Is something wrong?"

"I have to leave now, for Llywelyn's keep. I've put it off as it is, and now there are more messages for the prince—important business only I can impart, no doubt," he said sarcastically. "Evidently the man set out after me shortly after I left court. The weather held him up, and he's only now made it this far. 'Tis likely all an excuse to spy on me. The king's been hounding me, one way or another, ever since I failed to secure l'Eau Clair for him last year."

"I could go with you, if you'd like," Catrin suggested, toying with the ties of his shirt. "Llywelyn is my kinsman. I know him well."

He knew she'd offer, but as much as he'd like to accept, he didn't dare. "It's not safe," he said, seizing her fingers when she tugged at the curls of hair at the base of his throat. "Until we discover who attacked you, you shouldn't travel."

"I thought Ian had found the men." Since he continued to hold her fingers captive, she began nibbling at his chin.

"Catrin, enough! I haven't much time. As much as I'd love to strip off my clothes and climb into bed with you, I cannot." Lifting her and setting her beside him, Nicholas sat up. "Stop trying to tempt me. It's working all too well."

"How long will you be gone?"

"I don't know. Rannulf is going with me—"

"But Gillian just gave birth," she protested, placing a hand on his arm. "Surely he doesn't wish to go."

"He has no choice, 'tis by the king's command. I swear John has become suspicious of everyone. He tests us constantly. And ever since Rannulf married Gillian, the king has delighted in testing both Rannulf and me."

"I'll take care of Gillian and the babe as well as I can." Catrin wrapped a sheet loosely about her and stood.

Nicholas took her in his arms. "I know you will. Don't forget to take care of yourself. We'll be back before you've had the chance to miss us," he murmured. He took her mouth in a passionate kiss, then strode from the room before he changed his mind and stayed.

The king's command be damned!

Catrin pressed her fingers against her lips and watched him leave. Damn his king, and her cousin Llywelyn, too! Why couldn't they play their petty games themselves, instead of sending others to do it for them? Gillian and the child needed Rannulf here with them.

And she needed Nicholas. So much lay unresolved between them. It seemed every time they came close to speaking of all the things in their hearts, something or someone interrupted them.

Fearing she'd grow maudlin if she stayed alone, Catrin dressed in some of Gillian's cast-off clothing and tied back her hair. No doubt Gillian would be glad of company now, and Catrin wanted to examine her and the baby.

Her life had been a constant whirl since she set out from Gwal Draig. It would be a relief to rest awhile and gather her scattered thoughts and emotions. What better way to pass the time until Nicholas returned?

Ian left his horse—and his troop—in the woods outside Chester and motioned for Dai to accompany him. They set off down the winding track, heading toward an alehouse on the outskirts of town where he'd heard they'd find the men he sought. A dove cooed in the growing twilight, lending an air of peace to the evening that Ian hadn't experienced in far too long.

Doubtless it wouldn't last. Peace never did; it was as fleeting as a morning mist.

If he found the knaves who had attacked Catrin and Nicholas—and killed his men—peace would be the farthest thing from his mind. Once he got his hands on the bloody bastards he'd make them wish they'd never been born.

The tavern was a shabby place, surrounded by others in similar disrepair. When they ducked through the low doorway, they were assaulted by the sour smell of spilled ale mixed with smoke and the stench of unwashed bodies—the customary alehouse perfume.

A slatternly wench sidled up to them, her homely face lit by a smile. "Wot's yer pleasure, milords?" she asked, leaning her impressive bosom against Dai's arm when Ian glared at her.

She turned her attention back to him when he held a coin over her gaping bodice. "Do you know a man who's missing half his fingers? I've heard I might find him here."

"Ye mean Ralph? He's sittin' over there, by the back door." She pointed to a shadowy corner of the room.

He dropped the money into her gown and headed for the table.

Four men sat around a table, all drunk from the look of them. One man balanced a wench on his knee, one hand thrust down her bodice, the other under her skirts.

When Ian halted beside the table, the man dumped her off his lap onto the filth-strewn dirt floor, earning him a glare from her and a roar of laughter from his companions. "Ralph, what did ye do that for?" one whined. "Ye get yerself a woman and then toss her away...."

"I'd like ta toss her—" another cut in.

"Don't make sense to me," the first continued. "First there's that feisty wench with the sword—remember how Ned wanted her, even when she were dead?"

"Shut up, Will," Ralph snarled, swatting Will on the side of the head. "Can't ya see we got company?"

Ian tightened his fingers around the hilt of his sword, barely resisting the temptation to use it. But he permitted none of his frustration to show in his face. "I've been looking for you, Ralph. I've some work for you."

Ralph gazed at the two men measuringly. Evidently they passed muster, for he kicked a stool forward. "Have a seat, yer lordship, and we'll talk."

Ian sat down, Dai standing behind him, and accepted the tankard of ale someone pushed across the table. "I've heard you're not averse to a bit of robbery—or murder, if the price is right."

"That depends," Ralph said, his maimed hand toying

with an elegant dagger. "What do ya have in mind, mi-lord, and how much are ya willing to pay?"

"There's a woman I'd like to be rid of," Ian said. "You'd have to wait for her in the forest and set upon her party where no one will find them."

Will groaned. "Not that again. Christ, Ralph. Last time we lost some good men. And that Welsh bastard never did pay us, did he?"

"Cease yer prattle! His lordship and I got business. He don't want to listen to you flap yer jaws."

Ian and Ralph settled into negotiations, swiftly coming to an agreement. Listening to the lawless band, Ian found their complete disregard for life and law fascinating. At the same time, he wished he could cleave them all into tiny bits for what they'd done to Catrin and his men.

But they were simply tools. That much was clear. And once he lured them into his domain, he intended to discover who'd hired them, although he'd heard enough tidbits to confirm his suspicions.

Ralph and his men followed Ian and Dai out of the tavern and into the woods with a total lack of concern for their own safety, the fools.

Ian's men drifted out of the trees and surrounded them before they had a chance to draw their weapons.

"What's goin' on here?" Ralph demanded, struggling briefly against his captor's hold.

Ian ignored his question, instead watching as Dai disarmed each man and placed their knives and swords in a pile. 'Twas an impressive collection, ranging from a crude dirk to the elegant dagger Ralph had toyed with in the tavern.

Ian picked the dagger from the pile and looked it over, tossing it in the air to test its balance. "A fine piece for an outlaw," he commented, flipping it to land, quivering, in the ground between Ralph's feet. "Where did you get it?"

"I don't recall, milord," Ralph said, his eyes fixed on the bejeweled hilt.

"I wonder what it would take to restore your memory?" He searched through the pile for another knife, then flung it after the first. It sliced through the leather of Ralph's shoe, pinning his foot to the ground.

"Would you like your feet to match your hands, Ralph? 'Twould be simple enough. I could do it without getting any closer to your stinking carcass than this."

Ralph stared at his foot, seemingly amazed to discover that only his shoe had been cut—so far. He wriggled his arms, held behind him by one of Ian's men, but his captor didn't release him.

"He'll hold you till I carve you to ribbons, if I wish it." Ian chose another knife, tossing it from hand to hand.

Ralph stood enthralled, his eyes following the blade's sweeping arc. Finally he wrenched his gaze away. "What do ya want to know?" he asked, his voice resigned.

"Don't tell him nothin', Ralph," Will cried out.

"I always knew you for a fool, Will," Ralph muttered. He straightened and looked Ian in the eye. "'Twas from a knight we robbed in the marches. He was alone, easy pickin' for the lot of us."

A third knife thudded into the soil at Ralph's feet, this time slashing the threadbare fabric of his breeches on its way to the ground. "Fine, I'll tell you," he yelped. "Have ya ever heard of Lord Steffan? He's lord of Bryn Du, in Wales."

"You're holding my interest so far," Ian said, his fingers caressing the sword hilt at his waist.

"He wanted to be rid of his cousin. Told us we could keep the horses and such, so long as we brought her to him. But she died, so he wouldn't pay us. There really was a knight—a Norman, from the looks of him. We took his gear, as well."

Ian laughed. "You made a serious mistake, Ralph. Neither of them were dead, you see. And they lived to tell their tale. Unfortunately for you—" his gaze encompassed them all "—the lady is my sister, and the knight is a powerful Norman lord."

All of the men had lost their insolent looks, especially Ralph. "Tie them up," he ordered. "We need them alive for now. I can scarcely wait to see Steffan's face when I present you to him."

Catrin crooned softly to the child in her arms, holding her close to her bosom. "Where is your papa, Katherine?" Once again she felt the thrill of knowing the child was named after her.

Gillian finished weaving her coppery tresses into a braid and covered her hair with a veil. "It's only been a sennight, Catrin. You cannot expect them to rush in, hand Llywelyn a message and then ride away, all in an hour's time. Unfortunately, diplomacy is tedious and slow," she added, settling an etched copper circlet atop the veil.

"And it's been little more than a sennight since you were delivered of this child." Catrin placed a kiss on the babe's soft cheek. "I still don't think you should be up and tending to your household so soon."

"I couldn't stay in bed any longer. I'd have gone mad from boredom. If Rannulf were here, 'twould be a different story." Gillian's lips tilted in a saucy grin.

"'Tis much too soon to be thinking of that," Catrin warned, her face warm. Although she and Gillian had had some straightforward conversations about men in general—and their men in particular—she wasn't comfortable speaking so freely about lovemaking.

"I wish you could see your face." Gillian giggled and tapped Catrin on the cheek. "You never used to be so easily embarrassed."

"That's because I was never personally involved in any of the spicier gossip. It's not the same thing at all when you're a part of it."

Emma entered the room and held her arms out for the baby. Catrin handed her over reluctantly. Ever since the child's birth, she'd had a strong hunger for a babe of her own. Perhaps she already carried Nicholas's child in her womb, she thought, surreptitiously pressing her hand against her flat stomach. She found that the notion brightened her day.

Catrin picked up Gillian's polished steel mirror and gazed critically at herself while Gillian spoke with Emma. Plenty of food and rest this past week had put a bloom of health on her cheeks. Her back was healing nicely and the fever had gone.

All she needed to make her life complete was for Nicholas to return.

She missed him so! Would he like the improvement in her appearance? How could he not, she thought with a rueful chuckle. Thank goodness Ian had thought to have some of her things sent from Gwal Draig. At least now she was clean and well-groomed, with her own clothing to wear.

And no binder about her breasts. She couldn't bear the thought of trussing herself up in that contraption of torture, not when she considered how Nicholas's eyes darkened to that lovely shade of violet when he gazed at her curves. Simply remembering sent a stream of fire burning through her body.

She nearly laughed when she thought about how easy it had been to repress her womanly feelings after her experiences at Madog's hands. But now that Nicholas had shown her what beauty a man and woman could create together, she knew she could never return to that sterile existence. He had opened the floodgates of her emotions, allowing them to burst forth.

Her entire being had become sensitized. Not only was she aware of her own sensuality, but she reacted to her surroundings more strongly. The burgeoning scents of spring carried on a warm breeze, the delicate greens of the earth reborn—

They called to something deep inside her, reflecting her own resurrection from the cold, dark depths of her old life.

And like the awakening earth, Catrin wanted to bring forth her own new beginnings. Her life began anew with Nicholas. She'd wed him in a moment if he asked, go with him to Ashby and take up the challenges there.

There was nothing she wanted more.

"Do you like what you see?" Gillian asked, leaning over Catrin's shoulder to peer into the mirror.

Catrin started, her eyes focusing on the image reflected back at them. "'Tis an improvement over last week, I must admit." She placed the mirror carefully on the table. "Are you ready to go outside?"

"Yes. I cannot hide away in here any longer. Who knows what mischief everyone's been up to without my supervision?" Gillian laughed. "As if they really need it."

"Your household could likely run itself, 'tis true, but I'm sure life flows more smoothly when you're keeping a watchful eye over everything," Catrin said as they slowly descended the stairs and crossed the hall to go outside.

They hadn't reached the bottom of the outer stairs before shouts came from the guards on the gatehouse wall. A man, one of the villagers from the look of him, staggered through the gates and collapsed against the wall.

"Fire," he gasped. Catrin hurried closer, Gillian on her heels. His clothes were singed and soot-stained. He reeked of smoke. "There's fire everywhere in the village."

Gillian directed servants to find buckets and barrels and go to the villagers' aid. People streamed out the open gates and raced down the track to the town, Gillian and Catrin following as quickly as they could. A servant ran after them with Gillian's basket of simples, for there were bound to be injuries.

"Are you sure you should do this, Gillian?" Catrin asked, tugging on Gillian's trailing sleeve to stop her. "You've just risen from childbed. You've not even been churched. What if the villagers are so superstitious that they won't allow you to help? You'll have dragged yourself down here for nothing."

Gillian yanked her sleeve free. "I doubt they'll stop to think about whether the Church considers me unclean or not," she said tartly. "None of them are overly religious, truth to tell. Besides, I'm not certain the prohibitions extend to caring for the injured—or saving their lives." She rejoined the surge of people still rushing along the road. "Come along, Catrin."

Shrugging, Catrin resumed walking. Personally, she didn't hold with the Church's bizarre ideas regarding women who'd just given birth, but there were places where those constraints were closely followed.

Such trifles fled her mind as they topped the slight rise in the road and the village came into view. 'Twas like a scene from hell, cottages in flames and people running, shouting as they fought to save their homes.

Gillian grabbed Catrin's arm, her eyes filled with horror. "How could the entire village be engulfed so swiftly?" Seeing several people sitting or lying on the ground away from the buildings, they hastened to offer help.

Everyone in the group was hurt—burned, cut or badly bruised. The women set to work, tending their wounds. A small but steady trickle of injuries came their way as the castle folk worked with the villagers to salvage what they could.

During a lull the two women moved beneath the trees, seating themselves on cushiony piles of dry leaves. Gillian's face was pale and she looked tired, but Catrin knew better than to suggest she return to the keep.

"I doubt there will be much left to save," Gillian said, staring at the still-smoldering cottages. "Just so long as my people survive, I don't care. Houses can be rebuilt."

"What a noble sentiment." The sneering voice came from the forest.

Startled, Catrin turned and peered through the underbrush, her hand dropping to edge beneath her skirts in search of her dagger.

"Who is there? Come out at once," Gillian demanded. She slowly came to her feet as Steffan walked out from behind a large oak.

The comforting weight of her dagger filling her hand, Catrin rose and moved to stand between Steffan and Gillian. "What are you doing here?" she snarled. Looking back over her shoulder, she said, "Go for help, Gillian. Quickly."

Steffan folded his arms across his chest and smiled. "I don't think so, cousin." Catrin spun in time to see that

great oaf, Huw, grab Gillian's arms from behind and reach
up to muffle her mouth.

She turned back to face Steffan. "Let her go."

"Or what? Do you think to kill me with that trifling
blade on your belt?"

Catrin lunged at him with her dagger, wanting nothing
so much as to slash the smug expression from his face.
He reminded her of Madog—smooth, oily charm covering
the black heart of a snake.

Laughing in her face, Steffan grabbed her arm in mid-
slash, squeezing so tightly her fingers opened and went
numb, allowing the knife to drop to the ground. "You'll
not get the chance to try that again, you bitch," he
snapped, viciously wrenching her arm behind her. Pain
shot up her arm and across her shoulder, so intense her
knees gave way and she slumped against him.

Giving her arm one last twist, he let her drop to the
ground. "Tie them," he ordered, picking up her knife and
striding past her to Gillian.

Catrin refused to pay any heed to the man trussing her
arms behind her, instead focusing her attention on Gillian.

Huw finished binding Gillian's wrists and moved away,
a malicious grin splitting his face. Steffan grabbed her
chin and forced her head up, slipping off the rag Huw had
tied around her mouth. "Where is the brat?"

Seeing the raw fear in Gillian's eyes, Catrin answered,
"The babe is dead. 'Twas stillborn." Stalling for time,
she rose awkwardly to her knees and tried to adjust the
coarse rope tied round her wrists so it didn't hurt so much.
Where was everyone? Surely by now someone should
have noticed them.

But the activity in the village was centered away from
them, and they'd moved too far into the sheltering trees.

Gillian appeared ready to swoon. Catrin tried again.

"Leave her be, Steffan. Can't you see she's not well? She's suffered enough of late, without having to deal with the likes of you."

"No. You're both coming with me," he said, examining Gillian from head to toe. He grabbed at her breast and squeezed hard, laughing when tears began to run down her face. "You expect me to believe the Norman brat died, yet your breasts are full."

Gillian jerked back to escape his grip. "It has not yet been a week, Steffan. My body hasn't returned to normal." She took another step back. "Get off my land, you bastard."

"Oh, I'm leaving. But so are you," he said, his face alight. "Get them on the horse," he told Huw. "We've been here too long already. The fire won't distract them forever."

"You caused this?" Gillian shrieked. She kicked out at Steffan's legs, but lost her balance. She would have fallen if Huw hadn't grabbed her about the waist and tossed her over his shoulder.

"Let go of me, you worm!" Gillian's next words were inaudible as Steffan tied a rag to cover her mouth.

Guessing she'd be next, Catrin filled her lungs with air and opened her mouth to let out a screech, but Steffan cut off the sound with his hand before it became more than a squeak. "Don't abuse my good nature, cousin," he warned, wrapping a strip of fabric over her mouth.

What good nature? she wondered, trying to jut out her jaw so she could loosen the material later. She'd vowed this would never happen to her again. Rage toward Steffan threatened to cloud her mind, but at least it kept the fear at bay. The gag smelled like him, an overpowering scent of musk and sandalwood. The odor alone was enough to make her want to vomit—not wise under the circumstances. Sweet visions of mayhem, with Steffan as the victim, filled her mind as he hefted her up onto the horse behind Gillian.

Gillian looked over her shoulder at Catrin, her eyes filled with pain.

How could they escape this?

Catrin cast a last, hopeful look back toward the burning village as Steffan led them away, but no one saw them. Leaning forward, she pressed her cheek against Gillian's for comfort and hoped this desolate view of l'Eau Clair would not be their last

Chapter Twenty-Six

They journeyed through the forest for hours, stopping only once when Huw realized that Gillian and Catrin couldn't ride with their hands bound behind them. He adjusted their bonds, tying their wrists in front of them. Then they traveled deeper into the woods, following a path so faint Catrin could scarcely see it.

Huw and the three other men rode off a short time later—several hours into the journey, by her estimation—leaving them alone with Steffan.

Catrin had no idea where they were, or where they were going. Steffan hadn't spoken to them since they'd left Gillian's demesne. But he talked to himself constantly. She couldn't hear enough to understand what he said, but the tone of his voice and his odd mannerisms made her wonder about his sanity.

Not that she'd ever considered him sane. Even as a child he had possessed grand delusions and an arrogance far above his station. But he'd been a relatively harmless annoyance then.

Now he frightened her.

For the moment though, he ignored them completely, a blessing for which she was exceedingly grateful. This reminded her too much of her abduction by Madog. Simply looking at Steffan sent a shiver of apprehension running down her spine.

At first Gillian had been able to sit straight in the saddle, but Catrin could tell that her strength was gone. She slumped back, her eyes closed. Catrin suspected she'd fallen into an exhausted doze.

She bore Gillian's weight as best she could, but she could feel her own stamina fading away with the added burden. Surely even Steffan would have to stop sometime. The light began to fade into dusk, yet still they plodded on.

Suddenly Gillian sat up with a jolt, nearly slipping from the saddle. Catrin grabbed her belt—a difficult feat with her hands tied—and held on until she regained her balance. That strain, after Steffan's earlier roughness, made her arms feel as if they'd been wrenched from her shoulders.

Gillian looked about, confused, until her eyes settled on Steffan. She moaned behind the gag, drooping back against Catrin for a moment, then straightening her spine.

Since Steffan ignored them, she judged it safe enough to get rid of the gag. This was the perfect time to try something. Except for the fact that he continued to hold the lead rein, he seemed oblivious to their presence.

Besides, how could they decide what to do if they couldn't speak?

She rubbed her cheek against Gillian's shoulder, rolling the fabric down. Her mouth was dry, so she pushed at the gag with her tongue, finally forcing it out of her mouth. She nudged it down around her neck, wincing when the knot in the back pulled her hair.

"I think I can loosen your gag," she whispered to Gillian, her eyes fixed on Steffan.

After tugging at it with her teeth, the material finally came undone and fell to the ground.

"What I wouldn't give for a drink right now," Catrin whispered as she watched Gillian wiggle her jaw. Her mouth felt dry as dirt and tasted a thousand times worse.

"Do you think we could slip off the horse and get away?" Gillian asked.

"No. I considered it earlier, but I don't believe we could get enough of a start before he realized we'd left." She raised her hands and shoved at the hair hanging in her face. "I'm not certain whether we should try to untie ourselves, either. I don't know if we could. He seems demented, Gillian. Have you noticed?"

"No more than usual. But he hates to be crossed. When he took me before, he struck me so hard I fell against a stool and hit my head. And that was when he wanted to marry me." She eyed him nervously. "I didn't wake till the next morning. I'd rather try to get away. God only knows what he has in mind for us," she added, shuddering. "And Katherine needs me. How will they feed her when I'm not there?" A tear slipped down her cheek. "Perhaps we could overpower him."

"I don't think so. He's strong. When he twisted my arm, I thought I'd swoon."

"It's nearly night. The path is so dark, we'll have to stop once the sun goes down," Gillian said hopefully. "If we wait until then, mayhap we'll find a chance. He has to sleep sometime."

"Until then we should rest and plan," Catrin whispered.

Nicholas slumped in the saddle, his mount's bouncing gait doing little to counter his weariness. He and Rannulf had traveled like the wind to Prince Llywelyn's, observed the bare minimum of courtesies while passing on the king's messages, then ridden nearly nonstop back to l'Eau Clair.

He could imagine what King John would say when he heard about their whirlwind visit, but he didn't care. If there were consequences to this, he'd deal with them. No more would he seek to be the ideal knight; 'twas naught but a foolish quest, born of his shame. He'd allowed his life—and himself—to be ruled by the opinions of others for too long. No more.

From now on he'd live to please himself.

His horse sidled nervously, ears twitching back and forth. He scanned the area but saw nothing.

Then a gust of smoky air drifted by. Tension filled him. The acrid scent reminded him of battles, siege and death. "Rannulf," he called, foreboding lending a sharpness to his voice.

"I smell it," Rannulf replied, spurring his horse to greater speed. They galloped over the narrow track, their men thundering behind them. They were near l'Eau Clair. The possibilities racing through his mind made him curse even the short distance and the fact that they could travel no faster.

Wisps of smoke hung in the air like fog, and tendrils wove among the trees like gossamer silk. The closer they came to the village, the thicker the smoke. By the time they left the forest, they could scarcely see.

A man stepped into the road in front of them, startling the horses. 'Twas a wonder they didn't accidentally run him down.

"Lord Rannulf! Thank God 'tis you."

Edging closer, Nicholas recognized Sir Henry, the man in charge of l'Eau Clair's defense.

Rannulf leapt from the saddle and led Sir Henry out of the road. Curious, Nicholas dismounted and joined them.

Soot-stained and drooping with exhaustion, Sir Henry looked ready to collapse. "Lady Gillian and Lady Catrin are missing, milord," he said without preamble. "And someone set fire to the village."

"What?" Rannulf grabbed the front of Sir Henry's tunic.

"Were they abducted?" Nicholas asked, fear lending his voice a razor-sharp edge.

"Was the keep attacked? What of my daughter?" Rannulf's eyes were wild.

Sir Henry gave them both a stern look. "Milords. Let me tell you what I know."

Rannulf released him, but stood close by while Sir Henry straightened his twisted tunic. "It appears the women were taken, though we don't know by whom. I sent men to search the forest. No one attacked l'Eau Clair. And Lady Katherine is safe with Emma."

Rannulf looked ready to do murder. "Mount up," he said. "We'll arm ourselves for battle, then search for them ourselves." He vaulted into the saddle. "I'll be damned before I allow someone to take Gillian from me again." He spurred his horse on.

Nicholas silently echoed his words as they hastened through the smoke to the keep. Although he still didn't know who had attacked Catrin before, he feared they'd come to finish the task.

But why take Gillian? Before he left, Ian had hinted that he knew who was responsible for the assault on Catrin. According to Rannulf, Ian believed it was Steffan ap Rhys. Nicholas didn't agree, judging Steffan too craven for such a bold attempt.

He had never understood what prompted Steffan to

seize Gillian the year before. Perhaps he'd tried again and Catrin got in the way. Or maybe there was a lunatic roaming the marches, stealing their women, he thought acidly.

At this point all they had were suspicions.

However, someone had wanted Catrin before, wanted her badly enough to attack an armed troop to get her. His head spinning, he focused on the most likely answer. It looked to him as though someone wanted one of the women—or both—enough to destroy a village to get her. Sir Henry hadn't said, but the women were probably taken when everyone's attention was on the fire.

He'd get her back, he vowed. Catrin had become the most precious thing in life to him, a life she'd taught him to appreciate. He wouldn't rest until he held her in his arms again.

They found Ian standing amid the still-smoldering ruins of the village. As they halted their mounts he grinned. Was he demented, Nicholas wondered, to smile when his sister and cousin were missing and a village lay in shambles?

"Well met," he said, stepping forward and motioning to one of his men to take their horses. "Our timing couldn't have been better."

Nicholas grabbed Ian by the shirt. "What is wrong with you?"

Rannulf seized him from behind and tugged him away. "Enough, Nick. Give him a chance to explain," he said, although he, too, gave Ian a puzzled glare.

"Christ," Nicholas snarled. "Don't you care that your sister is missing—again?"

"Of course I care. But I'm glad you're here, as well." Ian gestured toward a group of men, sitting bound and gagged beneath the trees. "I've brought you a gift."

Impatient to be done with his games, Nicholas strode

past him. He stared at the group for a moment, until something about one of them caught his attention.

Lunging forward, he snagged the man by his tunic and lifted him up. "It was you. You son of a bitch. Why?" Ripping off the man's gag, Nicholas shook the whimpering coward until his head lolled on his shoulders. "Why did you attack her?" he roared, opening his fists and letting him drop limply to the ground.

He rounded on Ian when he received no answer from the outlaw. "Where did you find them?"

"Where I found them isn't as important as who hired them. 'Twas Steffan." Ian gazed at the fire-ravaged area. "This has the look of Steffan about it, as well. He must have waited till we left, then set his plan in motion. If we search for him, I'm certain we'll find Catrin and Gillian with him."

He shoved at the man Nicholas attacked. "I see you recognized Lord Nicholas, Ralph."

Eyes huge, Ralph nodded.

"I'm giving you and your charming band of followers to him." Ian smiled grimly at Nicholas. "Call it a gift for your impending nuptials."

He'd wondered what Ian's next move would be concerning Catrin. This acceptance was more than he'd hoped for; he'd expected something more along the line of swords and daggers, or a fistfight.

Instead Ian was giving him exactly what he wanted. "I thank you. I trust this means I may count on your support when I ask your sister to be my wife."

"I suppose I have little choice. But I advise you to approach her fully armed."

Rannulf watched this byplay in silence, but evidently his patience had reached its end. "This is all wonderful, I'm sure. And I congratulate you, Nicholas." Snatching up the reins, Rannulf swung onto his horse. "But unless we go after them soon, you may not have a woman to wed. It's clear Steffan has lost what few wits he had. I don't intend to leave Gillian in his hands any longer than I have to. As soon as I get more weapons and supplies I'm leaving. Are you with me?"

Nicholas jumped into the saddle before Rannulf finished his speech, and Ian wasn't far behind. Exchanging a worried look, they galloped up the track to l'Eau Clair.

As the last rays of daylight faded away, Steffan led Catrin and Gillian up a steep path through the trees. It soon became too narrow and rocky for the horses. Halting, Steffan jerked them from their mount together, so they fell in a tangled heap at his feet.

"Get up. We've ground left to cover before it's too dark," he said, poking at them with his foot.

Catrin had landed atop Gillian, and she feared she'd come to harm, for she lay still, moaning slightly. She tugged at Gillian's gown and tried to help her up, but she couldn't offer much assistance with her hands bound.

Arms folded, Steffan watched as they struggled to their feet, a strange smile on his lips. "Aren't you clever to take off your gags? No matter," he said with a shrug. "We're so far from civilization, you can scream all you want. No one will hear except me."

Judging from the look on his face, he'd enjoy it, too. But Catrin refused to give him the satisfaction—whatever he might do to her. No doubt Gillian felt the same.

"'Tis a pleasure and a delight to see you thus. I've dreamed of this—both of you here to serve me as I wish." He grabbed each by the arm and shoved them ahead of him. "Not long now," he said in an abstracted voice. He prodded Catrin in the back. "I grow impatient. Move."

She felt as though her blood had turned to fire in her veins as white-hot rage nigh overwhelmed her. How dare he steal them away from their loved ones and drag them out here? And for what purpose? It had to be something terrible, else he'd have taken them to the comfort of his own keep as he had with Gillian last year.

Exhaustion settled upon her, weighting her limbs until she could scarcely climb the uneven path. She couldn't imagine where Gillian found the strength to continue, unless 'twas fear of Steffan's anger that goaded her onward. She felt that spur herself.

Finally they emerged into a small clearing, faintly lit by the moon rising in the night sky. Steffan directed them to a crude hut and pushed them inside.

Catrin caught her balance against the rough wall, but Gillian fell over something, groaning as she tumbled to the floor.

"Clumsy bitch," Steffan snarled, ignoring her plight and striking a flint to light a brace of candles.

Catrin knelt beside Gillian and assured herself that she hadn't been hurt. But she sounded as though she'd reached the limit of her endurance. Catrin helped her lean against the wall, resolving to draw and hold Steffan's attention so Gillian could rest.

He moved about the hut, lighting more candles. The room seemed bright as day after the faint light outside.

A chill passed through her as she looked about the chamber, for it strongly reminded her of the accommodations in Madog's keep. A bed stood illuminated by several tall stands of candles. She'd swear she saw ropes looped at the head and foot of it. And spread out on the lid of the coffer at the foot was a bizarre assortment of objects. Catrin couldn't put a name to any of them, but she recalled the degradation and pain they could bring all too clearly.

Steffan met her stare with a blithe smile. "How do you like my little love nest? It's been ready for you for weeks, but those idiots who attacked you botched my plans completely."

Catrin struggled to contain her outrage while he ambled to her side. *He* had been responsible for the deaths of her men—just as much as she. More so, for their lives didn't matter to him. A cleansing wave of relief flowed through her. Although she was still accountable, her sin had been unintentional. But she harbored no doubt that Steffan had ordered his lackeys to kill her guard.

She could do nothing yet, but she'd find a way to send this fiend to hell if it killed her. Swallowing her rage, she stood silently while he traced his fingers down her neck, sliding them into the neckline of her gown. "They told me you were dead. But I knew they were wrong. You cannot die before I've had my vengeance on you."

He turned his gaze toward Gillian. "And you are an extra prize. I didn't know if I could get my hands on you, but fate has been most kind. I may gain l'Eau Clair after all."

"Not likely," Gillian snarled with surprising vigor. "Do you believe my husband will allow that? You're not fit to walk through the gates, let alone rule in my place—or Rannulf's."

Steffan's face darkened. "He's a man like any other, capable of dying. I care not whose body I step over to claim what is rightfully mine."

"You are mad," Gillian cried, pushing herself to her feet. "Whatever made you believe you have a right to l'Eau Clair? 'Tis a Norman keep, built by a loyal Norman lord. You delude yourself, Steffan. My father would never have approved you as a suitor for my hand.''

Gillian crossed her arms over her breasts, a slight look of discomfort on her face. Catrin had no doubt that by now Gillian's body ached, more than ready for her to suckle her child.

''Do you think I care what your father intended?'' Steffan sneered. ''I know 'tis my due. Once you're rid of FitzClifford you'll see I'm right. And if you don't, I don't really care, so long as I'm master of l'Eau Clair—and you.''

Grabbing a blanket from the bed, Steffan tossed it at Gillian. ''You might as well sleep. You're of no use to me yet.''

He turned to Catrin and seized the rope binding her wrists together. ''But I do have a need for you,'' he said, jerking her close. His eyes glittered viciously in the candles' glow. ''All our lives you've taunted me with your beauty, then spurned me when I honored you with my attentions. Arrogant wench!'' He dragged her toward the bed. ''And you ruined my plans to gain l'Eau Clair with your meddling ways.''

Catrin's mind went blank when he tossed her onto the bed and swiftly tied her ankles to the bed frame. 'Twas the nightmare of her past repeated.

She didn't know if she had the strength to withstand it all again.

But she'd be damned before she allowed that slimy worm to have his way with her. She'd tear out his throat with her teeth if necessary.

Steffan climbed atop her, his body pushing her deep into the soft mattress. His eyes eager, he pinned her wrists to the pillows above her head with one hand and crushed his engorged manhood into the cradle of her hips. She bucked beneath him, but she couldn't throw off his weight.

Her stomach heaved with revulsion. Gathering herself, she thought to try for one burst of strength to push him away. But before she could make the effort, Gillian moved quietly behind him, her still-bound hands clutched around the base of a candelabra.

She brought it down on Steffan's head with a sickening thump. His eyes rolled back and he slumped over Catrin with a groan.

"Thank you," Catrin whispered, her voice scratchy and faint. She squirmed out from beneath him while Gillian rolled him aside.

"Is he dead?" Gillian asked.

Catrin could hear him breathing. "No, unfortunately he's still alive."

"I've got his knife." Gillian tugged it from his belt. "Should we tie him up?"

"Let's not waste any time," Catrin said. "You hit him hard. He'll be sleeping for a while." She tried to sit up, but was brought up short by the bindings about her ankles. "Hurry, cut the ropes," she cried, frantic to get away. Gillian sawed through the cords and Catrin scrambled off the mattress. Pausing only to cut their bonds, they hurried to the door.

Catrin heard a faint sound behind her. Before she could yank the door open, Steffan grabbed her from behind.

Chapter Twenty-Seven

Steffan's trail had been easy to find. Nicholas, Rannulf and Ian wasted no time before setting out. Considering what both Catrin and Gillian had endured of late, neither woman was in any condition to be dragged through the woods by a lunatic.

And who knew what he might do to them?

Nicholas wondered what would happen once they caught up with Steffan. Although he had no doubt they'd free the women, the question of who would deal with Steffan had yet to be answered. They each had ample reason to challenge him.

Unfortunately, it probably wouldn't go that far. From what he'd heard, Steffan had managed to evade battles for most of his miserable life, the craven bastard. When faced with three bloodthirsty warriors, Steffan would probably slit his own throat, Nicholas thought with disgust.

The trail narrowed. Rannulf halted his mount and got down to examine the ground. After poking around a bit, he made a sound of triumph and raised his hand. He held a scrap of cloth in his fist. "Gillian was gagged—this cloth has her hair caught in it. Two horses took that trail—'' he pointed to a steep, barely discernible path "—and one horse carried a double load.''

He leapt back into the saddle. "We're getting close,'' he said, determination glowing in his eyes. "Come on.''

The sun set soon after. Nicholas hoped Steffan hadn't left the path, for they'd never know it. It was all they could do to keep going as the way narrowed in front of them and they had to dismount and walk single file between the thick growth of trees.

"Let me go!'' Catrin twisted her body in a vain attempt to break Steffan's grip.

Gillian flew at him from the side, his knife clutched in one hand, the fingers of the other outstretched to claw at his face. Her fingers connected first, and she raked her nails across his cheek, gouging him from cheekbone to chin.

As the blood ran down his face, he screamed and disengaged one hand from about Catrin's waist. Striking out, he caught Gillian in the side of the head with his fist. The force of the blow spun her around before she sank to the floor.

"It's your turn now, bitch,'' he growled, yanking Catrin by the arm and reaching toward her with his free hand. She evaded his grasping fingers, crying out at the wrenching pain as he twisted her arm again. "There's nothing like battling a woman to fire my blood,'' he said, his eyes wild with lust. "Perhaps once I sink my rod into you, you'll know your place.''

His words sent panic crawling up Catrin's spine. Redoubling her efforts, she fought him as he tried to drag her across the floor to the bed. Somehow she had to break free of him before they reached the bed, for she knew she'd be no match for his strength and weight once he had her pinned to the mattress.

Despite her resistance Steffan pulled her ever closer to the bed, past where Gillian still lay in a crumpled heap. The sight roused Catrin to greater fury. She kicked out, her foot jarring hard against his thigh, but she couldn't reach high enough to hit him in the vitals.

The blow had made him flinch, however, so she tried again. She battered at his legs with her foot, making her toes throb, and continued to struggle against his hold. In desperation, she sank her teeth into his hand.

Ignoring the way her stomach heaved, Catrin held on like a terrier with a rat, the taste of blood and sweat on her tongue making her gag. Steffan roared with pain, but she held on. With one last, frantic kick, her toes connected with his manhood. When he folded at the waist, hands dropping to cradle his injured parts, Catrin backed away and raced to Gillian's side.

Startling her with his resiliency, Steffan lurched to his feet and lunged for her again. Catrin had no choice but to abandon Gillian and lure him outside. Perhaps then she could hide and club him with a stick or a rock—anything to stop this madman.

She ran out of the hut into the moonlit clearing, Steffan hot on her heels. Shivering as much from fear as cold, she hastened into the shadows beneath the trees, frantically searching for anything she might use as a weapon. Her fingers closed around a broken branch just as Steffan caught up with her.

She struck out at him with the jagged end of the stick, poking him hard in the chest. "Come to me," he screeched, the sound terrifying. The moonlight washed the color from his face, making him a ghostly nightmare brought to life.

Panting, her heart pounding in her ears, she feinted with the stick, hoping he'd lose his footing. Instead he dived beneath her guard and carried her to the ground. The momentum of his body sent her skidding painfully over the rocky soil on her back, his weight atop her driving the air from her lungs.

Tiny spots of light flashed before her eyes against the night sky. She couldn't draw a breath. Her mind spinning, she felt consciousness slipping from her grasp. She groped alongside her for a rock—anything. But she found nothing.

By the time he lifted his weight off her chest, her fingers had begun to go numb. She gasped, air burning its way into her lungs.

Steffan sat back on his heels, straddling her, one hand holding both of hers above her head while the other tugged at her clothing. "I must have you now," he muttered, his eyes glinting in the moonlight.

He jerked her skirts up, bunching them at her waist. Raising his weight off her, he forced her legs apart and fumbled with his own clothing.

The searing heat of Steffan's manhood against her skin was the final indignity. Bucking, shrieking, Catrin fought with every bit of strength she could conjure up. She'd geld him before she was through, she vowed, if she had to use her bare hands to do it!

It seemed they'd been plodding along for hours, the night black as pitch, when Nicholas's horse began to whicker low in his throat. "They must be up ahead," Nicholas whispered, groping for a sturdy tree and wrapping the reins around it. "We'd better go on without the horses."

Stumbling over the uneven ground, they climbed up the

track. "Are you sure there was only one man?" Ian asked Rannulf.

"Aye. And I doubt there's an army waiting for us up ahead, either," he said wryly. "It's too remote. Who in their right mind would come out here?"

A scream split the darkness, bringing to a sudden end the muffled nighttime sounds. Nicholas could have sworn his heart stopped beating for a moment.

Moving as one, they raced up the path, slipping and scrambling for purchase on the weatherworn rocks. They burst out into the moonlit clearing as another shriek arose.

His mind working furiously, Nicholas took in the scene in an instant. The dark outline of a man's torso was silhouetted against the backdrop of the moonlit sky. He struggled with someone pinned beneath him, his victim's legs flailing wildly.

'Twas all Nicholas needed to see. He shoved past Rannulf, toward the pair writhing on the grass.

Leaping the last few yards, he hit the man—Steffan, he noted without surprise—square in the back, sending him flying.

In the brief moment before Steffan sat up, Nicholas stared down at Catrin. The silvery light washed the color from her face and highlighted the fear. Her clothes were nearly torn to shreds.

It was all he needed to stir him to a blood lust such as he'd never felt before.

Roaring his rage, he grabbed Steffan by the tunic and jerked him to his feet. Steffan didn't even have a chance to straighten before he planted a fist in his face and forced him to his knees. He grinned at the satisfying crunch of bone beneath his knuckles. "Get up, you coward," he snarled, motioning with his hands for Steffan to stand. "I've not even started with you."

Breathing noisily through his crushed nose, Steffan lurched to his feet and, clasping his hands together, swung them at Nicholas's head.

Nicholas evaded the blow easily, taking advantage of Steffan's momentum to knock him to the ground. There was no challenge to this, he thought, disgusted by the whimpering sounds stealing through Steffan's lips. He waited impatiently for Steffan to regain his feet, then stalked him around the clearing. "Fight back, damn you," he growled. "Or do you only hit women?"

His body swaying, Steffan simply stood and stared at Nicholas, his only response to the insult the fire flaring in his eyes.

"Do you know what I'm going to do to you, you miserable son of a bitch? Once I've beaten you bloody, I'm going to rip off your—"

Teeth bared in a terrible grimace, Steffan dived at him. *Finally.* Nicholas smiled, the exultation of battle rushing through him. There was no challenge —or honor—to pounding on a puling craven who wouldn't fight back. Steffan would die tonight, one way or another, for the things he'd done to Catrin.

Their hands at each other's throats, they rolled across the rocky ground, their struggle punctuated by grunts and moans.

Catrin stifled a whimper when Ian helped her to her feet. She absently tugged the remnants of her clothing over her nakedness, for she couldn't tear her gaze from Nicholas. Rage tautened his features, giving him the face of an avenging angel.

She wanted Steffan to pay for his sins, but she'd seen enough violence done tonight—and she didn't want any harm to come to Nicholas. She couldn't bear it if he should be hurt.

"Can't you stop them?"

"It's his right," Ian said. "Don't expect me to interfere—unless it looks like Talbot needs the help."

Rannulf looked around, his expression frantic. "Where is Gillian?"

Catrin grasped his forearm. "She's inside. Steffan punched her," she called after him as he raced toward the cottage.

Catrin gasped as Steffan rolled Nicholas toward the open edge of the clearing, where the earth dropped away into a steep ravine. She started forward, only to be brought up short by Ian's hand on her arm. "Let them go. Don't you have any faith in him?"

She didn't want to watch, but she couldn't look away. Every time Steffan landed a blow, which fortunately wasn't often, Catrin winced as if she felt it herself.

Steffan's hands closed about Nicholas's throat. Nicholas pried them off, then grabbed Steffan and flipped him away. Instead of coming back toward Nicholas for more, Steffan scrambled to his feet and suddenly backed away from him toward the ravine.

The moonlight showed Steffan's fear, and utter madness writhed in his eyes. As he stepped ever closer to the edge, Nicholas dropped his hands, offering no threat.

Steffan began to babble, disjointed phrases that made no sense, his voice rising with each word until he shrieked like a madman.

"Come away from there," Nicholas shouted, slowly drawing nearer to him.

Steffan's tirade abruptly ceased, the last shriek echoing wildly through the hills. "You'll never take me," he said, voice calm. He looked back over his shoulder as though judging the distance.

"Don't!" Nicholas leapt the few yards separating them as Steffan, arms flailing, stepped to the brink.

"Nicholas!" Catrin screamed. The two men lost their balance and pitched over the edge.

Her heart thrumming with dread, Catrin rushed to peer into the ravine, Ian at her side. The earth and rock had crumbled away, leaving a sparse fringe of vegetation hanging above the abyss.

Moonlight glowed eerily on Steffan's body, sprawled at an odd angle over the rocks jumbled at the bottom of the gully. He didn't move. But Catrin saw no sign of Nicholas.

A moan rising out of the shadows dappling the cliff face drew her attention. She lay on her stomach and leaned out farther, her fingers gripping tightly to the dead weeds hanging from the edge. She scrutinized the shadows. There—something moved, a mere trace of dark-on-dark motion halfway down the steep embankment.

"I think he's alive," she called to Ian.

Sliding carefully to the side, she made room for her brother to join her. "Nicholas," she called.

She inched forward to improve her view, then rolled back quickly when the earth began to crumble away beneath her. But the brief glimpse had convinced her 'twas indeed a man's shape draped over a narrow ledge far below.

She grabbed Ian's arm. "I see him. But I don't know how we'll get him up the cliff. Did you bring any rope?"

Ian crawled out for another look. "Back in my gear—" He gauged the distance. "But I don't think it's long enough." He rolled away from the edge and to his feet in one smooth movement. "I'll get Rannulf and the rope. You talk to Talbot, see if you can get him to answer," he said, heading for the cottage.

"Nicholas, can you hear me?" she called, crawling on her hands and knees to peer down again. "Answer me, damn you."

"If you don't move away from the edge," he replied, his voice rising faintly out of the darkness, "I'll wallop your backside when I get up there, woman."

"I just might let you," she replied, earning a weak chuckle.

She heard Ian and Rannulf behind her. "He's alive," she said, relief making her shake suddenly. She grinned. "He's well enough to threaten me."

His back pressed against the cold, damp rock, Nicholas pulled himself upright, dragging his right leg. He clutched it just below the knee, grimacing at the shafts of pain radiating from the joint. 'Twas only by God's mercy he'd been able to detach himself from Steffan's grip and grab the clump of bushes growing out of the rocks to slow his descent.

He'd stopped rather quickly, though, he thought with a grim smile, his leg twisting hard beneath him as he grabbed the bushes and swung onto the narrow ledge. But he didn't believe it was broken—it just hurt like hell.

"Ian's getting a rope," Catrin called. "Are you hurt?"

"Not enough to matter. Get me a rope and I'll be up there before you know it."

He heard the muffled sound of her voice as she conferred with the others, then the blessed slap of a rope hitting the cliff. "Can you reach it?" Ian asked.

Nicholas inched away from the wall and looked up. The end of the rope swayed enticingly five or six feet above him.

"It's close enough." He'd scaled sheer castle walls fully armed. He'd manage this.

Bracing against the rough stone, he stood slowly, trying to shift most of his weight to his left leg. When he looked down and saw Steffan, his body broken on the rocks, he didn't care how his knee felt.

He'd won. Catrin and Gillian were safe forever from that fiend—assuming Gillian was all right—and he'd survived.

He couldn't ask for more than that.

Gritting his teeth, he stretched as far as he could, but the rope dangled just beyond his reach. He crouched and then launched himself upward. The rough bite of hemp into his palm was a pain he'd suffer gladly, he thought, wrapping his fingers about the line.

Hanging by one hand, the muscles in his arm and shoulder protesting the effort, Nicholas pulled himself up and grabbed the rope with his other hand. Slowly he climbed hand over hand up the cliff, his right leg banging painfully against the weathered rock the entire way.

Rannulf caught him by the back of the belt and hauled him up over the edge. Before he had a chance to open his eyes, Catrin's sweet weight settled against his side.

"Thank God," she murmured, pressing kisses over his face. He opened his eyes when he felt a teardrop land on his chin. "I thought you were gone."

He raised one shaking arm and brushed his fingers over her cheek. "You should know by now I'm not so easy to be rid of." He sighed, holding her tightly against his trembling body. She buried her face against his chest. "Did he harm you, love?" he asked, dropping kisses on her hair. "When I saw him—"

"I'll be fine," she reassured him. "Just take me away from here." She began to sob.

"Don't, love. I cannot bear it," he whispered into her hair.

Raising her head, Catrin swiped away her tears on her ragged sleeve. "'Tis just that I thought I'd lost you."

He kissed the tip of her nose. "It would take more than the likes of him to keep me away from you," he murmured.

They lay huddled together for a time, listening as Rannulf and Ian conferred in low tones, then Rannulf hastened back to the cottage.

After a few moments he returned, carrying Gillian in his arms. "She'll be fine, with some rest," Rannulf said, setting Gillian carefully onto the ground next to them.

Catrin sat up and the two women clung to each other briefly.

His knee protesting the movement, Nicholas pushed himself upright. "Is that bastard dead?" he asked, tilting his head toward the ravine.

"I think his back is broken," Ian said. He coiled the rope and slung it over his shoulder. "Couldn't have happened to a more deserving wretch."

"Does anyone want to climb down there and get him?" Rannulf asked.

"Let him rot," Nicholas said. "'Tis no more than he deserves. Rescuing his corpse isn't worth risking our lives." Slowly rising to his feet, he let Catrin bear some of his weight, holding her tightly against him. "We've got far better things to think of," he said with a tired smile. "Let's go home."

Epilogue

Nicholas settled back in the thronelike chair in his chamber at l'Eau Clair, tightened his fingers over the heavily carved armrests and sighed. He couldn't help but recall how impressed he'd been by this chair when he'd taken the wardship of l'Eau Clair last year.

He'd been a shallow creature then, too easily swayed by the appearance of nobility...too stupid to know his own mind.

And his own heart.

Even when he left court for Wales—was it only a few weeks ago?—he'd cared too much for the opinions of others, of the king, and too little for his own worth.

Other men had protested the king's petty tyranny...and some had survived his subsequent wrath.

Nicholas grinned. He'd not be so compliant again!

Though he couldn't be sorry the king had sent him on this journey, for through it he'd gained his heart's desire.

From this day onward, he'd let the woman with a warrior's heart be his guide. If he followed her lead, he couldn't go wrong.

A light rap on the door heralded Catrin's entrance.

"Still lazing about, I see," she teased with a pointed look at his bandaged leg.

He rose slowly to his feet. "Not for long."

"Nicholas! Sit down at once!" She hurried to his side and tried to nudge him back toward the chair. "I didn't mean it—'twas a joke, nothing more."

He wrapped his arms about her, savoring the way she nestled into his embrace. "I cannot sit here, wondering if you…"

She poked him in the ribs. "If I what?"

"If you meant the promises you made to me, the last time we were in this room," he said with a glance at the bed.

Her cheeks flushed. "Nicholas—how can you speak of that now?"

His arms still around her, he limped back to the chair and pulled her onto his lap. "How can I not speak of that which is most important to me? You made a vow to me, Catrin. You swore you would be mine, be my love, the mother of our children." He cupped her chin in his hand and gazed into her eyes. "Will you honor your promise, milady—or will you be forsworn?"

Catrin stared into Nicholas's violet eyes, warmed to the depths of her soul by what she saw there. Love, respect, acceptance…this man—this warrior—knew her for who she was, and loved her in spite of it.

Or perhaps because of it.

A smile of joy rose to her lips, and her heart felt so light, 'twas a wonder she didn't fly about the room. "Aye, milord, I meant every word. I am yours, for good or ill—forever."

"Not till death…but forever?"

She answered his grin by stroking his cheek. "Yes,

forever. Be certain I'm what you want, Nicholas. You'll not be rid of me so easily."

He held her close and pressed his lips to hers. "Even forever isn't long enough."

* * * * *

Harlequin Historicals presents an exciting medieval collection

THE KNIGHTS OF CHRISTMAS

With bestselling authors

Suzanne
BARCLAY

Margaret
MOORE

Debborah
SIMMONS

Available in October
wherever Harlequin Historicals are sold.

Harlequin® Historical

CHRISTMAS MIRACLES

really can happen, and Christmas dreams can come true!

BETTY NEELS,
Carole Mortimer and Rebecca Winters

bring you the magic of Christmas in this wonderful
holiday collection of romantic stories intertwined
with Christmas dreams come true.

Join three of your favorite romance authors as they
celebrate the festive season in their own special style!

Available in November at your favorite retail store.

Look us up on-line at: http://www.romance.net

CMIR

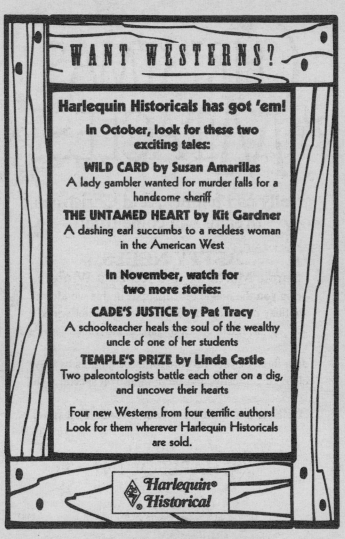

WANT WESTERNS?

Harlequin Historicals has got 'em!

In October, look for these two
exciting tales:

WILD CARD by Susan Amarillas
A lady gambler wanted for murder falls for a
handsome sheriff

THE UNTAMED HEART by Kit Gardner
A dashing earl succumbs to a reckless woman
in the American West

**In November, watch for
two more stories:**

CADE'S JUSTICE by Pat Tracy
A schoolteacher heals the soul of the wealthy
uncle of one of her students

TEMPLE'S PRIZE by Linda Castle
Two paleontologists battle each other on a dig,
and uncover their hearts

Four new Westerns from four terrific authors!
Look for them wherever Harlequin Historicals
are sold.

**◈ Harlequin®
Historical**

Coming in August 1997!

THE BETTY NEELS RUBY COLLECTION

August 1997—Stars Through the Mist
September 1997—The Doubtful Marriage
October 1997—The End of the Rainbow
November 1997—Three for a Wedding
December 1997—Roses for Christmas
January 1998—The Hasty Marriage

COLLECTOR'S EDITION

This August start assembling the
Betty Neels Ruby Collection. Six of the
most requested and best-loved titles have
been especially chosen for this collection.
From August 1997 until January 1998,
one title per month will be available to avid
fans. Spot the collection by the lush ruby red
cover with the gold Collector's Edition banner
and your favorite author's name—Betty Neels!

Available in August at your favorite retail outlet.

HARLEQUIN®